ERIFT'S JOURNEYS

Erift's Journeys

Book 1
Secrets of the Sealed Forest

by
J.T. Tenera

Book Design by Christine Filipak
Line and Copy Editing by Chet Sandberg
Proofreading by Ioanna Arka

ISBN: 978-1-7376827-0-7

2nd Edition

FOR ANYONE WHO HAS EVER HAD A DREAM TO CHASE. WHETHER YOU'RE YOUNG OR YOUNG AT HEART, ADVENTURE IS WAITING FOR YOU.

CONTENTS

ADVENTURE STARTS WITH A DREAM
NEVER STOP DREAMING

CHAPTER ONE

A LETTER AND A GAME

"LOOK OUT!"

A great orb of pulsing, black energy fell from the sky in Joseph's direction. It was a Dark Spell he couldn't defend against. He retrieved his sword from the nearby body of a shadowy soldier just in time to roll out of harm's way. The many faceless figures around him screamed as the forceful impact of the energy knocked them to the ground.

The blast sent him tumbling into a ditch and the jabbing pain of something sharp pierced his side. He removed his chest armor as soon as he stopped, then cringed at the large gash across his midsection. The discordant song of clashing swords and shrieking voices surrounded him from every angle while he clawed across the broken landscape. A familiar sight caught his attention.

"Eric!"

The figure looked up and grunted. "Joe...we can't hold them. I don't think we'll..." Eric grasped at a wound across his shoulder.

"Where are the others? Are they still alive?"

Eric's head fell to the ground as the thundering of an advancing attack washed over them. "No idea, but...I'm not sure I'll make it."

Joseph slammed the blade of his weapon into the earth and gave Eric a mournful look.

"I just need you...to do one more thing for me..." Eric breathed heavily.

Joseph swallowed and gave a solemn nod to his dying friend's last wish.

"I need...you to...deliver this chicken." Eric pulled a white fowl with a green beak from his satchel. "It's the last fetch quest before I finish the final side mission for the master weapon. Give it to the old lady..."—he panted with exertion—"...at the village farm."

Eric's final words echoed through his head like the chime of a bell, but they ultimately passed. His friend's head slipped to the side as the final breath left his lips. The chicken called out upon his death, and the lifebar above Eric's head hit zero.

Joseph shook him by the shoulders. His mouth was dry. "Eric?"

A soft voice gently pulled him from his grief.

"There is nothing you can do, so leave him be."

He looked up as a figure draped in robes of dark blue and white stepped beside Eric's body and knelt.

"What? You don't know that!"

"I promise your friend is fine. This is nothing more than a dream. You have an"—the robed figure's head tilted to one side—"odd imagination." The figure's voice was female and expressed concern.

Eric's white hen clucked, pulled a small sword from its sheath, then charged into the battlefield.

The girl passed her hand over Eric's body and it dissolved into the soil with a shimmer of white light.

Joseph staggered back and raised his sword. "What did you do to him?"

She gazed at him, her features hidden beneath the shadows of the hood. Only two details escaped the recesses of her hood—the soft sapphire glow of her eyes and the glint of her silver hair.

He stared directly into them, unable to move.

She approached. "I don't think Kilgan knows what he's talking about. There's no way someone like *you* can be part of this," she scoffed. "Magic has been asleep for too long. You're not awakened yet. You aren't ready, and you need to wake up! Wake up!"

"What?"

She gently shoved his chest and he stumbled backwards. As he hit the ground, the world shattered like a breaking mirror and the battlefield vanished.

Joseph Erift opened his eyes at the exact moment he tumbled from bed. He crashed to the floor with a thud. Rays of morning sunlight pierced the window and fell across his face.

He squinted and groaned. "I need to stop the late-night gaming. That dream was more vivid than usual."

He leaned back and blindly felt for the cell phone on the desk near his bed but it had fallen on the floor. The charging cable had also popped out, leaving him unable to turn it on.

"And that's why the alarm didn't go off." He sighed and rubbed his eyes, looking at the galaxy-themed clock on the wall.

It was close to seven in the morning.

He gasped and leapt up. *I'm going to be late!*

It was the last day of eleventh grade, and he didn't want to miss it. A mess of brown hair barely fell over his eyes in certain places, and aqua-hued eyes glanced at what could be described as a simple but sharp face as he passed a mirror in the hall. He always preferred to walk his own path in life, even if he wasn't the most social person around. It never bothered him as he was happy with the friends he already had.

After finishing in the bathroom, he ran back for a change of clothing. The jeans and t-shirt within reach would have to do. He glanced at the clock again and cringed. "Where's a fast spell when you need it?"

He stumbled into the bathroom down the hall and picked up a comb. The reflection looking back from the mirror appeared as if it was older than his seventeen years. It resembled him, but more mature. In a blink it was gone, and he shrugged it off. A few swipes of the comb did little to calm the jungle on his head.

"Eh, good enough!"

After plugging his phone back in to charge, he dashed downstairs to the kitchen.

He took a quick chug of orange juice from the carton and a bite of sandwich he didn't finish yesterday. The clock was ticking. He grabbed his backpack, stuffed some cash into his pocket, and was out the door.

He ran around the house and unlocked his bike from one of the pipes. The sun had just finished rising over Sethen County when he rode into the street. He turned into another driveway further down the road where he got off and waited. A pair of voices rose from inside before the front door was opened. His friend, Eric Castis, strolled out as he crammed the remains of a breakfast bar into his mouth and finished putting the last stroke of gel into his light brown hair. He always wore it highlighted in the front, where it was spiked up.

Even though Eric was a year younger, his best friend was in the same grade at the same high school as Joseph.

His buddy approached the garage and vanished inside. "Oh, come on! I know you're in here!" Eric shouted.

His friend had an attitude that often got him into trouble, but at his core, Eric was fun to be around—full of energy and ready to face most any challenge.

Curiosity got the better of him, so Joseph approached and waited as Eric rummaged through the piles of junk. Stray objects bounced into view, including a tire that rolled out onto the lawn.

He shook his head. "You know it would be easier if you cleaned it out, right?"

"Sounds like work." Eric struggled to remove his bike. "Besides, *someone* said they'd get a car once they got their license."

Joseph laughed. "I need a job to get a car. They don't let you walk up and take one off the lot."

Eric finally freed his bike and joined him. "So what's up? I thought you'd have left already."

"I overslept." He stopped at the end of the driveway. "You wouldn't believe the dream I had."

"Was it cool?"

"You'd have liked it. It reminded me of that game we played yesterday. Swords, magic…violence."

Eric grinned and tossed a quick thumbs-up.

"You were there. It looked like we were in some sort of battle. We'd been fighting these crazy shadows but they killed you. I also had to deliver a chicken for you because…" Joseph shook his head. "I don't even know."

"Oh, come on," Eric complained. "Why'd you kill me?"

"I didn't kill you."

"You could have at least shoved a potion down my throat or something. It was *your* dream."

He chuckled and nodded. The dream had been so real, its imagery still weaved in and out his thoughts. He hadn't even mentioned the strange female entity. That one still had him confused.

Joseph shifted on his bike as they rode off and the brisk morning air filled his lungs. The wind was at their backs as they left the suburban developments toward the school building. Buses were dropping off students as the groups walked in.

Joseph and Eric rode to the side of the building, bypassing the crowds to lock up their bikes. Class started at 7:30, so they hung out in their usual spot to wait for the bell. Joseph was still trying to shake the dream. The bike ride had helped.

Eric kicked at the ground as he folded his arms and leaned against the wall. "Our lives are boring, man. We do the same thing every day."

"One more year, Eric. College should be better."

Eric cringed. "Ugh, don't remind me."

Joseph set his backpack on the ground, slouched next to Eric and sighed as a familiar sight greeted them. A large black limo slowly weaved around cars and buses on its way to the school's front sidewalk. It stopped and the driver's side door opened. A man wearing a fine black suit got out and walked to the rear where he opened the last door. A young man clad in name-brand clothing stepped out. He ran his fingers through the slicked-back, perfectly combed style atop his head. The dirty blonde threads always looked like there was more hair product than actual hair, yet there were always stray strands that curved over his face.

"Why does Clyde still need to show off like that? It's the end of junior year. We get it—he's rich. This isn't an anime…" Eric's expression perked up at the thought, as though it was the first time he considered it. "I kinda wish it was, though."

"Like you wouldn't do the same thing," Joseph teased.

Eric shrugged. "I bet every neighborhood has someone like Clyde. Maybe in an alternate universe it's you or me stepping out of that limo and Clyde's leaning against this wall complaining about annoying rich kids. Weird to think about, isn't it?"

Joseph shook his head and smiled. "Whatever you say, Eric."

Clyde had moved to their city four years ago. Though he boasted, and a sort of smug self-satisfaction oozed from his every word, they knew little about him. The Foristen name had acquired a powerful reputation in the neighborhood, even if the exact nature of their business had remained under wraps. They were just another part of the odd social elite. Joseph never had a problem with Clyde, so he never let the snide remarks and snickering laugh get to him. However, he had to admit the tension between him and Eric always made for an amusing performance.

As if Joseph's thoughts had summoned him, Clyde made a sudden turn and headed in their direction.

He stopped and gave them each a nod. "Look what the bikes dragged in. Still on two wheels I see. Must be hard passing that driving test." He flashed an insincere smile. "I've never had to use them, but I hear the buses give a plenty comfy ride."

"You're a funny guy. I'll pass it when I'm ready," Eric casually replied. He pointed at Clyde but looked at Joseph. "Ever notice how his mouth moves a lot without him saying much of anything?"

Joseph enjoyed the show. Moments like this made him wish he could make popcorn appear from thin air.

"Envy looks petty on you, Eric. I know it eats you alive that my channel has more followers." Clyde tossed his hair before folding his arms. "You're more than welcome to join them. You might never catch me, but I don't mind if you want to watch." He shrugged. "You might learn a few tricks of the trade. I might even toss you some mentions if you ask nicely enough."

"The only reason your channel has more viewers is because you get access to all the new games first! In a fair fight, I'd come out on top. My page will always have more style."

Clyde's frown was fake. "It looks like you'll remain one step behind me, then. Hate to see you as a middle-aged man flipping meat patties at Mach Burger, but not everyone has natural talent."

Clyde gave Joseph a quick look before turning to enter the school.

"The only natural thing about him is his ego," Eric muttered.

"Don't let it get to you. He thrives on the attention."

"Why isn't he in private school with the other rich jerk-offs so we don't have to deal with that?"

Joseph laughed. "Maybe they don't want to deal with it either." The bell for class chimed as he said it. "Come on. Don't wanna miss homeroom."

The hallways were overflowing with bodies trying to get to their rooms on time. "See you at lunch, man!" Eric gave a quick wave and was out of sight.

Joseph started for the upper floor but as he turned the corner, he met with an immovable object and his backpack fell, tumbling the contents to the floor. An elderly gentleman in a dark green suit gave a soft, hearty laugh as he shook his head.

"Terribly sorry about that." He smiled, stroking his fingers through the long ivory beard on his kind-looking face. The old man adjusted the round frames of his glasses. "I sometimes lose focus when I'm lost in a thought. There's always so much that requires my attention. I'm sure you know the feeling."

"Don't worry about it." Joseph knelt to pick up his things and stuff them back into place.

The stranger bent at the waist and came up with one of Joseph's books. "Ah yes! The Wand of Time and Space. This is an epic tale of fantasy and adventure. Have you read much?" The man offered him the book and Joseph put it away.

"I just started reading it."

"The beginning of a new voyage is always thrilling, is it not?" The man nodded as he folded his arms behind his back. "They often come into our lives when we least expect it. Of course, those are just fictional stories meant for our enjoyment."

Joseph cocked his head and squinted at the man after he adjusted his backpack. "Are you a teacher here? I've never seen you before."

"You could say that, but I'm better described as a guide who helps enlighten others." The man stepped back to allow Joseph room to pass. "I should let you be on your way. You don't want to be late on your last day, do you?" The man winked. "Besides, you have something very important waiting for you at home." He gave Joseph a reassuring tap on the shoulder. "Every adventure starts with a dream." He then disappeared around the corner, and it was as if he'd never been there.

Joseph paused before he chased after the old gentleman. "Hey, have you—"

Be he was already gone. In the hallway, fellow students flashed him confused looks. Joseph's cheeks became warm as his self-consciousness mounted. First the dream, then the odd old man. He shook his head and climbed the steps to the second floor so he could deposit his belongings and take what he needed.

His first class awaited him, causing his feet to drag like lead bricks on his way to the room where Mrs. Moyers taught Advanced Algebra. He was never a morning person, and he tried not to fall asleep as he progressed to World History and finally to an elective Astronomy class—the only one he found interesting.

It wasn't that he hated school, but he craved freedom, and his mind often wandered to other, more interesting places. Rich fantasy worlds continuously called to him from the hidden recesses of his mind, and whenever he had a moment, they drew him into their seductive embraces. Sometimes that got him in trouble.

His mood lightened as lunch time approached.

This was the only time of day Joseph could check in with Eric. Once seated, he glanced to the table where Clyde sat on the other side of the room. The rich kid always showed off the lunches his family's personal chef prepared for him, and he was always surrounded by his closest acquaintances.

"Hey Clyde, how about sharing some of that?" A brown-haired kid named Bob Stenner practically drooled over the presentation as he flashed a wide smile. "You can't really eat all of it, can you?"

"Yo, Clyde, we got any plans tonight?" asked another by the name of Keith Kithney as he messed with the dreads of his black hair. "We need to get in some game time before your trip, man."

Another kid with dyed blue and aqua hair named Brian Harris blew the strands from his eyes before shaking his head. "Last day...what a drag."

"Bunch of suck ups!" Eric muttered before stuffing his burger into his mouth.

There had been times when Joseph had to forcibly prevent his friend from hurling food at Clyde and his sycophantic entourage. Eric had a tell, though. As his irritation mounted, he'd scrunch up his face while letting his fingers play with his lunch. Joseph watched his friend carefully, and he always pulled his friend back down before he could complete the act.

But Eric wasn't up for it today. He sat silently and occasionally lifted his head to glance at them with narrowed eyes.

They finished their meals and parted ways. Joseph's day continued with eleventh grade Language Arts, which was followed by a course in animation he had elected to take. Part of him always wondered how video games were made and the class was fairly interesting. The last part of the day was a game of softball in Gym. Even if purely by luck, Joseph's day ended with a proud moment when his hit helped score the win against Clyde and his team.

The day was finally over. Summer had officially begun.

Joseph almost knocked over fellow classmates in the rush to his locker. He emptied everything into his backpack before slamming it shut, then practically skipped out the door. Outside, Eric was already leaning up against his bike waiting for him.

"My time has been served and I'm out on bail!" Eric cheered as their hands met in the air with a clap. "You ready to tear up this summer?"

Joseph nodded. "I might look for a job too." Joseph unlocked his bike from the rack. "Question is, what do we do first?"

"We game until the sun rises! And pizza; lots of pizza!"

They each laughed, the expressions on their faces becoming more hopeful as each new second of temporary freedom accumulated.

Someone grunted from behind them.

They flashed knowing looks at one another.

"So, what do the two of you have planned over the summer?"

Joseph tried to ignore it.

"I asked you a question, and I don't feel like repeating myself." Clyde sighed.

Eric rolled his eyes. "He must be tired—not a single insult in that sentence. I'm kinda impressed."

Joseph turned. There stood Clyde, with Keith, Brian, and Bob standing behind him.

"We're not begging you to talk to us. We'll gladly not talk to you all summer." Joseph leaned his bike to the side. "But I'm curious. Why do you want to know?"

Clyde's face took on a strangely vulnerable look before it shifted. "Hmph, I was going to invite you guys to check out my game stream this coming week. I'm flying out on vacation to handle some of the arrangements." Clyde tried to act casual. "I thought you'd be interested, but..." The rich kid shrugged. "It's just a preview stream for Dying Nightmares. I'll be the first one to play it."

Eric huffed and turned away. "That game is nothing but jump scares. I didn't plan on playing it."

Keith chuckled with a confident grin. "Someone sounds envious."

"Tch, envious of what? It's another fad game that'll die off in a month!" Eric replied, perhaps too forcefully.

Brian shook his head. "Bad at hiding it, too."

"The only thing I'm hiding is my secret weapon. Watch for it this summer. I'm going to have the most amazing video uploads." Eric's eyes lit up. "It'll blow you all away!"

Bob jumped into the conversation. "C'mon, you're just bluffing. Clyde gets all the best stuff first."

Clyde raised a hand to silence his friends. "It's a shame you won't accept. One of the developers will be watching and answering people's questions in real time. It's a great opportunity."

"I don't need your handouts. One of these days you'll be asking to hang out on *my* channel!" Eric put on his best salesman's smile. "You know, you might want to jump on this train while you still can."

Clyde's grin was confident as he nodded. "Don't be shy should you change your mind. You can't say I never offered."

"I'll offer you something, all right," Eric muttered.

"Your choice." Clyde dismissed him with a wave as Eric argued with the others. He then turned to Joseph. "Why do you bother with him? You can do so much better in your choice of friends."

"Because he's my best friend." Joseph smiled. "Enjoy your summer, Clyde."

Clyde smirked and snapped his fingers, drawing his friends' attention. He turned away and nearly fell as they retreated.

"Need help there? One foot in front of the other, man. It's not hard!" When Clyde didn't acknowledge him, Eric pressed further. "See you almost...next fall...or, uh; whatever!"

They hopped onto their bikes as Clyde and his group left without further incident.

"Nice comeback at the end there." Joseph laughed.

Eric pedaled faster until he gained enough speed to take his hands off the handlebars of his bike then pretended to wave a wand. "I'm a wizard with words! When I'm rich and famous, they'll call me Eric Superstar Castis, just like my video channel. I'll be in movies!" He steered his bike close to Joseph and winked. "Clyde is going to regret everything, then."

Joseph smiled. Even when Eric was faced with Clyde's insults, his confidence never wavered.

A few minutes later, Eric turned into his driveway. "See you later, man. Make sure you call in about an hour so we can plan out some awesome stuff!" He rolled his bike into the garage and walked inside.

The bicycle crashed in the back shortly after, causing a small pile of items to roll into view.

Joseph rode alone until he reached his own home, then rolled his bike to the side and walked through the front door. His mom came out of the kitchen when he entered.

"How was your last day of school?"

"Okay, I guess. It was a strange day." Joseph almost mentioned the old man but let it drop instead.

"Three months break—that should be plenty to settle your aura," she said. Her blonde ponytail bounced as she readied dinner. "Never too early to start planning for college, either. You might wanna look into a part time job over the summer. The apothecary shop near the center of town is hiring."

Joseph cringed. "That's okay. I have a few ideas." He walked into the kitchen to get a snack.

He wasn't looking forward to sorting through what seemed to be an endless pile of college applications.

"Oh, I almost forgot," his mother said as she chopped some vegetables. "You got something in the mail today. I left it on the kitchen table for you."

"Thanks, mom." He closed the refrigerator door and walked to the table, searching through the pile of scattered papers to find it. He took the large envelope to his room and once there gave it a quick glance. It had no return address.

"That's weird."

The ordinary brown packet was labeled with his name and address. Something else was odd though. The postmark read June 7th. He tore open the top and removed the letter nestled inside. Two pieces of paper and a CD case were also tucked into the delivery, but he left them alone to focus on the letter.

To Joseph:

First allow me to present to you this special invitation. After much consideration and study, you, as well as a few others, have been specifically selected due to your talents to participate in a special viewing of the entertainment of the future! As a result, you have qualified for an all-expense paid vacation to the lovely tropical resort islands of Murean to attend a professional demonstration of this brand new release.

Joseph stopped reading. "What in the world? This is a joke, right?"

The letter made no sense. The details were vague and reminiscent of some cheesy online advertisement.

Right now, you are most likely thinking to yourself: What is going on here? Hold on tight, because I can tell you it is something sensational! If you enjoy the world of fantasy and action, then you would be a fool to pass up such a chance! This is quite possibly the opportunity of a lifetime, and a grand honor! However, instead of spoiling the fun and telling you what wonders await you, I have enclosed two plane tickets for you and your friend, Eric Castis. He has also managed to wiggle his way into this elite selection. I have also included a demo of the game we would like you to review. Your plane departs at one in the morning on the 8th of June. I will show you the rest once you arrive. Prepare your mind for the most amazing trip into the world of science and adventure for tomorrow's leaders!

> *P.S. Please tell no one...*
> *Sincerely,*
> *Professor Benjamin Thessit, PhD*

"The 8th? That's tomorrow..." Joseph glimpsed into the envelope where the two pieces of paper and plastic case were nestled. Just as the letter indicated, they were plane tickets to a place called "The Murean Islands," and on the jewel case was written "Call of Echoes 3: True Honor."

"Huh...this isn't supposed to be released for another year."

Joseph had never heard of the place. Could it be real? The letter was so convincing and serious. If anything, the idea of such an elaborate prank amused him. He leaned over and pulled his laptop from where it rested beside his bed. Once it was powered on, he ran a search of the islands mentioned in the letter. Results came up, but they contained little information. The maps he found came with warnings that they were only speculation on the location, and most maps placed them randomly at different places in the Pacific Ocean.

"Does this place even exist?"

He tried running a search on the name in the letter, but there was nothing. It wasn't until he typed in a search for the game and the islands together that he got a recognizable result. He clicked the link.

The website that came up was exactly as the letter had described. After a short animation of the game's logo, it revealed an exclusive showing and demonstration for a secret reveal on the Murean Islands to be hosted by one Benjamin Thessit. He was listed as the company's head of research and testing. There was a lot of evidence to support the strange letter.

Though a force nagged at the back of his mind, another part laughed at the idea. It could be Clyde playing a joke on him, especially after the statements he'd made earlier.

The letter had also mentioned Eric. Joseph sighed. His own computer wasn't powerful enough to play the game. It left him with only one option. He put the letter, tickets, and case into his pockets and ran downstairs.

"Be right back, mom!"

He dashed out the front door and was on his bike before his mother finished her reply. Joseph pedaled down the street to Eric's house and hopped off just before he crashed, then stumbled to the front door and hit the bell.

"I'm coming!" a voice shouted from inside just before the door opened. Eric held half a sandwich and he struggled to speak around a mouthful of food. "What are you doing here, dude?" He shifted his eyes to the sandwich. "Uh, I didn't make two. Sorry."

"Don't worry about it." Joseph pushed around him through the open doorway. "You *have* to see what I got in the mail."

Eric dropped his sandwich on the table as Joseph pulled out the letter. He unfolded it and handed it to his friend, who took it with a puzzled stare.

"Just read it," Joseph urged.

Eric rolled his eyes and focused on the letter. He gave a short laugh and flicked the paper away once he was done.

"What's so funny?" Joseph picked it up from where it had landed on the ground.

"That's a terrible joke, dude." Eric licked his fingers as he finished his snack. "I mean, whoever wrote this needs to work on their acting. There are two obvious problems with this whole prank. First of all, *no one* has access to this game, not even the company staff. I bet *Clyde* doesn't even have anything for it yet. Second, I didn't get my own letter, so that throws this right out the window. If they wanted to contact the best gamer, I'm the obvious choice, right? Thirdly, if they wanted to make this letter sound more believable, they could have at least changed some of the words and sent some fake plane tickets and a game or made the destination someplace that was real. Normally they hold these events in New York or California. Japan would have been a great choice too." Eric looked as though he was trying not to laugh. "I might have fallen for it, but c'mon...someone's playin' us."

Joseph presented the tickets and CD jewel case. "Like these?"

"Dude, are you serious?"

Eric grabbed the items from Joseph's hand and gave them a good look. The longer Eric looked at them, the more the expression on his face brightened.

"There's no way this is real, but if it is...oh man, we've gotta try this out. Come on!"

Eric ushered Joseph to his room as he plunged into the chair by his computer and put in the disc. They waited as the game installed and loaded up.

Eric rubbed his hands together. "This is so cool! We're gonna play *Call of Echoes 3* a year before anyone else." He sighed proudly. "Glad I just upgraded my computer—wait till my fans see me playing *this*!"

Joseph raised an eyebrow and laughed. "You don't have that many followers."

"Yeah, yeah; it's a bit slow right *now*, but when people see me playing this, my popularity..." Eric's eyes got wide. "Fame and fortune, here I come!"

The game, an action-shooter, started, and Eric played through the first level. It was exactly as the letter described. Once the demo ended, he was able to pull Eric away from the controller to show him the website that matched the location on the tickets.

"Everything makes sense. The tickets are right here and the game is real."

"This is crazy. You know that, right? Look at these little hologram thingies. You can't fake those. This guy must have seen my videos. Not sure why he sent this stuff to you, though. That's weird."

"I don't know if that has anything to do with it." Joseph took the tickets back. "Clyde was taunting us about this earlier. Don't you think it's a bit...strange? It's not that I don't believe it, but—"

"Dude, think about it. If these tickets are real, it stands to reason everything else the letter says is real as well. And if all that is real, then it's seriously *real!*" Eric grabbed Joseph's shoulders. "Think about it, man—a *real* vacation! We get to travel across the world and play the full version of a game no one else gets to see for another year. We'll probably get to meet some of the folks who worked on it—and don't forget the beach!"

"We need to bring it up to our parents, though I already know what mine will say."

"No kidding. Mine freaked out that one time we stayed out too late for a movie." Eric frowned. "You know, the letter says to tell *no one.* I bet they want this top secret so it doesn't leak all over the internet. You're not gonna let our parents stop us from having the most amazing summer ever, are you?"

It was good that Eric's parents worked late—otherwise they'd have easily picked up on the excitement in the air.

"Okay, let's say the Murean Islands exist and we somehow make it there. Then what? What if it's a scam or something?"

"Who in the world would do such a dumb thing? You saw the website, and the game actually works! Think about it, man! I mean, *really* think about it! We're old enough not to need our parents anymore." Eric's face softened. "Come on, it'll be fun. When will we ever get another chance like this? Watch, we'll turn it down and some other lucky guys will take our places. In this time and in this reality, we're... the chosen ones!"

Joseph couldn't shake the strange feeling he'd gotten earlier. It was like a string tugging at his mind. They'd have to leave home without permission from their families to take the risk, but Eric had made a convincing argument. It was the chance of a lifetime. All the pieces of the puzzle were there; all he had to do was put them together.

"Come on, man—you *want* to go!" Eric wriggled his fingers in a scheming motion but couldn't stifle a chuckle. "You're under the spell of this amazing game, and it commands you to follow it!"

Joseph folded his arms and sighed. "It wouldn't hurt to check it out, I guess. We wanted an exciting summer, right?"

"Now we're talking." Eric extended his hand in a celebratory fist-bump but abruptly pulled short, leaving Joseph hanging. "Wait, how will we get to the airport? Even by car the city's a long trip."

"We can get there by bike in a few hours, just gotta leave early. We'll sneak out tonight, when our parents go to bed. We should leave a note so they don't worry too much, though."

"Ah, an excellent idea, old chap!" Eric said with a fake British accent. "We'll let them know we snuck halfway around the world for a sneak peek at a video game. They'll totally understand." His voice then returned to normal as he pointed at his friend. "You just watch—they'll find a way to ground me while I'm at college."

"I just want to cover all our bases. If something goes wrong, it'll give us a chance to explain."

"Yeah, a chance to explain how we ditched the rules." Eric shook his head. "Whatever. So, are we doing this? No backing out?"

Joseph stared at the tickets, keenly aware of their texture as he rubbed them between his fingers. His excitement outweighed his nervousness. "It looks like we're going on a vacation."

"Awwww yeah!" Eric bumped Joseph's fist with his. "What time should we leave?"

"Let's try to make it out by ten, just to be sure."

Eric nodded as he turned to the display on his monitor, giving a crack of his knuckles. "So long, boring summer; hello, epic opportunity!"

Joseph sat down as Eric restarted the game. Something important truly had been waiting for him at home.

The old man at school had been right.

CHAPTER TWO

SNEAKING OUT

Night came and the late hours drew near. Joseph had waited until his parents were asleep to sneak downstairs, leave his note, and slip out the door. He'd mentioned the video game demo and promised he'd text them later.

He now stood outside Eric's house. The lights were still on, and he worried that his friend couldn't get out.

"Eric?" Joseph whispered. "Can you hear me?"

He carefully made his way around the perimeter, peeking through windows to see if anyone was there. He finally spotted Eric and gave a gentle tap on the glass to alert his friend.

Eric jumped and rushed to the door.

"Be quiet—we're not alone."

"Yeah, I saw the lights were on." Joseph peered inside. "What's going on? Are you ready?"

His friend let him in. "Getting there. My dad fell asleep on the couch and I don't want to wake him."

"Good. Grab your stuff and let's get going."

Eric glanced back to the living room. "I can't yet. My music player is under the couch."

"You don't need it. Besides, don't you have your phone?"

"You know how quickly my phone eats up its battery? We don't know how long this trip is going to take. This adventure needs a soundtrack and I only have so many chargers," Eric pleaded.

Joseph rubbed a hand down his face and sighed. "All right, let's see what we can do."

Eric pumped his fist. "Sidequest initiated."

He tiptoed into Eric's living room, where Eric's dad was lost in slumber on the couch. The occasional snore rumbled through the room like that of a sleeping dragon. He lowered himself to the floor and felt around underneath the sofa, but found nothing. He stood and gave his friend a shake of his head.

"Oh, look in the closet. You can use the broom."

Joseph rolled his eyes and crept to the closet. The door creaked as it opened, and he quietly pulled out the broom. The television had been left on, and it masked most of the noise. Even with the yelling and explosions of the war movie blaring, Eric's dad didn't stir. Joseph pushed the broad end of the broom under the couch, and the object slid into view.

"There it is!" Though he still whispered, Eric's voice had gotten louder with excitement.

Eric's father shifted.

Joseph stopped breathing and held perfectly still. Eric's dad rolled on the couch, mumbling a few inaudible words before falling back asleep. The coast was clear; he followed Eric back to the door.

"I can't believe I did all that just for you to have music." Joseph shook his head. "Is that everything?"

Eric stuffed the player into his bag. "I owe you one for braving the snoring giant."

Joseph grabbed his things as they closed the door and went to the garage for Eric's bike.

"Good thing I"—Eric made finger quotes in the air— "*accidentally* forgot to close the garage!"

The familiar sound of objects crashing to the ground filled the air as Eric retrieved his bike.

"How much time do we have?" Eric asked as they started on their way.

Joseph checked his phone. "About two hours."

"Plenty of time. I once stayed up for three days without sleep. I'll carry the energy for both of us!"

Joseph had never been the nocturnal type. "I'm glad one of us can."

"We could totally pick up some food and energy drinks on the way."

Joseph gave Eric a lethargic nod.

Their ride through Sethen County went without incident. The occasional car drove by, but the night was otherwise quiet. Joseph had been to the city a few times but never by bike. Their adventure already featured a new experience.

An hour later, their route took a wrong turn.

"Crap, my phone must have gotten thrown off when the signal cut out back there." Eric sighed as he made the front of his bike skip.

Joseph pointed to the glowing neon lights of an open gas station. "Stop over there. We can rest and figure out where we are. I'll see how my signal is."

They set their bikes near the entrance and went in for something to drink. Joseph opened the GPS on his phone and waited for it to find their location while Eric bought food. They'd strayed from their path but were still on track to reach the airport on time. Eric came out holding a drink in one hand and a hotdog in the other.

"So, Columbus, where are we?" Eric took a bite of his snack.

Joseph got back on his bike. "We're about half an hour from the city."

Eric finished his meal and they pushed on.

The rest of the trip dragged on. Eric nearly fell asleep a couple times, and Joseph had to ride over to pull him back out of the street. The sights of Terance City soon welcomed them into their concrete embrace. The roads' gradual turns had given way to sharp angles at every corner. Lights and skyscrapers guided them as they left the suburbs behind entirely. It was a setting Joseph never saw himself living in.

They kept a steady pace, and signs for the airport appeared. The sound of planes taking off and arriving overhead was enough to jolt Eric from his drifting state.

Joseph put his phone away. "We're almost there."

"Remind me to remind *you* to get that car for our senior year. No more bikes after this."

They turned off from the highway. It wasn't long until they approached the airport's massive parking lot.

Joseph pointed to an area where they could chain their bikes out of sight. Once they were secured, they walked to the front of the building and stepped inside the airport.

"Look at all these people!"

Joseph laughed. "The world never sleeps, even if you can somehow nap while riding a bike."

Eric stopped to stretch his arms. "Hey, that wasn't sleeping. I was riding with my eyes closed. Pretty impressive, huh?"

"You were snoring and falling behind."

Eric rolled his eyes as they got in line.

Joseph handed the man at the counter their tickets when they were there. "Could you tell us where the plane heading for Murean departs?"

The man looked at the tickets and glanced up.

Joseph cleared his throat and adjusted his stance as the man began to type on his computer.

The man shook his head and stood. "Please excuse me a moment."

The clerk departed into the back room and was followed by a muffled conversation. He returned and handed the tickets back to Joseph.

"My apologies; I simply had to check something regarding your destination and passage. Your IDs, please."

They both presented their identification.

"It's against company regulations to let minors board without the consent of an adult. Are your parents here?"

He handed them back.

"They're waiting for another one of our relatives to arrive and told us to go ahead. It looks like the cabs run slow at night, don't they?"

He gave Eric a push with his elbow to lead him into the story.

"Huh? Oh yeah! You wouldn't believe how long our aunt takes to pack her suitcase," Eric added with a goofy smile. "She takes forever to waddle her lazy—"

Joseph gave him another quick shove.

"Right...well the entrance to your flight is near the other end of the building. Just make sure to follow the directions mentioning Port 124 and you should find it easily. And here, take these." The man handed them two identification badges bearing a symbol and number. "According to the status of your tickets, you'll need those. I've never seen them before, but my manager insists you'll need them. Just wear them and you'll be fine. I'll be sure to give them to your parents once they arrive. Is there anything else I can do for you?"

Joseph hoisted his bag. "No, thank you."

Joseph thought he saw the old bearded man from his school standing in one of the rooms behind the counter. Only this time he wore a professional suit and tie. The man waved, but before Joseph could wave back, he was gone.

Joseph glanced at his badge. "That was strange."

"Who would have thought our flight came with special perks? This event must be serious."

"Just make sure we stick to the story. We need to be convincing if someone asks again."

Eric pretended to slick back his hair and gave a dramatic pose as they walked. "You haven't seen anything yet. Set the stage, and I'll take the lead."

They followed the signs, fighting through a crowd of people busy on their cell phones. The second sector led them to take a right. The security check lay just down the path.

Joseph pulled Eric to the side.

"I don't remember seeing a detour. What's up?"

"Act normal. The stranger we act, the more they'll suspect something."

"Yeah yeah, I get it already. We're on the clear list, remember? This will be a piece of cake with these sweet indentification badges."

Joseph took in a deep breath as butterflies fluttered in his stomach. It was too late to second-guess their choice, but they'd come to a cross in the road. He didn't know what to do if they failed to make it through.

Everything went smoothly, even if they got a few concerned looks. Those expressions faded from the staff at the sight of their special tags, and after a single phone call, security allowed them to set their bags on the belt and approach the scanner. Joseph fidgeted, trying his best to look calm.

A female voice chimed on the intercom. "Flight 124 will be departing momentarily. All passengers should now board. Thank you."

Joseph twinged when he heard the announcement. His bag rolled into sight and he snatched it up.

"Join you in a sec." Eric turned to the lady at the belt and held up the tag. "You always need to double check the VIP baggage, don't you?" He grinned and twirled the badge between his fingers. "You ever watch gaming videos online? I'm a bit of a celebrity."

Joseph shook his head. As expected, the young woman ignored his friend's awkward attempt to show off. When Eric's bag made its journey along the belt, the computer next to it beeped and its travel came to a halt.

Eric tapped it with a finger. "Uh, why did it stop?"

The same woman turned her head to look at the personnel at the scanner. "Is there a problem?"

"The system found something of interest in this young man's bag."

The woman waved Eric to the side. "Over here, sir."

Joseph's heart rate spiked, and his friend seemed to turn white.

"U-uh, okay." Eric hesitated. "You know I was totally kidding about the celebrity thing, right? Haha, just trying to lighten the mood, you know?"

"Eric, what's in there?"

His friend shrugged.

Joseph watched as the officers began to check around Eric's supplies, making sure to carefully examine each item.

The intercom came on once again. "This is the last call for flight 124. All those boarding should be on the plane and seated immediately."

It was taking too much time. Their flight could take off and leave them stranded at the airport. Their only choice would be to return home. They couldn't let that happen.

They couldn't miss their chance.

CHAPTER THREE

TOURING AN ISLAND PARADISE

The officers searching Eric's bags finished, and Joseph sighed as they handed them back and allowed Eric to pass through without a problem.

"What happened over there?"

Eric struggled to close the top of his carryon over the sheer mass of electronic devices inside.

"Did you really need to pack all that?"

"Some people live for technology. I need technology to live. There are backups for my backups, and then plans A through G for every occasion. This is a big trip!"

Hurrying as fast as they could, they bolted down the long hallway. Joseph glanced to the side as planes took off and vanished into the night sky. He feared theirs was one of them.

The woman at the gate stopped them. "Tickets, please."

Joseph fumbled to take out his ticket, while Eric made a showing of it as he flashed the special badge between his fingers.

"Told you. We're VIP."

"Thank you, Mr. Erift and Mr. Castis. The flight will depart in a moment. Looks like you made it just in time. Please take your seats."

They rushed to their flight, but Joseph hesitated.

"What's up?"

Everything was so new. They'd left home, ridden to the city, traversed the airport's security, and were about to fly to a strange new location far from their families.

He sighed and shook his head. "It's nothing. We made it through, right? I guess we're on our way."

They boarded. There was no turning back now.

"This is the coolest thing ever. What if my page views are climbing as we speak? I could be a celebrity right now and not even know it! I like this Ken guy—he's got good taste in talent."

"His name is Ben. Professor Benjamin Thessit."

Eric shrugged. "I didn't know you needed a PhD to watch people play games, but whatever."

The plane was surprisingly vacant, and only a few other passengers joined them. One among them, a man in a black suit and shaded lenses, briefly shifted his attention to them before looking away. The whole situation made Joseph uneasy. He sat by the window while Eric rummaged through his bag.

"Did you just steal the window seat?"

"Hah, yeah. You missed your chance. You can have it on the way back."

Eric wasn't willing to argue. He agreed, put his bag in the upper storage bin, and sat down with a heavy drop.

The pilot came through on the intercom.

"Good evening. Welcome to our nonstop flight to the Murean Islands. The plane will take off shortly. All electronic equipment must be turned off or set to airplane mode, and your seatbelts must remain in use until the plane has reached cruising altitude. We hope you enjoy this sixteen-hour flight over sparkling oceans and spectacular cities."

Eric sat up. "A sixteen-hour flight? What are we supposed to do? I'll die of boredom."

"You brought enough entertainment to satisfy an entire classroom. How can you get bored?"

"I can only listen to the same music, play the same games, and watch the same movies for so long. I can't do that kind of thing. I'm not even including battery power."

"Relax, Eric. You'll be fine."

Eric groaned and fell back into his seat.

The engines rumbled as the plane rolled down the runway and into position. It traveled forward and picked up speed as the nose lifted to greet the night sky.

Eric gripped the sides of his seat. With one final jolt, they were airborne. Joseph watched out the window at the buildings and streets below as they shrank into the distance. The details grew less apparent, until only the shimmering lights were visible.

As they continued to climb, clouds blocked the presentation, so Joseph sat back to relax. He glanced at Eric, who still clenched his eyes shut. Smirking, Joseph reached over and tapped him on the shoulder.

Eric jerked and opened his eyes.

"What happened to the fearless celebrity known as Mr. Castis?" Joseph joked.

Eric tried to brush off the reaction and cleared his throat. "Hah...you uh, totally fell for it. I guess my acting is getting better."

In mock admiration, Joseph teased. "Yeah, I really thought you were scared for a moment."

"The point is, we're on our way to a wonderful vacation in a beautiful paradise far, far away, with private access to the game of the year while it's in development. And you thought I was worried. Pffft...yeah right."

The plane's warning lights blinked off and Eric put on his headphones.

With little else to do, Joseph brought out the book he'd packed. The pages flew by as he disappeared deep into the science fiction worlds of the novel. Strange stories of magical space odysseys dotted his tired mind with each completed chapter. However, it wasn't long until the events of their trip started to take their toll. Unable to keep himself awake, he drifted off.

When he opened his eyes, Joseph was in his own bed at home.

He rose and went to the window. The full moon was out, and it was like nothing had changed. There was no plane, there were no tickets, and his belongings all appeared to be back in place.

He scratched his head as he pondered the situation. "Was it only a dream?"

There was a knock on his bedroom door, so he turned to open it. The moment he did, complete darkness surrounded him. It was as if he'd released a shadowy mist that reached out and devoured the room.

Joseph ran, shouting out into the black void, hoping anyone would answer him. Turning in every direction, he panicked, though nothing was there. Then a voice called to him.

"Stop panicking and relax. It can't harm you."

It was the same female voice from the battlefield dream.

41

"This isn't some kind of game, so I hope you take it more seriously once you arrive. I'm not sure what Kilgan is planning, but I hope he knows what he's doing. I hope you know what you're doing as well. Now wake up!"

Something was shoved against his back and another voice broke the darkness.

"Oh wow, check this out!"

"W-what?"

"We just got over the ocean and you have to see! It's incredible!"

Joseph's mind came back to him, but he didn't open his eyes right away. What he thought was real had been nothing but a dream, and what he thought had been a dream was the reality. He turned his head and opened his eyes. Below them lay the vast ocean. The reflection of stars sparkled along the water's surface like thousands of diamonds in the night. Painted clouds floated gently over the picture. It helped him relax.

"How long was I asleep?"

"Maybe two hours. You started to jerk around like you were having a nightmare. Good thing I saved you, huh?"

Joseph put a hand on his head to collect his thoughts. "It was strange. You remember the dream I told you about the other day?"

Eric nodded, appearing to half pay attention.

"It felt like it was real. There was this girl and—"

"Hold that thought! It looks like meal time."

Joseph forgot about it and pulled out his tray. Maybe a meal would help keep his energy floating. He felt like he'd run a marathon. Despite his best efforts, Joseph drifted back into slumber a few minutes after they had finished eating.

There were no dreams to greet him this time.

He woke sometime later. Everyone on the plane, including Eric, now snored in their seats. All the window shades were closed except his. Having little else to do, he opened the book he'd started reading earlier.

He lost all track of time to his reading, and he'd consumed more than half the book before Eric woke up. Joseph looked out the window. A large, crescent-shaped mass of land rose in the distance, dotted by many smaller islands trailing the water's surface. In full view, the sun hovered near the beautiful landscape. Joseph put away his book and tapped Eric on the shoulder.

"I think we're almost there."

Eric opened his eyes and grunted before turning back over in his chair. "Ugh, I won't let Clyde win. There's still two hours left for the competition, isn't there?"

"It already ended. You lost."

Eric didn't respond at first, but then he bent forward and stretched his arms before leaning to look out the window.

He shoved Joseph's face to the side and into the glass. "Holy crap! Look at that."

The pilot's voice soon overcame Eric's tone.

"Good evening. This is your captain speaking. In a moment we'll be approaching our destination, and it is necessary for you to fasten your seatbelts while we make the decent to the airport. We hope you enjoyed your flight on International Skyline."

Eric pulled away from the window. "Did you hear that? We're here. We're actually here! I can't wait to get off this plane and check it out. Oh man, this is so cool!"

A few of the other passengers glanced at Eric's excited display.

"That's great." Joseph's voice was muffled. Eric's hand still held his face against the window. "Think you could move so I can breathe again?"

"Oh, yeah. Sure thing."

His face freed, Joseph gazed out the window as the plane descended. He could now make out each separate building, as well as some enormous pools for the resort hotels. Joseph hastily packed the book and the few other things he'd used back into his bag and waited for their flight to land. After a rough touch-down on the runway, they'd arrived.

Eric nearly bounced as he stood. "I can't wait to explore the city. I don't know about you, but my legs are begging to get out and explore, and these hands are dying to get a few rounds of game-time. What should we check out first?"

"We need to find Professor Benjamin Thessit to figure out the arrangements. I'm not sure how any of this is supposed to work."

Joseph had taken money with him, and Eric must have as well, but he worried about how far it would take them.

Eric grabbed his backpack from the top storage bin and started pushing his way between everyone. "Our island paradise is waiting."

Joseph waited until things calmed before making his way out. When he set foot into the airport, he quickly searched for Eric. He found his partner in crime checking out one of the food shops.

Joseph chuckled. "Where do you put all of that? We just ate."

"Some people's eyes are bigger than their stomachs. My stomach is bigger than my eyes." Eric opened the sandwich. "I haven't eaten anything for a few hours and I'm starving. Good thing they accept American money here. You want some? It's some kind of local dish! Maka...Muah...something or other. Whatever, it's a fish sandwich!"

Fried bits and pieces of what appeared to be fish were oozing out from between the pieces of sweet bun.

Joseph smiled. "Uh, no thanks, Eric. I know how hungry you are."

Eric threw the bag over his shoulder and followed Joseph as they strolled down the airport's walkways.

It felt like a blast of fire scorched right across his face when they found the exit.

"Phew, someone's bringing the heat," Eric said and set his stuff down to stretch. "I didn't know it would be this hot here. Should have worn shorts."

"You've always wanted to go on a tropical vacation. Beaches aren't usually cold," Joseph joked.

"It's not that. I just didn't know I should have brought sunscreen and shades!"

"We'll check out stores once we take care of business."

Joseph turned, only to collide with a figure that had been standing behind them. He tumbled back from the surprise.

"Hey, sorry about that! I suppose I shouldn't have been standing so close, you know?" a voice responded.

Joseph looked up to see a young man wearing a straw hat with an aqua band, a tie-dyed t-shirt, baggy brown shorts, and a pair of sandals.

"Need a hand?"

Joseph accepted his offer and dusted the sand off his clothes. He was about Joseph's height, with bronze skin.

He handed Joseph his bag. "Hey, you two must be new to this isle."

"Is it that obvious?" asked Eric.

"It's the way you're dressed," he replied with a considerate chuckle. "Most tourists forget to dress for the trip, so they stand out, you know? We don't get too many new faces, so it's easy to point out the fresh swimmers." He pointed to Eric's sandwich. "Gotta say, though, most tourists don't go for the Maku'ah Mawah on their first day. You must have a real taste for fried fish innards."

Eric paused in the middle of his next bite. "I...what..."

"Maku'ah Mawah is a local favorite here, on the Murean chain. Its base is taken from the innards of a fresh local fish that are served up fried and sweet. Don't usually see first timers diving in so eagerly."

Joseph tried not to laugh as Eric's face seemed to turn green. His friend took off for the nearest trash can without a single word.

"It's nice to meet you..." Joseph paused, not knowing the name of their new companion.

"Hey, James Le'ah Carnella is the name, but friends and family call me Jam. I have a bit of the music in me, you know? And you're Joseph Erift." He reached out, grabbed Joseph's hand, and eagerly shook it.

"How did you know? Are you part of the gaming presentation?"

"Gaming presentation?" Jam cocked his head. "Hey, you must mean Professor Thessit. He asked if I could show you and your friend around the isle while he prepares for your arrival."

"You know him?" Eric asked once he returned. His sandwich was nowhere to be seen.

"Hey, the man's a respected researcher around these parts. He told me to make sure you were shown the way. He said you'd be fish out of water."

"The man has good tastes. That's why I'm here."

Jam smiled and took off his hat to wipe back his black hair. "He keeps to his research, you know? He's a good soul, though."

"What kind of research?" asked Joseph.

46

"Hey, you should ask him when we get there, you know?"

Jam picked up the pace and motioned for Joseph and Eric to follow.

"Since you already know my name," Joseph pointed to Eric as they followed. "this is—"

"Hey, Eric Castis, right?"

"Bit of a know-it-all, isn't he?" Eric whispered.

Jam faced them while they walked. "I'm just the messenger, here to show you what's what, you know?"

A loud rumbling filled the air, causing them to stop. Joseph looked up just as a large ship soared over the tall buildings. A massive red balloon swayed above the wooden body, while loud propellers carried it over the city. As it zoomed over them, a rush of wind followed in its wake and blew through the streets as it passed. The giant structure creaked and turned around the back of a large hotel before it headed out over the ocean.

Eric tried to capture it on his phone. "Whoa...that looked just like an airship. I wonder if they sell tickets to ride it!"

It faded into the distance, and Joseph turned back to Jam. "Is that common here?"

Jam laughed. "Hey, looks like someone is testing out the Professor's inventions for him, you know?"

A car horn broke their trance, forcing them to keep moving.

The island city was busy. The beach was packed, the streets were full, and the shops were plentiful and crowded with shoppers. Palm trees and summer skies were all capped by a sparkling ocean. Tropical island music, complete with the chime of steel drums, filled the air.

"So Jam, do you watch game videos online? I'm starting to become a thing on the internet. You might have heard of Eric *Superstar* Castis. I've covered a lot of games, you know."

Joseph chuckled.

"Hey, I don't do a lot of stuff online. I don't even own a phone, you know?"

"Off topic, but do you know anything about this?" Joseph took the envelope from his pocket and handed it to Jam.

After he finished, Jam gave it back to Joseph with a soft hum.

Joseph put it away. "Something wrong?"

"Hey, there are a couple things I haven't filled you in on." Jam shook his head. "I don't think it's my place to tell you, though, you know?"

"Maybe he's a mad scientist calling people in from around the world to harvest body parts! And he's gonna cut off our heads and stick them on a robot for research."

Joseph and Jam blinked at Eric's suggestion.

"What? You never know."

"Hey, it's nothing like that. He's just passionate. It's nothing you need to worry about. There's nothing wrong with a man who loves his work, you know?"

Joseph found little comfort in the island resident's words. Even if their friendly greeting was more than he had expected, it did little to resolve their situation.

"Tell us more about yourself," Joseph asked their new guide.

Jam tipped his hat. "What do you want to know?"

"Do you live here?" asked Eric.

"I live in Hawaii with my parents, but they thought it would be good for me to come here during the summer and work at my aunt's shop. Can never have too much experience, you know? It's like my own private invitation. Even with seventeen years' experience, I still have a long road to travel."

While Eric and Jam took in their discussion, Joseph looked down the road. A massive building caught his attention, which had been drawn by the sun's reflection off its gleaming surface. With the exception of the tall hotels that dotted the city, it had to be one of the most impressive structures on the entire island.

"Hey, no worries about walking, you know? The city offers lots of different transport services. You two are rather lucky for getting the chance to visit. It's not an easy task to accomplish, you know?"

"I hope they have jet skis!" Eric grinned as he snapped some photos with his phone.

Joseph raised an eyebrow. The busy city contrasted with Jam's comment about their luck at being able to visit.

They continued down the sandy streets as Jam occasionally pointed out important places and Eric kept asking him questions about the island and what they'd be doing.

"Here we are." Jam pointed to a building.

It was the same structure Joseph had spotted from across the beach during their tour. The only difference was that, up close, the building looked as if it had suffered substantial damage. Whether it was from a natural disaster or a manmade one was hard to tell.

"Jeez, what a dump. Where's the gaming center?"

"It looked more impressive from a distance. What happened here?"

"Hey, no worries," Jam said with a wave. "The professor is into some heavy research. There's bound to be a few hiccups now and then. Just give him a chance. Either way, I need to head back. I have some things to take care of at the shop."

"That's it? You're just going to leave us here?"

"The least you could do is introduce us," said Joseph.

"Hey, you two will be just fine! It sounds like you're here for a great thing, so just give it a chance, you know? Get on the board and follow the surf. We'll catch up later!"

Jam gave his farewell and made his way back down the long cobbled pathway into the city.

Joseph sighed as he rubbed the back of his neck, glancing at Eric.

"At least he didn't charge us."

Joseph smiled and grabbed his things. "That's good. We don't have much money."

"I wonder if they'll have a convention setup. I'd love to buy some cool merch."

They faced a large entry. The metal frame was bent and slightly charred. Joseph hesitated to knock. Everything inside the letter had been true so far, and now he faced its source.

The moment of truth was upon them. With a steady grasp, Joseph raised his hand and pounded on the door.

CHAPTER FOUR

AN ENCOUNTER TO REMEMBER

Joseph whistled as they waited but there was no answer.

Eric seemed restless as he threw his bag over his shoulder before circling around. "I'm gonna go look for the demo building. You wanna come?"

He tried to walk away, but Joseph grabbed his shirt to keep him in place. "We're not going anywhere until we see this guy. He's in charge, so he'll know what's going on." Joseph raised his fist and knocked on the door again. This time his effort was rewarded.

A bellowing explosion rattled the building and the surrounding ground. Joseph and Eric jumped away as the doors flew open and a coughing figure hurried into the open with smoke trailing behind him.

"My goodness! That was *much* more power than I anticipated! I didn't know that amount of electrical output into those crystals could cause such a reaction."

He was a man slightly taller than Joseph. A pair of large goggles covered his face, and thick dust coated his brown and gray hair. It had been blown upright and singed on one side. He fumbled around in the pockets of his dirty white lab coat to pull out a cloth to wipe his face clean. Joseph kept his eyes locked on the man, unable even to tell if he glanced at them.

"Where in the world does he"—he removed the goggles and blinked—"well, bless my soul." His humble brown eyes carefully studied their features as he walked rings around them. "You must be Joseph Erift!" He pointed to Eric. "And you must be Eric Castis! Wonderful to see you have decided to take this first step on your own."

Eric cringed. "I'm starting to regret that choice."

"I trust you made your flight with relative ease? I made sure the proper arrangements were in order while I monitored your travel."

Joseph had a feeling this was the man who got them through airport security. However, neither he nor Eric said anything right away; they simply gazed at this odd older gentleman. Joseph cocked an eyebrow as the man seemed to notice his own disheveled appearance.

"Oh, goodness, forgive me. I was in the back trying to...well, you can't always expect tests to run smoothly. Sometimes things just blow up!" The man gestured to the inside of the building. "Please, do come inside."

He and Eric exchanged confused looks before they followed him in. The smoke cleared as the man opened some windows. The first room was littered with tables covered in glass beakers bubbling over with strange, glowing liquids. Boxes lay piled up on the floor, and odd contraptions of all sorts had been placed in random points of the room. Every bit of the building was brilliantly illuminated by the open glass ceiling to create a bright yet odd atmosphere. It wasn't the first place someone would think of for a game presentation.

They stopped by one of the large tables in the back. The strange researcher looked at the items on it before wiping them onto the floor, filling the air with the crashing sounds of shattering glass. After cleaning his sleeve, he walked behind the table and faced them, presenting each with a cup of coffee poured from a nearby pot.

"Would either of you boys like a cup of coffee?"

They both shook their heads.

"Well, I always have some at the ready should you change your minds. Now then….Joseph…Eric. First, let me welcome you to the wonderful southern Pacific islands of Murean and to my modest research labs." He threw his arms into the air as the contents of his mug splashed. "I am Professor Benjamin Thessit, but you may refer to me however you please."

Words still didn't form for Joseph and Eric seemed equally confused by this eccentric man. Joseph glanced at the dirty, overcrowded room. Did the man hate cleaning, or was he too busy?

"Is something wrong?"

"Yeah, we're a little confused right now. How did you know who we were and where we lived? I don't know why something like this has to be such a secret." Joseph pulled the game disc from his pocket. "We're here for a game presentation, aren't we?"

"Ah yes; about that—I suppose I have some explaining to do."

Eric stepped forward. "Got that right! I don't see any computers or controllers, so what gives? Obviously you've seen my talents on the internet. You got us some sweet game time. So as long as you hook us up, I'll let this all slide."

The man shot Eric a wry smile. "I'll get to that soon enough. It has been a very long day." The professor wiped more dirt from his face. "Before I explain, I need to clear up a few other things, then I can answer your inquiries. I'm sure you have many, and I will address each as best as I can."

"We're listening."

Joseph leaned back in a chair to put his feet on the table.

Eric copied Joseph's pose. "Yeah, let's hear it."

He nodded. "Right, I'll tell you what I can for the time being. Unfortunately, a wrench has been thrown into today's preparations."

Eric groaned. "So we don't get to play today?"

"Yes...about that. You see, there is more going on here." Professor Ben cleared his throat. "While I do intend to show you a grand demonstration that will certainly impress you, I regret that my statement was somewhat false. While the disc I sent you was real, there's no full demonstration for it in my possession at this time."

Joseph sighed. "So this is all a setup? What about the website we found?"

"No way...please tell me you're just messing with us for some sort of comedy video." Eric slumped where he sat. "All right, where's the camera? Very funny, guys. The show's over!"

"I dislike saying this, but I'm afraid it was all part of my attempt to bring you here. The website is a fake I created myself. I needed evidence to support my claim. So, please, give me time to explain. If you're not fully convinced of the predicament after I elaborate on the scenario, you need not concern yourselves any further. You can walk away without another word."

Joseph relaxed into his seat. It wouldn't hurt to hear the explanation. It wasn't like they had many options.

Eric rested his chin on his hand.

Professor Ben walked nearby. "Now then."

Joseph tried to eye the professor's movements, but as he moved behind them, he rapidly reached out and plucked a hair from Joseph's head. He did the same as he walked by Eric.

Eric jumped to his feet and threw out his fists. "The hell? What's your problem?"

Joseph remained silent and moved his hair back into place. He kept glancing at the shattered clock on the wall. It felt like time had fallen still.

"There's no need for concern. I only pulled the single hair I required." Professor Ben showed his hand to Eric.

He held a small bundle of Eric's hair between his fingers.

"Oh, goodness...I'm truly sorry. Here, I only need one of these."

Eric huffed as he clenched them tightly. "Gee, thanks! Now where's the glue?"

Professor Ben didn't seem to understand Eric's sarcasm as he pulled a small, suspiciously glue-like bottle from his desk.

Eric ignored the offering and rolled his eyes before he tossed the hair into a nearby garbage can.

"What was that about?" asked Joseph.

"That shall be a topic for another time."

After producing two small bottles, he placed one hair in each before labeling them and putting them in his pocket. He then took a hearty swig of his coffee.

"Can you please explain what's going on?"

Eric gave him a stern look. "I demand a warning before you start drawing blood. We were *supposed* to be playing video games, not playing lab rats."

The professor frowned. "I was wrong to falsify the topic for your journey, and I will make it up to both of you. Tomorrow morning we can move right into my reasons for doing this."

The man poured himself another cup of coffee and took a sip.

Professor Ben's lack of focus made Joseph's head hurt. He was prepared to speak up, but Eric beat him to it.

"So, there's no game and now you're pushing us off? Where are we supposed to go until then? Do you want us to sleep on a bench like bums? No, I demand satisfaction. This is unacceptable!"

"Don't worry about that." Professor Ben reached into his coat pocket and offered them a paper with a warm smile. "There will be no bumming on the beach. I have booked you a room in the Murean Grand Hotel for the duration of your stay."

Joseph took the slip—a fully paid registration.

His friend was quick to snatch the paper as his enthusiasm returned. "Huh, well it's not *Call of Echoes 3*, but I guess staying in a luxury grand hotel at a tropical paradise will uh…have to do." His ever-present smile had returned.

"Please think of it as an apology for not being straightforward about why I brought you here. Just give that to the clerk at the front desk, and you should be all set. I promise my reasons for this whole charade will be crystal clear to you in the morning. I would elaborate on the missing pieces at this very moment were I not so pressed for time. Another event requires my attention."

Eric headed for the door. "You suck for lying to us, but whatever. We have a room to check out. I'll see ya in the morning, doc!"

Eric waved goodbye and walked outside.

Joseph went to follow. However, the professor stopped him.

"I want you and Eric to get a good night's sleep. You're going to need it for tomorrow." Professor Ben patted him on the shoulder and gave Joseph a broad, friendly smile. "Be sure to enjoy your stay."

With that, the professor leisurely walked away, and disappeared into the other room.

Joseph didn't like the way the man spoke. It was like there was some underlying meaning in those words. He didn't know what to expect, so far from home in a bizarre world filled with even more colorful characters and strange questions. They didn't need to play a video game; it felt like they were living one.

"Just like a fantasy." He walked out the door and back into the tropical evening.

"Hey, we're over here," Jam called from where he and Eric stood.

"I was just telling Jam how everything was a lie."

"Hey, sorry I didn't let you in on the situation. I was asked by Professor Thessit to wait until he was finished before I show you the hotel, you know? It won't take long. How about a quick tour around the boardwalk? It has the best sights and shops around."

Jam led the way. The cobble path quickly detoured onto the beach and smooth seaside streets.

"This is the Murean Boardwalk," Jam said as he lifted his arms. "Around here you'll find plenty of good places to eat, great souvenirs—lots of interesting things to do. Jet skiing, surfing lying around on the beach—this is the place to hang, you know?"

They stopped now and then to check out the stores and other offerings. Beyond the horizon, the setting sun painted the sky in a beautiful, fiery violet. Then a familiar sound emerged, and Joseph stopped dead in his tracks. He hoped he was hearing things.

Eric and Jam also stopped and flashed him a curious stare.

"What's up? You look like you've been shot."

"I thought I heard a voice. It sounded familiar, and not in a good way."

"Only voice I hear is my stomach telling me it's meal time. We were lied to and tricked into a tropical vacation. Other than being hungry, I'd say we're breaking even at this point."

He motioned for Eric to be quiet so he could listen between the bustling crowds.

Eric complied, and his eyes widened. "No way…"

"You heard it too, huh?"

"Hey, what are you two talking about?"

A familiar figure walked in the distance. Joseph shook his head in disbelief, yet he wasn't entirely surprised. How had they ended up at the same vacation resort as Clyde Foristen?

"Why is he here?" Eric spoke through gritted teeth.

"This must be the vacation Clyde was talking about. Didn't he mention streaming that game? What if he got the same letter from Professor Ben?"

"No way! First we don't get to play it, and now this?" Eric clenched his hands. "I swear if that's what's going on, I'm gonna give Ben a piece of my mind!"

"Hey, are you two talking about a friend or foe? Don't leave me in the dark, you know?"

Joseph pointed. "See that blonde guy with the goofy shirt and shorts?"

Jam squinted and folded his arms. "Hey, that's strange. The professor didn't say you two were bringing a friend."

"The day I call him a friend is the day I burn my online channel to the ground." Eric spat on the ground and sneered. "That's Clyde Foristen, professional snob and all time annoyance."

"You aren't on good terms with one another?"

"Clyde's from our hometown and comes from a wealthy family. He likes to flaunt it. Not sure if he does it on purpose or if he's just unaware he's doing it."

Eric cracked his knuckles. "I'm getting to the bottom of this."

"Wait, if Clyde sees us, he'll—"

His friend was already on his way to face Clyde, and Jam was right behind him.

Joseph took a step forward, but the atmosphere seemed to shift, as if time had slowed around him.

"Hm hm hm, you seem to have a talent for running into interesting characters, don't you?"

Another familiar sight met him—the stranger he'd encountered at school. His presence confirmed Joseph probably did see him at the airport. He stared in disbelief. This time the man presented himself in a dark green shirt with tan shorts instead of the casual suit from before.

"Ah, yes, you seem perplexed by my presence. I can tell by that curious look in your eyes."

The crowds around him moved in slow motion while a hazy silver light roamed between the bodies.

"What's happening? Are you doing this?"

"Don't worry. It is a simple Slow spell and it'll fade away momentarily. I desired a word with you."

"A slow...spell?" Joseph shook his head. "I knew it...this really is a dream."

The man took a bite from the dripping bar of ice cream in his hand. Some dribbled into his white beard. "What a delightful creation this is. This iced cream is truly remarkable." His amusement at the treat faded at Joseph's confused expression. "Fear not, for this is no dream. Have you made much progress in that story of yours?"

"No I...what does that have to do with anything?"

The man smiled. "You remind me of an old acquaintance when he was your age. He was full of determination, but doubt always seemed to plague him. He forgot that sometimes it's better to follow the flow of fate rather than to fight its current. While we all wish to carve our own way, it can never hurt to embrace what is given to us. Our minds are always best kept open."

Joseph frowned. "I have no idea what you're talking about. Are you part of Professor Ben's event?"

A soft smile overtook the man's face. "Do excuse the ramblings of an old man. Once again I find myself lost in recollections of things long since passed. I simply wish to inform you that tomorrow will be an...*interesting* day. However, I'm afraid I've grown weary from using that spell. Hopefully, we'll see one another again once I've regained my energy." He took another bite of the frozen treat before pointing at something behind Joseph.

The silvery light started to fade as the movement of time returned to normal. When he turned around, the man was gone, leaving Joseph speechless.

Eric and Jam had approached Clyde, so he hurried to join them.

Clyde nearly fell over when he saw them. "This isn't possible! What are *you* doing here?" Clyde pointed a trembling finger at Eric's face. "One of you better start explaining!"

"Move that finger before I put it somewhere you won't like," Eric threatened.

Clyde frowned as he gritted his teeth and lowered the offending digit.

"None of your business, Clyde," Joseph calmly replied. It wouldn't do any good to feed the fire of Clyde and Eric's conflict.

Clyde's tone shifted. "Hmph, tell me something, Joseph—how could you afford a trip to this lovely paradise? I know your parents can't afford such a lavish vacation, and if I recall, neither of you work." He tilted his head and narrowed his eyes. "How do you even know about this place?"

"We work plenty. We work our awesome brains playing video games, while all you work is your mouth! You know what else? You see that big building out there? Oh yeah, that's totally where we're staying!" Eric crossed his arms and grinned.

Joseph winced, but it was too late now.

Clyde's mouth dropped open and his eyes widened like a scorned puppy's. "You two are staying at one of the finest, most expensive hotels in the world?" He shook his head. "I refuse to believe it."

"It's true, and it's totally free! Is that jealousy I see, Clyde? Is someone jealous he's not the most impressive person around anymore?"

Clyde lowered his head and kept it there for a quiet second before he began to laugh.

Eric's smile faded. "Wait, why are you laughing? That's not supposed to be funny."

"Hah...why am I worrying about something as stupid as you two being here? It's only a poor choice of timing. You might have received some awfully good charity, but that doesn't matter." Clyde ran a hand through his hair. "You still can't hold a candle to my flame."

"You might be a candle, but I'm as cool as the ocean. You hear that?" Eric pointed to the ocean. "Is that tsunami coming for you, Clyde?"

"Hey, I can see what you mean," Jam whispered to Joseph. "A clam with a mouth big enough to swallow a whale, you know?"

"Hm? And who might you be?" Clyde demanded.

"James Le'ah Carnella," Jam formally introduced himself as he reverted back to his friendly attitude. "Allow me to welcome you to—"

"Save your breath, island meat. I don't need to hear your welcoming speech." Clyde shifted his focus to Joseph. "I know there's something going on here. You can't hide it from me, so if I were you, I'd watch your backs. Take one step out of line, and I'll be the first to know. This isn't a place where you can walk around unnoticed."

Clyde turned around, nearly losing his footing as he stormed off and faded into the crowds.

Joseph looked down and let out a sigh of relief.

"Oh, I'm so scared!" Eric mocked once Clyde left. "What are you, a spy?"

"He's just messing with us, Eric."

"Tch. I wouldn't be surprised. I bet he hacks all those video games. Wait, no—that's giving him too much credit."

"Hey, now that we got that out of our systems, how about we get you two to the hotel, you know?"

"Sorry about that. It's been a long day," replied Joseph.

"Hey, it's all good. Let's get you two settled into your home away from home. We can catch up on all the things we missed some other time!"

"Sounds good to me!" Eric rejoiced.

Joseph nodded, and they resumed their trek to the hotel. They'd already left most of the boardwalk and were now on the shore of the beach. With each step, their shoes sank into the sparkling sand, and Jam pointed out the large structure in the distance.

"Hey, there you have it," Jam said as they walked onto the street. "The Murean Grand Hotel is the prime estate of the Murean Islands. You won't find a nicer resort!"

"Pinch me…or I might start crying…"

Eric's voice drifted off, and his expression made him appear lost in a dreamy state.

"Hey, that's the last thing I want, unless it's tears of joy, you know?"

Joseph smiled. Jam and Eric's optimism nearly made him forget the unpleasant encounter with Clyde.

They approached the large building and climbed the front stairs. The hotel's interior proved even more astonishing than the outside. It was full of elegant furniture, and graceful pictures decorated the finely designed walls. A glamorous crystal chandelier over the central fountain accented the grand entrance.

Joseph blinked as Jam waved his hand back and forth past their astonished faces.

"Hey, if you two are done admiring the scenery, I best get going."

"Yeah, thanks for the help," replied Joseph.

"Anytime you need anything, just ask the professor for me and I'll be in touch, you know?" He walked away with a cheerful wave.

Eric was still staring off into space. Joseph snapped his fingers to get his attention. "Come on, let's get our room."

"Oh yeah, that's right."

When they got to the front desk, Joseph set his stuff down and pulled the paper out. The man at the counter watched curiously as Joseph unfolded the parchment, then offered it to him.

"A man by the name Professor Benjamin Thessit told us to give this to you. He said everything should be taken care of."

The desk clerk took the paper and examined it. When he was done, he let out a slight chuckle before tossing it in the trash.

Joseph hesitated to breathe. "Is everything okay?"

"Of course," the clerk said as he handed Joseph a set of keycards. "The professor is always one to give such amazing entertainment. You'll find your room on the seventh floor. We hope you enjoy your stay."

Joseph picked up his bag and walked over to Eric, who was preoccupied with deciding what he wanted from a vending machine near the restrooms. After making a choice, Eric took out a candy bar from the bottom of the machine.

"Whoa!" his friend said as he jumped back. "Don't scare me like that."

"Had to get the taste of fish guts out of your mouth?" Joseph teased as Eric tore into the wrapper.

He took a bite. "Don't remind me."

"You seemed to like it before Jam told you what it was." Joseph smiled and held out one of the keys. "Anyway, we got our room."

Joseph was excited, but he did his best to contain it as the elevator ascended to the seventh floor. His smile was obvious by the time they stopped and the doors opened. Eric bounced as he walked halfway down one side of the hallway, looked around the corner, and ran back down the other end.

"This way!"

"The number on the key says 742!"

Joseph refused to run after him. He was too tired and his mind was too jumbled by recent events. He couldn't remember the last time he felt so wiped out, yet his legs kept moving, fueled by anticipation. When he looked up, Eric had already unlocked the door and pushed his way inside.

"Whoa. We just hit the jackpot!"

Joseph staggered into their room. Eric jolted by in a hurry and poured his frantic energy into the atmosphere.

"Look at the size of this TV, and check out the size of this bathroom! Look at these beds! They're huge!" Eric leapt onto the first bed and sighed. "So this is what it feels like to be rich. Yeah, I can see myself getting used to this."

"I can't believe Professor Ben paid for a suite."

Joseph dropped his bag and walked to the balcony.

"What's with the disappointed look?" his friend asked as he jumped up.

Joseph opened the sliding door to step outside.

"I'm fine. I'm just tired from all the traveling today. It's been a lot to take in, and I'm worn out."

Joseph placed both arms on the edge and gazed at the view. The sun was nestled right on the edge of the ocean as the brilliant gleam over the waves grew darker. He had to admit it was impressive, and the fresh air blowing across his face gave him a sense of relaxation amidst the changes.

"Wow..." Eric's voice was hushed as he gawked at the view. "I never thought I'd see something like this. It's seriously amazing, isn't it? It almost makes up for Ben messing with us. It still sucks we don't get to play the full game."

"Yeah, it doesn't seem real," Joseph whispered. "I'll probably wake up any minute now."

"If this is a dream, I never want it to end."

"I guess we'll have to see what happens next." Joseph tried to hide his tone with a laugh.

"All right, what's up? You always seem to get all weird and silent when something's bothering you."

Joseph tapped his finger on the balcony and closed his eyes.

"Don't you think any of this is a little...strange? We got a package in the mail, and the man who sent it just admitted it was all a lie. The whole situation is bothering me."

"Yeah, but look at this place. It's awesome!"

"You're not worried about what's *really* going on?"

His friend laughed. "Man, you and I are total opposites."

Joseph looked at him. "Like how?"

"I don't like to think about the consequences. If it's something I want to do, I do it. But you like to think about things so hard you give yourself headaches. You also have common sense to spare. It probably makes you the smarter one."

He flashed his friend a slight smile. Eric was trying his best.

"Weirdly, that makes me feel better...somehow."

"Good, since I was starting to make myself sick." He pretended to throw up as he finished his sentence but then waved to someone below. "Jam, look up here!"

Eric hurried back into the room.

"Where are you going?"

"I wanna see the nightlife. I bet there's all sorts of parties here! This way you can have some privacy to kick it and relax." Eric snapped his fingers and threw open the door.

"Well, just—"

His friend left before he could finish.

"Never mind."

Joseph looked back at the ocean. The great orb of fire was dwindling to a dull ember as the light ebbed along its watery grave. He couldn't help but think of their hometown and their families. What were they doing now? Were they searching for him? He was sure they were. Out of curiosity he pulled out his phone. There were many missed calls and texts, but he couldn't bring himself to look.

"I'm probably just overthinking everything. Even if we were lied to, there's no reason I shouldn't try and enjoy it...right?"

He strolled back inside and wandered into the bathroom. "Wow, this place really is amazing."

Being there made him feel like he'd taken on the role of a celebrity. He gazed at the large bathtub and the giant rooms. None of it came out of their own pockets. He took a towel off the shelf and ran some water to clean his face. His nerves more relaxed, he turned into the bedroom and threw his body onto the comforting surface of the second bed.

After bouncing a few times, he let his head down. "I wonder what Professor Ben will tell us tomorrow. I can't wait to hear his reason for all of this. It can't be too bad. Although..."

His mind wandered, seeking answers to every possible question he could come up with. Exhaustion finally made him drift into a heavy sleep.

The dreams were always waiting for him.

CHAPTER FIVE

RISKS AND REASONS

A massive sword met Joseph's blade and knocked him to the side. He turned, facing the figure of Sky Strafe, the hero character from the RPG game *Timeless Fantasy*.

"You're a novice. You could never hope to handle a real-life journey," Sky said with a toss of his spiky hair.

Joseph dodged the next swing but was knocked back by Sky's fire spell. A rapid barrage of lasers assaulted Joseph, forcing him to face the new onslaught. He blocked two of the blasts with his sword, but it was knocked from his hands by the next attack.

The Chief, another playable character from the space shooter *Haven's High*, approached. "You should have stuck to the video games, kid. Real life will get ya killed."

A kick to Joseph's back then sent him to the ground. He rolled and sprang back to his feet.

Rika, a main fighter from the *Alley Brawler* series, folded her arms. "You shouldn't have left home. What kind of training do you have? What were you thinking?"

Why were his favorite video game characters attacking him? Their insults echoed from all directions. He prepared for their next round of attacks, but a hooded figure dove into action to defend him.

"You need to stop with these crazy dreams—it makes it hard to talk to you!" She danced between each attack, knocking Sky off his feet with a swipe of her staff and then using it to reflect a laser back at The Chief. "I'll try again some other time. Get out of here and wake up already!"

He heeded her words and ran. He didn't get far as he bumped into Professor Ben, of all unlikely people.

The smiling researcher held up a pot and poured the contents into his mug. "Care for a cup of coffee?"

He kept pouring. The intense overflow washed under Joseph's feet and swept him away. He screamed, falling back into the flood of coffee as the world faded to white.

The sun was shining directly in his face, chasing away the nightly chill, but also blasting his eyes with its rays. He pulled the covers over his head to block the glare.

"That's a new one..."

There was nothing but the sound of crashing waves and the gentle laugh of the crowds below. The music of a steel drum band drifted up from the street and chased away the chaos of his dream. He felt more relaxed.

Until the phone on the nightstand underwent its chaotic gyrations, indicating a phone call. That broke the sense of harmony he'd only barely obtained. He rolled onto his side to answer.

"Hello?"

"Good morning. This is a wake up call for room 742. It is 8:00 a.m. Thank you for using the Murean Grand Hotel's automated phone service. Have a pleasant—"

Joseph hung up.

He stared at the ceiling, waiting to fully wake up. Then it hit him—he ran to the balcony, nearly tripping over the blankets. Everything was still there; he pinched his arm to be sure it was real.

"It wasn't just another dream. I'm still here."

He went back inside to change his clothing and straighten up.

"Did Eric ever come back?" Scratching his head, he was about to search when the harsh sound of snoring drifted in from the main room. Further inspection revealed the sleeping body of his friend lying face down in the cushions. It was an amusing sight, made even more so by the garland of fake flowers around his friend's neck.

He nudged Eric in the side with his foot. "Time to get up."

His friend didn't budge.

"Move it already," he said in a louder tone.

Eric covered his head with a pillow and mumbled. "Just give me a few more minutes. I was out all night...need more sleep...homework can wait..."

"Room service is here. They brought up some breakfast," Joseph whispered. "They have waffles, pancakes, bacon, and eggs."

"Can't it—wait, breakfast?!" Eric leapt off the couch. "Why didn't you tell..."

Joseph smirked as his friend realized where he was and what was happening.

"Oh, come on, that's just cruel."

"Haha...sorry. We can grab something on the way to Professor Ben's." Joseph strode to the door and motioned for Eric to follow.

After a flurry of activity as Eric rushed to get ready, they were out the door.

"How was the night life?"

"Aw man, you'd have loved it! I asked Jam what there was to do around here—parties, celebrations, that sort of thing. He said there's a party of some sort almost every night here during the summer, so I had him show me around. You should have seen it. I totally hit it off! I bet everyone here knows me as the party king by now."

"Nah, that's okay. You can have all the party scenes to yourself."

"Dude, seriously. Tonight I'm gonna show you the ropes for partying 101. It'll be crazy, it'll be fun and you're gonna love it."

Joseph smiled and shook his head as they stepped inside the elevator.

"Did Ben call and tell us to meet him?"

"No, but I have the strangest feeling he wants to see us." Joseph laughed.

When they exited the elevator and were on their way outside, a sign on their route grabbed Eric's attention.

"Hey, check this out!" Eric ran up to where it was posted by the door. "There's a breakfast buffet open from 7:00 a.m. to 11:00 a.m. for hotel guests only...that's totally us."

"We should probably grab something quicker and just eat it on the way."

"There you go again. You're trying to be all serious and don't want to do anything exciting. Have you forgotten we're on a vacation? Besides, *someone* owes me breakfast after this morning! Stop worrying and relax, man."

Eric had a point. It was really his fault, and he had promised a meal. "Okay. We'll grab some breakfast and then"—he pointed to the exit—"straight to Professor Ben's."

"Time to refuel!" Eric dashed for the guest dining room.

Eventually, the growling of Joseph's stomach reminded him he hadn't had anything to eat since they got to the island. He sighed. "No point in wasting a free meal."

After filling their stomachs, they left the dining room, Eric walking unsteadily behind Joseph in a lethargic waddle.

"Oh man...that was...so good." Eric burped as he followed Joseph out the door.

"I told you to slow down." Joseph chuckled.

"But it was so amazing!" Eric sat near the edge of the curb. "Food tastes so much better when it's expensive and you don't have to pay for it."

Joseph nodded. "Let's keep moving. We don't know how long this meeting will take."

Eric staggered to his feet, and they traveled toward the lab at the end of the city.

Joseph could only shake his head as every couple of steps Eric let out a belch and then a sigh of relief.

"Phew, that's better!" Eric said, and the pattern repeated itself the entire walk.

The city was full of activity. Bike riders zipped along near their sides, while cars slowly crawled down the main streets. Surfers had their boards out to catch the morning waves, and tourists of all sorts took in the morning sun. Soon, the smooth roads became cobbled paths, and they followed the line of palm trees to the outer laboratory.

"Finally." Eric gave one last burp. "Nothing like a morning walk after a good meal."

"Glad you got that out of your system." Joseph pounded his fist on the door. "The last thing we need is for you to belch the alphabet for Professor Ben."

Someone grumbled from the other side of the metal barrier.

"What is—?" Professor Ben started to shout, causing the pair to jump back. "Ah, yes. There you are. I was just about to phone the hotel again. Please, come on in!"

"I had a feeling that was you calling this morning," Joseph said as he and Eric followed him.

The professor laughed. "I must apologize. The moment you two left, I realized I'd forgotten to inform you about our meeting time." He took a sip from his mug and smiled. "My mind has been all over the place as of late, and I can't seem to locate it!"

"You should have found it before you lied to us." Eric sighed as they were led to a table.

Joseph elbowed his friend, making him groan.

"We're hoping you'll tell us what's going on," Joseph corrected as they took a seat. "Why did you do all this?"

"Rest assured, you will leave this room feeling entirely enlightened!"

Without another word, Professor Ben turned away to pull a pile of books off the shelf behind him. He carried them to the table and without warning dropped them with a loud smacking sound. Joseph glanced from the books to the professor and raised an eyebrow.

"Please, do open them," Professor Ben encouraged, pointing to the books.

He looked at Eric as they each opened one.

"Now look carefully at what is written inside," Professor Ben instructed.

"Didn't think there'd be homework on this trip," Eric muttered.

Joseph glanced over the first few pages. He flipped through them, unable to read a single word. The symbols and apparent sentences were entirely unrecognizable. Was it a different language or something else entirely?

"Do you see it? The writing?" the professor asked in an excited tone.

"I do, but I don't know what it is," Joseph admitted. "It's just a bunch of symbols."

"Yeah, I don't get it." Eric slammed the book shut and tossed it back onto the pile. "Had I known this was a test, I might have studied. Can we go to the beach?"

The professor sighed. "I expected as much."

"Do you know what they are?" asked Joseph.

"Of course I know what they are. I have devoted most of my life researching the information in these books!" Professor Ben shouted as he picked a book from the pile and flipped through its pages. "Every phrase within these pages has been my guide through this task. Every last sentence within is a deciphered mystery long lost to this world. They have been my life!"

"Yeah, cool. That sounds totally interesting." Eric yawned. "Really, I'm glad you're so excited, but unless these are plans for the next big game release, I don't see how this is a big deal."

"What do you *mean* it's not a big deal?" Professor Ben gasped as he threw the book onto the table.

"I uh...I just meant...ahah..." Eric's words faded away.

Joseph's expression was one of concern. "Maybe, if you explained it to us first, we could better understand it." He looked at his friend. "Right, Eric?"

"Yeah, something to that effect, I guess."

"Oh, yes, of course." The researcher cleared his throat. "I apologize. I didn't mean to get so angry. I am very...*passionate* about my research." He took in a deep breath and retrieved the book he'd dropped as he sat across from them. He poured another cup of coffee and sighed. "Joseph...Eric...what I'm about to tell you must never, and I mean *never*, be told to anyone else unless I instruct you to do so. Is that understood?" He gave each a somber look. "I am sorry to make such a large demand so soon after meeting, but if you require answers, this is the way it has to be."

Joseph shrugged. "I guess."

"Just get on with it." Eric rocked back and forth in his chair.

"Excellent." Professor Ben took in another slow breath as if to gather himself. "Each of these books I have collected during many years of exploration and study. They have come from many places across the globe, yet they all share one common denominator. You may not know this, but inside each of these tomes...I suppose I should just be blunt and cut right to the chase. What I'm trying to say is that my research revolves around one thing and one thing only. It involves a truly powerful and ancient force known as...Magic."

Joseph didn't know what to think, and it appeared Eric felt the same way. Those words had come out like the professor expected them to immediately believe them.

"Magic?" Joseph asked.

"There are unbelievable powers that have been hidden from the world for many, many years. Possibly even before records of time were kept. To put it more simply, my field of research is gathered around the study of this force and extracting it," Professor Ben explained. "My role is to gather the powers lying dormant in the artifacts of this existence and to process them through the means of science!"

Joseph cocked an eyebrow. "I don't get what you're saying."

"Magic is not some form of science-fiction, as this world would have us believe," Professor Ben desperately tried to clarify. "It's as clear as the sun in the sky or the ground beneath your feet."

"You're telling us you believe Magic is real."
Joseph pretended to understand. "And there are others like
you who do this sort of thing?"

"I am but one person in a massive organization that
functions on these levels. However, if you're asking if
others study Magic, the answer is mostly negative. No one
else outside this group knows of these discoveries or that
you two are even here. Do you have any questions or
comments before I continue?"

Joseph glanced at Eric. His friend shrugged before
rolling his finger in a circular motion next to his own head.
He then made a slight motion to the door.

With a nod, they stood.

"Wait, where are you going?" Professor Ben
appeared startled as he chased after them.

Joseph strode to the door. "I think we've heard
enough."

"Yeah, you must have used Magic to escape from
your straightjacket," Eric added.

Professor Ben lunged forward and slammed his
hand onto the door in front of them. He rushed to the latch
and locked it.

Joseph stumbled back, eyes wide. "What are you
doing?"

The professor grabbed him by the shoulders.

"Please, you can't leave! You haven't given me a
chance to finish explaining." He looked at Joseph and
shook him violently. "I need to elaborate on why you two
are here!"

"Let go of me!" Joseph tried to squirm free of the
man's grasp.

Professor Ben let go and got down on his knees.
"Please!" he begged. "Just give me an opportunity to show
you what I'm talking about, and if you still do not believe
me, I shall pay for you to stay here for a whole week and

give you anything you desire to buy on this island. You two are the *only* lead I have. You just need to give me a chance."

Joseph sighed as he looked down to the man. It seemed every fiber of the researcher's life hung on their acceptance of his plea. He turned to Eric. "What do you think?"

"I think he's crazy. But hey, if he's willing to pay for us to stay a full week, I don't see a problem. It beats going home empty-handed," Eric replied as he became distracted with his phone.

Joseph looked down at the professor, who appeared defeated. Though his words seemed like the rant of a madman, compassion tugged at him to see such desperation in the older man's eyes.

"Okay, we'll see what you have to say." Joseph made sure his stance on the matter was known. "I'm not ready to trust you...not yet. All of this sounds crazy."

Professor Ben jumped to his feet and grabbed Joseph in a tight hug. "Oh, thank you." His death grip tightened. "Thank you, thank you, thank you!"

Joseph struggled for air and tried to get away. "Could you...let me...go now?"

"Oh yes, of course." The professor shot him a joyful yet sheepish look. "I'm truly sorry."

The man released him and Joseph gasped. He brushed off the dirt Professor Ben had left on his shirt.

"If we decide to leave at any time, we're out of here." Joseph's look was stern.

"Yes, yes, I have not forgotten the deal. Now let me show you exactly what I've been talking about!" The older man rejoiced as he led them to the back room.

Joseph looked back at Eric and motioned for him to tag along, even if his friend's eyes never left the screen he was typing on.

"Are we going to get paid for this or something?" Eric asked.

"That all depends on how you view currency." The professor chuckled. "As far as I'm concerned, knowledge is the highest value of legal tender."

"That sounds like a no. Oh, look…Clyde's showing off the game *he* was able to get!" Eric grumbled as he showed Joseph the screen. "Can you believe him?"

Eric gasped as Professor Ben plucked the phone from his hand and dropped it into a small metal box.

"Dude, what are you doing?!"

The professor touched a button on the box, causing the small glowing container to shrink enough to fit into his coat pocket.

"Worry not—you can have it back once my demonstration is finished. I need your full attention," Professor Ben kindly replied.

"Seriously? Come on, just give it back. It isn't even paid off yet!"

The researcher showed no intention of answering the demand. He moved around a large shelf and pushed it to the side, revealing a large metal door. The man approached a keypad on the wall and entered a code. A pressure valve was released from the frame, allowing him to open the gate to another large room. He motioned for them to follow.

The walls were covered with the same kind of writing that Joseph had seen in the books. Every inch of the chamber was decorated in runes drawn with chalk. Below their feet, the floor had been etched and painted with pictures of planets and stars that all glowed in the light of the sun from the glass ceiling above.

Eric perked up as he looked around. "I think we just stepped into some kind of weird alternative universe."

A loud buzzing object flew across the room unexpectedly in their direction, crashing into a nearby wall before it exploded. Joseph and Eric leapt away as metal parts rained onto the floor.

"And this alternate universe is trying to kill me. What in the world was that?"

"Oops. I must have forgotten to turn that one off. That was one of my first attempts at a magical storage unit. The darn things cannot seem to handle the pressure. That was the third one this week."

Joseph shook his head as Professor Ben shoved the ruined parts to the side with a broom.

"Now if you would follow me, we have much to do."

Joseph glanced at the broken object on the floor. The machine was strange but by no means magical.

They followed Professor Ben through another door into a room that wasn't as big as the previous one, and it didn't appear to contain anything special. They stopped by the entry as the professor approached the corner and took a long wooden rod from its holder. The stick had a crystal at the top and stood as tall as the man wielding it. He moved it around in his hands before he looked at them.

"You two are about to be amazed. However"—the professor waved them back—"you might want to stand back a ways. I'm still trying to work on my aim."

"I can't wait to see this," Eric joked.

It looked like nothing more than a stick, leaving Joseph unimpressed. "What is that?"

"This is my very first successful attempt at Magical Containment!" Professor Ben boasted. "What you see in my hands is a real Magic Staff that combines the workings of ancient powers and brings them to life through the wonders of science. It took me years just to get this far with it."

"What does it do?" asked Eric.

The man smirked as he held the staff's clear crystal to his head and went into a state of deep concentration. They watched him, curiously at first, but more out of concern. Soon, the clear material of the stone glowed a bright red. A spiraling light danced along its surface, and Joseph could have sworn a soft chime sounded right as the top flashed.

Professor Ben held it out with a firm thrust. "Erif!" he shouted at the top of his lungs.

The glowing of the stone intensified as it burned hotly. Joseph looked onward, shocked when a fiery energy formed around the stone. Within seconds, it gathered into a ball and launched a seething orb of fire forward. The heated blast crashed into the wall and burst into a small explosion. The flames scattered along the metallic surface for a short while before vanishing into a cloud of dark smoke.

The professor twirled the staff, blew once on the tip, and tapped the bottom on the floor. "Now then, would you not say that was pretty far out?"

Eric ran to see it. "That was *so* bad-ass!"

Joseph couldn't believe what he'd seen, yet a part of him remained doubtful. "It shoots fire?"

The older man shrugged. "There are a few bugs to work out of the containment system." He looked over his creation. "Essentially, to answer your question, yes—it *does* create fire. However, the fire it manufactures is largely dependent on the one in control. We haven't been able to install more than one arcane energy at a time."

Joseph placed a hand to his chin. He couldn't judge it just yet. "Can I see it?"

"Oh, well...I suppose there is no harm. Just be careful."

He took the staff from the nervous hands of the professor and examined it.

"What are you looking for?" Eric frowned.

"I'm trying to see how this thing works." Joseph scanned over every detail. "For all we know, he might just be pressing switches and using a spark to set the fire."

"Hey, that's right. How do we know this isn't just another machine?" Eric faced the professor. "Someone already invented the flamethrower, Ben."

"You will find it is nothing of the sort," Professor Ben insisted.

Joseph looked at the staff one last time. An idea struck him. "I've got it."

"You finally understand what I have been trying to show you?" the man asked.

"Yeah, I know how to solve this mystery."

Eric clapped his hands together. "Awesome, so what did you find?"

Joseph held the staff firmly in his hands as he brought it into the proper position. Without giving Professor Ben a warning, he placed it at an angle against the floor and slammed his foot into the center of the staff.

CHAPTER SIX
MAGIC OF THE MIND

Joseph's kick snapped the wooden staff in two, drawing a gasp from its owner.

The older man panicked. "What are you doing?"

A flame-colored mist dispersed from the broken halves. Joseph grasped the two pieces and examined the broken ends.

There was nothing out of the ordinary.

Eric peered over his shoulder. "See anything?"

"No...there's nothing here."

He got another idea and smashed the crystal top into the ground, causing Professor Ben to shriek. Joseph sorted through the pieces, desperate to find anything to explain what they'd seen. He spotted an odd metallic item under the shattered crystal.

"Found it!" He showed Eric and the professor. "What do you call that?"

"That, Joseph"—Professor Ben sighed as he carefully took back the shattered remains of his creation— "would be the trigger used to ignite the Magic once held inside the crystal. Willpower and fantasy alone are not enough to create the flames you saw."

"So it's all fake?" asked Eric.

"That would be far from the truth."

Joseph folded his arms as Professor Ben cleaned the mess on the floor.

"Magic is a force long dormant in our world. However, science has proven a key factor in its revival. Better yet, science has slowly led me to the discovery of powers that may still be burning bright. We simply can't see them. Even so, Magic can't simply appear from nothing without a trigger, whether that trigger be human or artificial."

Joseph blinked. The professor made it seem like much more than a magic trick.

"I don't understand what you're trying to tell us."

"I had my reasons for bringing you here, but an unexpected visitor threw off my schedule." The man frowned. "At least he was not intent on destroying my research. Come to think of it, I suppose stealing it is just as bad." Professor Ben cleared his throat. "But I digress."

Joseph rubbed the back of his neck before running after the researcher. The statement made him curious.

"Wait, what did you mean by that?" Joseph pushed his way in front of the professor. "Who is this other person?"

Professor Ben gazed out the window of his lab. "That was the other thing I needed to explain to you." He turned around to face them. "There is a lot more going on than you might think. I'm afraid this is now much more than a simple show-and-tell demonstration."

They took a seat as he motioned to the table.

"Before you arrived, I had an encounter with someone else who I now wish could be present at this meeting."

"What happened?" asked Joseph.

"I was recently tasked with making a concentrate from a peculiar piece of magic stone once discovered during my younger days. If my studies were correct, that stone was formed from the essence of a dark soul. This other person, a misguided young gentleman, stole it before I could properly test it. He obsessed over the power it might bring to life. I should have known better by the look in his eyes, but I dismissed my apprehensions as warrantless. I was blind."

"Smooth move, Ben."

"You couldn't stop him?"

"I tried, but I was powerless. Perhaps part of me didn't want to stop him." He shook his head as he paced back and forth. "It was as if he knew exactly what was going on. He barely blinked an eye at my hypothetical explanations. Before I knew it, I woke on the floor, and the solution, along with a few of my other possessions, had vanished along with him."

Joseph sighed. "When did this happen?"

"It was yesterday. That was why I did not wish to engage the two of you then."

"Seriously, call the local authorities or something. You probably promised him a video game demo, too. In fact, I'm disappointed by the lack of gaming on this trip."

"I take full responsibility for luring you here. Yet you must believe that I called you for a much deeper purpose."

"But you don't know us, and we certainly didn't know you before we got here."

"The pieces of this puzzle are far more complex than you might think."

"Then tell us already!" Joseph slammed his fist on the table. A deep breath followed. He rarely lost his temper, but the professor's long-winded explanations were trying his patience.

Silence claimed the room.

Professor Ben nodded to Joseph's request. "Eric, if you would help Joseph move these tables to the side of the room. It's time I come clean."

Joseph and Eric each grabbed a table to clear an opening in the center where their host requested. When they were done, the professor approached a lever near the door and pulled it down.

"You might wish to relocate."

They changed their position as the lab shook. The floor in the center of the room shifted until the segmented plates left a massive hole. Professor Ben pressed more buttons on the panel near the lever, and a large metallic tower rose from the opening. Its peak nearly reached the ceiling, which had started to close above them until the room was left in near darkness. The transformation continued as joints extended from the tower's center and shifted into a pyramid-like shape. Once in place, the limbs rotated, picking up speed until a gentle hum produced a barrier of light.

The glowing shell rapidly expanded. It rushed past them, planting its illumination on the walls around the room, diminishing the darkness. The core of the device released rays of light, generating small spherical images all over. The runes on the walls reacted to the demonstration, glowing with an otherworldly light.

Eric ran around the room. "Wow, the graphics on this are better than the current consoles!"

"Indeed, it's quite beautiful but also dangerous," Professor Ben advised. "Those arms are spinning so fast that you would lose your hand in an instant!"

Eric quickly withdrew his arm and instead busied himself with taking pictures.

The professor gave Joseph a look of concern. "Are you okay?"

Joseph gazed into the rotating optics. The lights, the rays, and the machine in the center all seemed unreal. His voice came out so softly he barely heard his own words. "It's incredible."

"This is the device I used to locate you. I am glad you are impressed by my work."

Digital displays glimmered in every corner of the room. Some of the brilliant models floated right in front of him. They appeared as miniature planets that danced through an array of illuminated stars and galaxies. Small moons circled their hosts. It seemed real enough to touch, and when Joseph did, the object floated away from him. His eyes wandered the room, taking in the incredible exhibit.

"Those are planets, stars, and even entire galaxies," Professor Ben explained as he enhanced each of the features, bringing them to life. Every floating image gained new appearances and details. "They are taken from our own Milky Way and beyond. Every small point of the universe we have discovered can be viewed here, ready for me to study at any given time."

"I still don't understand how this helped you find us."

"It probably has one of those built-in internet maps," Eric whispered.

The older man chuckled. "Joseph, do you see that one over there? The one moving near the window?"

Joseph nodded once he located it.

"Go take a look at it."

He walked over to investigate the small green and blue orb. Flowing white clouds circled its surface. "It looks like Earth."

"Correct."

Able to direct the digital items with his hands, the professor grabbed the display of Earth and moved it to the center of the greater galactic image. Using his fingers, he enlarged the sphere until the details of their home planet came into view.

"This is pretty impressive, professor." Joseph moved his hand through the image, watching in awe as it fuzzed through. "How did you build all of this?"

"I have found many things in my years of travel and research, which is how I came across such amazing artifacts and knowledge of the old world. Combining ancient Magic with modern technology has produced what you see before you. Though, allow me to answer your previous question. As you are well aware, I can enlarge a specific object and investigate further into its finer details such as things living on the planet, if there are any, as well as their current state and life cycles."

Eric poked a few of the displays. "Wait, you found life on other planets?"

The professor laughed. "I have not, but you never know what Magic can help us discover." He opened the center console, revealing to them a magical glowing core of green light that came from a small gem at its heart. "This allows me to obtain the information I seek. By accessing the memories scripted into the living blueprints on these artifacts, I can replicate their recordings. Magic is an element that is pure, concentrated knowledge. Memories, thoughts and information...all of it exists and swirls together as a single powerful force that draws out our deepest determination. While Magic is not tangible on its own, the driving willpower of those who use it can come together and create unimaginable energies. Think of it like the formation of water. We know the components exist, though we cannot see them. Yet when they come together, they create an element that is essential to all life on our planet. Magic flows through our universe every day, and it carries the collective information of the world with it. Using this machine, I can peer into this cycle, and it creates this wondrous display before you. There are so many things in this world we do not understand. If people took the time to look around, they would see so much more."

Joseph gazed at the picture of Earth floating over their heads. There was so much he didn't understand, but an itch had formed in his mind. Space had always captured his attention, and he was struck by an intense desire to learn all the things Professor Ben was explaining.

"Now, on to how I discovered both of you. As you can see, the planet looks just how it should—filled with bright colors and teeming with life. But this is only the outer shell of our planet. Its life energy looks much different, much darker than its outside form. It's almost as if the power that thrives in these places can sense problems dwelling within its creation."

"Life energy? Sure you're not a gamer, Ben?" Eric teased.

"Allow me to demonstrate." The professor opened a small hatch next to the controls and pushed a button hidden below.

A lens fell over the beams of light where the projections were born, giving the planet a strange aura. A beautiful flush of bright greens appeared over the model of Earth and danced like the lights of the northern skies.

"What's that?"

"That is the planet's life energy. See the lively green colors? This is how the Earth's living force looks when everything is normal. At least, that is what I have come to understand. However..." He pushed another button, and the colors around the Earth changed to a dark swirl of interlaced black and red that sprang from the core. "That is the event causing much alarm as of late."

Eric waved his hand through the image. "It looks sick."

"What's wrong with it?" Joseph did the same as his friend, and the evil hues began to swirl away from the Earth, where they raced through the stars beyond.

"I believe life on this planet senses a disturbance. It is as if the very souls that cycle in and out are performing a strange calling." Professor Ben sighed. "I have seen references to it in a book we have uncovered. Perhaps in our dig for knowledge and answers we have unearthed something else? I can't be certain."

"Are you saying the *planet* feels problems around it?"

"If not the planet, then the souls it carries—they are certainly distressed. I have seen that state begin in multiple life forms in the universe, only to watch helplessly as they are devoured by it, never to be seen again. Its meaning is unclear, and I have yet to reveal its reasons. Then again, if I knew the answers, there would be little reason for our meeting. I do not know what our connection to one another is yet, but I believe there is a basis for everything."

Eric waved his hands around the murky swirls. "How do you know the machine isn't broken?"

"The makings of this technology might be far from perfect, but its results are quite precise. Our organization has tested every possible outcome."

"Good." Eric shrugged. "So tell this mystery organization of yours to fix the planet problem."

"The planet is in trouble? I still don't see why it has anything to do with us."

"I believe it extends beyond this planet. A while back, when I was studying the map of our world, everything just—" the professor held up his fists and opened his hands. "Poof! Everything went dark. The item powering it reacted in a way I had never seen before! Many different points of light lit up, most of which were embedded onto the Earth's surface. I studied the globe, trying to mark them, but they appeared and vanished so swiftly. However, two of the points were nearly atop one another, so they drew my attention first. They were the only ones I managed to calculate in time. So when I homed in on these specific points—"

"It brought you to us?"

Professor Ben tapped his nose as he further enlarged the image of Earth. The digital display rushed by them until they stood directly over a three-dimensional view of their street. "That would be correct. By combining this device with satellite images gathered via database, I was led to both of you. Magic remains a big mystery in our world, but these events must somehow connect. I believe that within the weavings that create this energy, the souls of you, Eric, and many others are tied together."

"Did you tell the organization you work for?"

"Joseph, nothing has gone as simply as I just explained it. Indeed, I did pursue the matter with my employers, however, they didn't take kindly to the details I gave them. They do not believe an event lacking credible evidence should warrant further investigation. It was cataloged, but"—the professor shook his head out of frustration—"it ceased there."

"I bet they're already planning a cover-up. That's probably why he won't tell us where he works," Eric murmured.

Professor Ben shut down the invention, and the lights faded from the room. The ceiling reopened and the machine receded into the floor as it closed.

"Professor...that other person you mentioned...who is he?"

The older man hesitated. "His name is Ryan Morter, and he is a troubled young man with his own agenda. I believe he's seven years older than you, Joseph, yet he is still misguided."

Ryan Morter...you probably know a lot about what's going on...

"I'm unsure if he knows how to use the solution he stole. If applied improperly, nothing in this world can help him." Professor Ben lowered his head. "He knew a lot more than he led me to believe, yet no matter how I reasoned with him, he refused to halt his reckless behavior. I know this was not what you hoped for, but I wish to enlist your assistance in finding him. I fear our time has grown thin on that matter as I suspect he has inside assistance."

"You tricked us into coming here just so we can play hide and seek in the city?" asked Eric.

The professor searched through his papers. "I doubt you would find him on the islands. He made it quite clear he had no intention of listening to me, so staying here would not benefit him in the slightest."

"Where would we even start?"

"Before his departure, Ryan took a few of my other findings with him—ancient texts that described old haunting grounds for magic drawing ceremonies. Many of these locations have become idle over the years, but they still contain the markings of their old users." He stopped searching and smiled. "Ah, yes...here we go." He pulled out an old book. "More importantly, these places might still hold keys to immense seals that lock the boundaries of Magic away from our world. I researched the area in my younger days, though I'm certain we missed some important discoveries."

Professor Ben reached for his coffee mug, sighing when he found the cup was empty.

"You want us to find Ryan before he uses that potion you made?" Eric groaned. "I hate fetch quests."

"There is one last thing I need to show you before we proceed." The professor walked over to another wall. "We have much to learn and discover, but not much time."

Professor Ben typed another code into the wall panel and a new passage on the floor slid open.

Eric shook his head. "Got a lot of free time, don't you, Ben?"

The man smiled and pulled out the same compact box from before, pressing on the small object as it enlarged. He retrieved the cell phone he'd confiscated earlier and tossed it back to Eric.

"Oh, thank goodness—she's okay!" Eric hugged the handset.

The man's chuckle echoed down the narrow metal corridor as they descended. "As for my free time, you are not wrong, but more than that, I also wish to keep my prized belongings safe. It is curious that Ryan located them so easily."

The empty sound of their steps echoed into the darkness ahead, but flickering lights emerged to guide their way.

At the end of the corridor stood a door. Professor Ben typed another code into a panel next to it. The frame shifted and rose open with a series of sharp beeps.

"Quickly—I put a security timer on this one!"

The moment they passed under the door, it slammed shut behind them, sealing the room in a blanket of vague shadows. Professor Ben spoke quietly to himself, and lights flickered, swiftly illuminating everything. It took a moment for Joseph's eyes to adjust, but when they did, what waited for them nearly knocked him over.

Eric gasped. "That's the same ship we saw when we got here!"

The gigantic vessel had the body of a wooden ship, but floating above the base was an enormous balloon made of blue fabric. Metal bands securely wrapped the balloon, which was then locked to the body by chains, causing the entire ship to float. It swayed gently in the air above them, emitting soft groans from the forceful weight it harnessed.

"Eric's right. We saw a ship like this when we got to the island."

Professor Ben sighed. "I have no doubt you did. Ryan took my prized prototype. What you see here is my second model—revision B. It might come as a surprise, but these vessels can reach speeds of more than two hundred miles an hour." He pressed a button on the remote, causing a ladder to unfold from the edge of the ship. "Powerful, fast, and more importantly, it travels the skies faster than any bird! Through the clouds and beyond. It was a design lost to the ages long ago, yet through my studies...well..." The professor winked. "Let us just say the Skyship might find a new log in the history books!"

"Skyship? Don't you mean *airship*?"

"Not according to the ancient records." Professor Ben started to climb.

"Let's go, Eric." Joseph nudged Eric in the shoulder and followed the professor up the ladder.

Once aboard the deck, Professor Ben led them to the stern. After ascending a short set of stairs, they arrived at the ship's controls.

Joseph tapped the deck with his foot. "How does this thing stay in the air?"

The professor smirked. "A little bit of Magic goes a long way with our modern technology. Boys, allow me to introduce you to the Nightmare 27—or NM27 if you prefer. The thing was a nightmare to reconstruct without my original plans and took our small team twenty-seven attempts. The name is well deserving." He chuckled. "It is a fully functional, durable mechanism that defied the laws of nature during its time of creation. You have your own sleeping and living quarters in the lower cabins, too. Even more amazing is that it requires no fuel and you never have to purchase a ticket."

Joseph folded his arms as he circumnavigated the deck, running his hands over the smooth railing. "This machine existed before the first flight?"

"*Long* before that time. For many centuries these machines roamed the skies. Magic was regarded a miracle in its era. Fantasy was just as real as those who wielded its power. From the dense woven material of its gas-filled levitation chamber"—he pointed to the blue balloon—"to the sleek, lightweight body." He spread his arms indicating the lower body of the vessel. "It took me many years to discover the lost texts describing its mechanics and a massive team to put all the pieces in their proper place. The wheel functions just as you would expect. As for this lever here"—he pointed to one that was right beside it—"you use it to change speed and shift gears, much like driving a standard car."

"Now we're talking!" Eric leapt forward to gawk at the controls. "I can't wait to test drive this thing! We get to fly, right?"

"Is this *legal* to fly?"

The professor smiled at Joseph. "Do not concern yourself with that. I assure you all required paperwork is in order."

Joseph shook his head and walked to the edge.

Eric looked over at him. "What's wrong, Joe?"

He wasn't sure where to begin. "This is all way too much at once, and I don't understand any of it. Magic that can sense danger and make fire? Flying machines that were never discovered and potions with dark powers? It doesn't make any sense. I'm not even sure if this is real or not." It made his head hurt.

"Some things are not meant to be understood." The professor approached him. "Destiny is not entirely compatible with a proper reason. There are so many wonderful paths through life. Whichever road you are on is the very same one you were meant to follow."

Joseph hit the railing with his fist. "How is it *my* destiny if I didn't choose it? We thought we were coming to play a game demo, and now you've thrown us into something entirely different."

Eric nodded. "Yeah, what Joe said. You've given us the worst tutorial so far."

Professor Ben frowned. "Hmm...let me try to clarify this." He tapped his head. "I work for an organization that studies and revives Magic. During my studies, an event alerted me to a potential crisis that guided me to the two of you. I knew you would not come if I simply asked, so I created the game presentation. However, Ryan Morter has stolen some of the things I wished to show you. I now believe you stand here for another reason. Perhaps I was meant to bring you here to help me find him. However, I can't force you to aid me."

"This sounds like a crazy anime...and we're the stars heading off to save the world." Eric smirked. "I can roll with that."

Joseph leaned against the railing of the ship. He and Eric didn't want a boring summer, but this was almost too much. But wasn't it the stuff of their dreams? A real-life adventure was tempting.

"You really think we can help you?"

"Sometimes you need to trust your instincts—and yes, I believe you can."

Joseph gazed up at the balloon. "This ship can really go over two hundred miles an hour?"

Professor Ben snapped his fingers. "Get me a pot of coffee and I shall make it even faster!"

"Won't the wind blow us off?"

"The bow is designed to divert the air current. You will feel little more than the invigorating rush of wind and the thrill of flight. Though I suppose the engine's core also plays a key role in protecting its passengers."

Magic, a wild search, and everything else Professor Ben told them about sounded like the ramblings of a madman. But at that very minute he stood on the deck of an ancient flying contraption brought back to life in the modern world. They'd been lied to, but it opened a chance for them to journey on their own. Who knew what they might discover?

Joseph smiled. "I hope you know where Ryan went. I can't imagine you'd expect us to start searching the entire world for him."

"By all means, I—" Professor Ben paused. "Wait, does that mean what I think it does?"

He nodded and moved away from the railing. "We're already here, right? Besides, I want to know what we have to do with it."

It was insane, but at the same time he couldn't resist. It felt right in its own odd way.

"Sign me up, too! We get a free vacation, we'll get to learn how to fly, and we get a *real* adventure? This summer will be epic! We're practically living our own video game." Eric narrowed his eyes. "As long as it's more than fetch quests."

The older man gave Joseph a hearty slap on the back. "Excellent! Now is the time to free your spirit of exploration, my boy."

Joseph gave Eric a sincere look. "Why are you so excited? When he said there was no demo event, you didn't seem interested at all."

His friend grinned. "Eh, I'm still not happy about that, but this might be just as good. Besides, check this out." He pulled out his cell phone. "Almost twenty missed calls, and close to thirty text messages. Guess who they're from."

He knew exactly who they were from. His own phone had gone off multiple times, and he'd ignored it. That thought made his heart sink. "Our parents..."

"Bingo!" Eric nodded as he pocketed his phone. "I'm not exactly eager to be grounded for the rest of my life. Might as well enjoy our freedom while we can, right?"

"Get over here, you two!" Professor Ben shouted. "Time to show you how to operate the controls!"

"Wait, *we* get to fly it?" Eric rushed to the professor's side.

Joseph looked at his phone, thinking over the messages he hadn't answered. After his friend hurried to join the professor, he opened his mother's message and replied without reading what she'd said.

"Eric and I are okay. I'll bring you and dad something cool. See you guys soon."

He hit send and put away the device.

Professor Ben was making sure everything was set as Joseph joined them. The man's fingers flew across the

97

panel, pulling levers and flipping switches. The harsh grinding of gears quaked beneath as the engines roared to life. Joseph followed his friend to the side of the ship just in time to see the ceiling open beyond the top of the balloon. The bright blue sky welcomed them with open arms.

"Would you mind coming over here?" Professor Ben asked Joseph.

He dashed back to where the professor stood.

"All you have to do is remove this cover." He removed a small portion of the canvas tarp from his side of the steering wheel. "You then turn this switch to remove the ground stability." The man pushed it to the side and the deck shifted beneath them. "Once it is unlocked, you simply pull that chain over there. That will fire up the power core to get us fully airborne!"

Joseph put his hand on the chain Professor Ben had motioned to. "This one?"

The scientist nodded.

He tugged with both hands, and a wave of heat spread over them as the burning fire in the heart of the ship awoke at his command. The propellers whirled at the back, whipping the air behind as slowly the working hum of the machine lifted it higher.

"All right, everyone, hold on!" The professor gripped the wheel to steady the ship.

The vessel accelerated, and the force was strong enough to send Joseph and Eric sprawling to the deck. The ship sailed through the opening in the ceiling and continued its ascent into the sky. Once his balance returned, Joseph staggered to his feet, though he had difficulty steadying himself.

"Are you sure this is safe?"

"I would not be here were it not!" Professor Ben replied as he kept his focus firm.

Joseph ran back to the side of the ship, and for the second time he watched the earth shrink beneath them. He peered into the distance; they weren't far from the city, though their location put them just beyond the outstretched hillsides and cliffs at the back. Soon, the crescent island became little more than a beautiful green mass floating in an endless sea.

Eric had also come over for a look. "You have to wonder if the people on vacation are used to seeing this sort of thing. Not everyday you see airships in the sky."

"Yeah, it sure is different."

"What changed your mind about doing this?" Eric asked. "Was it this awesome"—he wiggled a loose board on the railing—"but *rickety* ship, or"—he grinned and lowered his voice—"the fact he'd probably stalk us home if we didn't?"

"To tell the truth, I don't know what made me change my mind. I'm not even sure I *have* yet." His words came out in a concerned whisper, barely audible over the sound of rushing wind. "It's still hard to accept, so I don't know."

Eric waved off his response and continued to gaze at the ground. "This is so much better than watching a screen. Forget the fantasy—this is real life now."

That was exactly it. It was nothing more than a wild, out of control fantasy.

"Get over here, you two!" Professor Ben called. "It is time for flying lessons to begin."

They left the side of the ship and joined the professor at the controls.

"We've reached a safe altitude, so there is no need to worry about steering for the time being." He wiped his brow. "Make sure you pay close attention. To start the ship, you remove this piece here and turn the lever clockwise. This gets the engines running. Then pull on this chain here—it starts the thrust propellers in the back and heats the core. Once you are airborne, use these controls to fly." He pointed to the levers on the board of the steering wheel. "This stick controls the speed. The different colors on the side indicate how fast you are going. Oh, and before I forget, do not use the black lever under the wheel there. It is an accelerant, and I have not fully tested it. It's not quite stable and needs more testing."

Joseph listened to the elaborate explanation as best he could over the rushing wind and roaring engines.

"Any questions?"

"Tch, almost too easy," Eric bragged. "I could probably fly this thing in my sleep. I once placed fourth in Super Star Kart for a local tournament."

Professor Ben gave a confused expression. "Let me show you into the cabin area." He directed them down the back stairs leading to the middle of the ship. The man bent and pulled a section of the floor up to uncover the entry leading inside. "In we go!"

The ship's interior was spacious. Along the wall ran windows that let in sunlight from the outer body. Tables and chairs had been positioned around. If there were ever a floating mobile house, it would be the closest comparison. From the plush carpet to the bedrooms and bathrooms, it was conspicuously extravagant.

"The outside might look like junk, but this is amazing. Do you have a stereo in here?"

The professor snapped his fingers. "Of course. I spared no expense bringing this wonderful craft back to life."

"You put a lot of work into this, but won't all the furniture get tossed around while flying?" Joseph gave one of the tables a kick and raised his eyebrows when it didn't move.

"Most of the important items have been bolted to the floor. Now we shall delve into the wonders of flight."

"Player one is ready!" Eric was back up to the deck before the others could say a word.

The scientist chuckled. "You think he is excited for this new experience?"

Joseph smiled. "He loves this sort of thing. Hopefully, he isn't already trying to fly on his own."

"We'd better get up there before he gets carried away. The last thing I need is to have him knock this machine out of commission before we start our journey."

Professor Ben ran after Eric, and Joseph followed. When they got to the controls, Eric was holding the wheel, passion gleaming in his eyes.

"Glad to see you waited for us. I was worried for a moment." The professor gave a sigh of relief.

"I didn't want to show my skills until I had an audience." Eric smirked as he pulled out his phone and snapped a selfie of himself at the wheel. "Oh, yeah, that's a keeper!"

The professor walked over and grabbed the steering wheel. "We shall start by having you two gain some hands-on experience. Joseph, would you mind?"

Joseph stood next to the wheel. "You sure about this?" He cringed at the thought.

"Don't let your nerves get the best of you. Take the bull by the horns! Let the thoughts come as they will, but meet each challenge head-on. Trusting in oneself raises strength and courage, and you will need plenty of both!"

Plenty of both? What does that mean? Joseph took a deep breath and grabbed the wheel. Through the wood, he felt it jerk to the side from the forceful currents.

"Let me know when you are ready, and I shall shut down the autopilot," the older man said.

Joseph closed his eyes, let out a long breath, and tightened his grip. "All right—I'm ready."

Driving a car was one thing, but to be in control of such a large ship flying through the sky was almost too much.

Professor Ben shut down the controls, and the ship rolled to the side as Joseph let go of the wheel, throwing everyone off balance.

"You have to keep the wheel steady. It might also help to open your eyes!" Professor Ben shouted.

"Y-yeah…I know!" Joseph clenched the wheel and straightened their course. He hadn't realized his eyes were shut. He peeled them back open to anxiously observe the effects his actions had on the vessel.

The ship slowly returned to a proper position, and the shaking stopped. Joseph tried his best to calm his nerves, but his hands trembled. The professor walked back to where he'd been standing and observed over Joseph's shoulder.

"Good. Now that you have the ship under control, I want you to try changing its direction. Take the wheel and turn the ship to the right," the scientist instructed.

Joseph turned the wheel as far as it could go. The instructions from his driving class did little to help him with an airborne vessel. The ship turned, as expected, but its angle was too sharp. He panicked when the ship threw Eric and Professor Ben to the side, and he had to grip the wheel to stay in place.

"Too fast, Joseph!" Professor Ben scrambled to keep himself from falling off the edge. "Turn the wheel back in the other direction!"

"Come on, dude, you've got this!"

Joseph grit his teeth as he turned it back, but this time he did it much more slowly. The ship straightened, and Professor Ben once again approached the controls.

"I guess I should have said this sooner, but keep your rotations deliberate. The ship can adjust itself but only if given time. It takes practice, but you will get there. It's not much different than driving a car."

"I know, I just...lost it for a moment there." Joseph sighed heavily, then swallowed the lump in his throat.

"Relax. Take it one step at a time. The Skyship can be intimidating at first, but with practice comes a fine understanding. Its operation will become easy, like a second nature for you. It requires a steady guide of the flow," Professor Ben promised.

Joseph nodded and this time kept his wits together. The ship was nothing more than a vehicle, however oversized and airborne. Each time Professor Ben gave him an instruction, he listened. Thankfully, the pace was slow. Before he knew it, the way the NM27 functioned seemed less threatening. He completed a full circle around the island and stood proudly at the controls with a breath of relief.

"See? Nothing to it!" Professor Ben cheered.

"I guess not, it's just...*nerve-wracking*."

"Can I try now?" asked Eric.

"By all means. Joseph, if you have gotten the hang of it, let us see how Eric handles the controls."

"Finally. Move over, Joe! Let a professional show you guys how to fly in style." Eric shoved Joseph out of the way. "I bet this will be better than *Airstrike Counter 2!*"

Joseph admired Eric's enthusiasm. Maybe he needed to follow his friend's example.

The professor addressed Eric. "As I told Joseph, this is nothing more than a massive automobile. Flow with the controls, like the clouds."

"Yeah yeah, I know. Let me handle it!" Eric grabbed the wheel.

While Professor Ben lectured Eric, Joseph looked around. He descended the steps and walked to the front of the ship. Once there, he grabbed one of the heavy cables holding the balloon and hopped on the upper platform.

When the wind blew across his face, all Joseph's uneasiness broke free. The rush was exciting as he looked over the landscape. The sparkling ocean below resembled an exotic postcard. The way light reflected from the Murean Grand Hotel caught his eye. He pulled out his phone to take a picture. Even Professor Ben's eccentric ramblings didn't detract from the view. Closing his eyes, Joseph inhaled deeply to take in the fresh sea air.

An unexpected shaking cut his moment of peace short; the craft jolted to the side and sent him tumbling to the deck. A loud burst of steam erupted from within the vessel, and the noise hissed over the rushing winds.

"That didn't sound good."

He leapt up and ran back to the helm, where Professor Ben had taken back the wheel.

Eric backed away from the wheel with his hands up. "It wasn't me, I swear."

Joseph braced his body against one of the poles in the center of the ship before their platform tilted. Another explosion followed from the engines below. Professor Ben fought to gain control.

"Whoa, look at all that smoke." Eric looked over his shoulder to the source of the noise. "It's not supposed to do that, is it, Ben?"

"The engine's processors must have overheated!" Professor Ben yelled. "Joseph, hold the wheel steady."

He moved as fast as he could to take Professor Ben's place at the controls. As he did, the older man dashed inside the ship.

"We're gonna die, we're gonna die!" Eric paced from place to place, frantically running from one side to the other. "We're gonna crash, die, and then blow up on a tropical island." He stopped to shrug. "Honestly...not a bad way to go."

Joseph kept every ounce of his focus on trying to keep the ship stable. No matter how hard he tried, the machine fought his control as it began to tip forward, its nose aimed at the surface. The island below grew closer and closer.

Professor Ben rushed back moments later, out of breath and shaking his head. "The power core ruptured a fuse in the engine. There's no way I can fix it up here."

"What the hell are we supposed to do?" Joseph screamed.

The wheel jerked out of Joseph's grip, and he struggled to regain his hold.

"Aim for the water. Our only hope is to glide through the surface and pray it does not fracture the body!" the professor advised. "We can sail her home if we accomplish that!"

"What do you mean, *if?*"

They had no more time to contemplate the situation. Professor Ben ordered them to brace their footing and in slow motion, their skyward ship plummeted toward the sea. Their speed grew rapid, and the island buildings appeared larger in the distance. The vessel swooped over the residential areas, rocking uneasily through the gushing winds as it sailed beyond the cliffs toward the ground.

The front of the NM27 crashed nose-first into the waiting ocean below, forcing a wide spray of white water to erupt from the bow. The impact threw Joseph's head forward, and it smacked firmly into the front of the wheel before he fell to the ground. The rumbling stopped, but he didn't know if the landing had been successful. The caressing sound of the waves carried his mind away as the alarmed seagulls faded into silence.

CHAPTER SEVEN

LOST IN FANTASY

"**A**re you okay?"

Joseph groaned at the sound of the concerned female voice. It took a moment for the robed, hooded form to appear—seemingly from thin air—as she knelt where he lay.

"Looks like you really smacked your head on that one. Maybe it'll knock some sense into you." The figure laughed softly. "I'm sorry this all feels so sudden. It's never easy when someone's life gets flipped upside down or things don't work how they hoped." She placed her hand on his head. "Laeh."

A gentle warmth radiated from her palm, and Joseph's headache subsided.

"What was that? What did you do?"

She stood. "Your path will be tough, but Kilgan believes in you. Just don't let it go to your head or get yourself killed, okay? The man helping you seems to know a few things about Magic. I guess it wasn't sleeping after all."

"Magic…is real?"

"You'd be surprised how real, but it's time to get up. Try not to get hurt again."

She gently slapped him on the cheek.

He blinked. Things were blurry, but the pounding in his head was gone.

"Sweet! You're not dead!" Eric said as he approached.

Joseph winced. "Good to know. I was worried there for a second. Where's Professor Ben?"

"In the engine room, checking out the damage. I had a feeling this piece of junk would crash. It's probably held together with tape and glue."

Joseph rubbed his head where he'd been hit. There was no pain or wound. Though he was thankful, it was getting harder and harder to separate his dreams from the real world. He stood, looking over the edge of the ship.

"We're already back?"

"Yeah, Ben sailed us to the island while you were out. Been a few hours. I guess this thing can float *and* fly. Though I think we freaked out locals and tourists alike when we flew over the resort."

The professor returned, looking exhausted. "The energy balance was slightly off. I had to adjust the flow of power, but everything should be functioning normally now. I shall give it a few tests throughout the day to make sure everything is working properly before we set for the sky again. Are you okay, Joseph?"

He nodded. "Just a bump on the head. Not too bad."

Professor Ben smiled, then led them to the ship's exit and down the ladder to the sandy beach. They'd come to rest near the back of his research lab.

"I'm glad everyone is okay. The last thing I want is for you to sustain an injury before you even depart. I'm truly sorry for the results of this test. Rest assured, everything will be perfect to go come morning. For now, I would like you and Eric to return to the city and rest up. I will have everything prepared by tomorrow. We can meet then."

"Sure. I guess we'll see you later?" Joseph waved as they set off.

The professor remained with the ship as Joseph and Eric trekked back to the city. The sun had passed its high point, putting midday behind them and beginning its descent toward early evening. Once immersed in the bustle of crowded streets and towering buildings, they did little but take their time exploring Murean.

"Wanna get dinner?" Joseph suggested as they passed a line of food trucks outside a cluster of shops.

His friend smiled. "You read my mind! All that science talk wore me out, and we never even got to eat lunch."

Joseph chuckled. Eric would never turn down a chance to grab some more grub, whether they'd lunched or not.

After passing a few seafood places, they settled on a local Asian restaurant. They made bets about who could eat the fastest using chopsticks. Though it resulted in more food on the ground than in their mouths, they laughed like the teenagers they were, and unlike the school cafeteria, no one forced them to stop and clean it up. As they ate, the upbeat music of a local band played, and a familiar form caught his eye.

"Isn't that Jam?"

His face stuffed with food, Eric glanced up, and together they watched the local commotion in the distance. Accenting the steel drums and fast, hearty strings was the lighthearted melody of the flute their recently acquired island friend was playing. Seeming to move without his conscious command, Joseph's foot began tapping beneath their table. Eric seemed to enjoy the sounds of the tropical atmosphere, too. A crowd gathered and began clapping to the performance. Then Joseph noticed something strange.

It wasn't clear at first, but the longer he watched, the more certain Joseph became he wasn't imagining it. Around Jam's feet, the small pebbles and mounds of sand shifted, as if dancing to the music. He'd thought it was simply the movement from the composition and tremors from the feet of the audience pounding the ground. Right at the finale, when the beat hit its peak, those same stones rose from the terrain and gently swirled in the air before dropping back to the earth. Even the strong vibrations from the band couldn't have caused that.

Was that real?

The crowd gave a round of applause before dispersing into the streets. Jam and the rest of the band packed up their things and vanished as well.

Joseph stared at his friend. "Did you see that?"

"Yeah, Jam wasn't kidding when he said he had the music in him. That was pretty cool!"

Eric slurped in a mouthful of noodles.

"Yeah..."

He still wasn't sure if it had actually happened. Maybe Professor Ben's rant on Magic was getting to him.

"Now all I need is a few good hours of sleep, and I'll be ready to head out in the morning, bright and early." Eric yawned and stretched.

"Like when you got ready for school?"

"Trust me. If we had field trips like *this* every day, I'd be waiting outside the door!"

Joseph laughed as they finished dinner and headed back to the hotel. Through the hotel's revolving doorway waited the air-conditioned entrance, which served as a refreshing contrast to the stifling outdoor heat. When they reached the main stairway, Joseph gasped and pushed Eric to the side.

Someone was waiting for them.

"Dude, why the sudden tackle?" Eric fixed his shirt, oblivious to what had caused Joseph to push him.

"Shhh, look!" Joseph flattened himself against the wall and peeked around the corner.

Eric poked his head out and searched the room as well. "I don't see anything."

"Look who's standing by the front desk."

Ahead of them, Clyde leaned against the stairwell railing. His eyes occasionally scanned the foyer of the main entryway as he tapped an impatient foot on the floor.

"Ugh, now what does he want?"

"You *did* brag about us staying here."

Eric cleared his throat and smiled. "Hah…yeah, I guess that's my bad."

"We can probably sneak around him."

His friend nodded, and they crept through the lobby, keeping their bodies low to the ground.

"Hey, there you guys are!" a friendly voice called.

Jam waved at them from the hotel entry. Clyde was quick to notice.

"Or not! Hit the escape button!"

They rushed by Jam on the way to the elevators.

Eric quickly bumped fists with him. "Hey, Jam. Bye, Jam!"

Neither elevator door opened when Joseph hit the button, which meant that both were on other floors.

"We don't have time to wait!"

"Looks like we're taking the stairs," Joseph said with a sigh.

They pushed through the doors and hurried up the stairwell. Clyde wasn't far behind.

Joseph's heart pounded as they left the stairwell on the next floor. They rounded the edge of the hallway right as the exit opened behind them. To their left, there was an open room being cleaned, and outside sat two large bins filled with dirty towels.

"Quick, get in."

Joseph desperately pulled piles of towels from the first container before he jumped in.

"Oh, man, this is nasty." Eric groaned as he shuffled into the second bin. "We went from the top of the world to the bottom of the bin in a single day."

Once Eric was settled, the only sounds came from the maid cleaning the room. Footsteps approached as the noise of heavy breathing came from above. Joseph held his breath, making no sound until the threat had passed.

"I know you two are here!" Clyde wheezed as he spoke. "I don't know what you're doing, but I *will* find out, one way...or the other. You can't pull these tricks on a Foristen, Joseph. We're well connected. I'm sure once your families discover what's going on...oh, won't that be fun."

Joseph winced. He dreaded returning home.

Clyde gave a discouraged grunt and his steps faded.

Joseph cautiously rose to check their surroundings. "I think he's gone."

Eric leapt from the basket and danced around the floor in a circle, flinging towels in all directions. "Disgusting. Get these things off me!"

The maid gasped and dropped her supplies at seeing them. Smiling sheepishly, Joseph grabbed Eric before they shuffled out of sight of the confused woman.

Eric pulled a stray cloth from his shirt and threw it to the ground. "Quick thinking on your part, even if it was disgusting."

"Keep it down. We don't know where Clyde is."

"You'd think he'd have better things to do than stalk us. Doesn't he have his fancy video game stream to work on? And why does he want to ruin *our* vacation?"

"I'm not sure we can call this a vacation anymore." The coast was clear as they entered the elevator. "It's hard to enjoy anything with Professor Ben rushing us around all the time."

"Yeah, he needs to lay off the coffee, but aren't you excited about tomorrow?"

Joseph shook his head as they proceeded to the room. "I was excited...until I remembered this isn't a video game. We could have died in that crash, and there's no respawning after that." He slid their key and entered the room, then he walked to his bag and pulled out the novel he had been reading. "Magic and adventure come from books and video games. It doesn't happen in real life."

Eric narrowed his eyes. "What about the fire Ben started? What about the computer with all the planets and stars? We even got to fly in a ship. How is none of that real?"

"I want to believe all this, I really do. Part of me *does* believe it, but what's next, dragons and time travel? We might as well have aliens land and tell us we should believe in them as well—just for good measure because life is apparently crazy now."

"Come on," Eric playfully punched Joseph in the shoulder. "You're taking this too seriously. Lighten up and have some fun. How often does stuff like this happen to someone? It's like we won the lottery. We have the chance to do something seriously awesome."

"I think you're being a bit…gullible." Joseph let the book drop to the floor, where it made a loud smack. "This isn't a video game, Eric. We're not going to become heroes and save the day. We've been tricked, and that's all there is to it."

"Yeah…right." Eric's drop of excitement matched the trajectory of the dropped book as realization dawned and his head drooped.

Joseph sighed and frowned. "Sorry. I guess I don't know how to handle this. My brain is all over the place. Maybe I'm just tired."

Eric shrugged as he took out his wallet and walked to the door. "Eh, who cares? You're right. It's been a super long day. I'm gonna head out and see what else is going on. I'd rather deal with Clyde and his bull-crap if it means I get to enjoy myself. I'll catch you later."

Eric left without another word, and Joseph let his back fall hard against the wall behind him. In frustration, he knocked his head against the surface a few more times before he let out a long sigh. "Eric's right…maybe this *is* something I should be excited about. I love fantasy and video games…but that's not real life…is it?" He shook his head. "And now you're talking to yourself, Joe."

A knock on the door interrupted him. He assumed Eric had forgotten something. "Did you—"

He couldn't believe it. The elderly man he'd seen at his school and the beach was there, dressed as a hotel steward.

"You've gotta be kidding me."

"It seems our paths cross again. Funny how that keeps happening, is it not? I did however bring the tea you requested."

Joseph was stone-faced. "I didn't order any tea."

The man sported a wide smile that beamed from within the long white of his full beard. "Well, then I suppose this one is on the house." He pushed his way into the room, wheeling the cart in as he did. "You look like you need something to relax."

"I need a lot more than that. Between you and the professor, I hardly know which end is up anymore."

"You're not happy with how things are turning out? I'd have assumed you'd love a real-life fantasy adventure."

"Happy?" he scoffed. "I can't tell if I'm dreaming or not. Nothing has gone the way I expected. We came here to play a video game and now...I don't even know what's going on."

"Patience and trust come with a reward of their own. I suggest you offer both to the professor. It sounds like he's under a great deal of stress. Give him a chance to sort things out and your own worries should be resolved as well. Perhaps you should put yourself in his shoes and have some faith." The old man held out his hand, rubbing his fingers together.

"Wait, you want a tip for bringing me tea I didn't order?"

The man chuckled, tipping his hat. "You can't blame a man for trying. I mean, you never know until you try." He was about to leave but paused. "Speaking of which, I'm sure you will be departing in the morning. If I may offer some advice?" He paused again, then continued when he had Joseph's attention. "You should jump three times when you find the mark on the cliff."

The strangely specific advice wasn't what he'd expected. "What?"

The man nodded. "You'll know when you find it. Now, if you'll excuse me, I have other deliveries. I hope your dreams are more pleasant tonight." With that last gesture, he turned and left.

Joseph chased him, but the elderly gentleman had already vanished from the hallway.

114

"Maybe that's all this is—nothing more than a dream. I'm not crazy." He shook his fist. "I just need to wake up!"

He cleared his throat after a few other hotel guests opened their doors to look at him.

Joseph rubbed his eyes, then closed the door, grabbing a change of clothes on his way to the bathroom. After wiping the foggy mirror, he stared at his own reflection. The image gazing back didn't seem like him. After his unexpectedly discouraging response to Eric, he was more lost than ever.

"What am I doing here?"

Frustrated, he finished and returned to the other room, then eyed the cart with the tea. *As long as it's here, I guess.* He poured a small cup and drank. It wasn't anything special, just tea with a hint of calming herbs and honey.

The tea was real, right? It wasn't a dream.

Once the tea was gone, he crashed face-first into the sheets of the bed.

Later, a familiar vision returned to him.

He awoke at home, in his own bed, when that same knock at the door broke the stillness. Upon answering it, the scenery crumbled, and he fell down into the abyss. It swallowed him as it had before.

He fell, spinning in every direction like he couldn't tell which was was up, until suddenly he stopped midair. He glanced around, though nothing but the darkness embraced his body, seeming to compress him on all sides in a chilling hug.

When he tried to plant his feet on the ground, there wasn't any. "What's going on? Get me out of here!"

The nightmare drove him crazy; it had full control over him. He gripped his head, covering his ears. The response to his demand was a horrid mash of noise. A loud screech blew in from every direction, and the sounds of metal scraping and disembodied screaming voices assaulted his senses.

The female voice returned as her figure materialized before him. "Relax…it's trying to break free, but it can't yet. Breathe deep."

She laid her hands lightly on the sides of his head and whispered a strange word.

"Mlac."

A strange blue aura encased his body and his muscles and nerves relaxed. The whispers and voices faded away.

"You're a bit of a pain to keep an eye on. Stop stressing yourself out, because I can't keep saving you like this. It's time to wake up."

He floated away and after a time opened his eyes. He lay on the floor of the hotel room, tangled in the bed sheets.

Joseph turned and looked at the clock. It was already past 7:00 a.m.

He sighed. "Getting tired of these dreams..."

A painful twinge gripped his back as he stood, but he worked it out after a few stretches. How much had he tossed and turned? Judging by the ringing in his head and the state of his bedding, he'd twisted and flopped all night. When he approached the other room, Eric was nowhere in sight.

The tea was still there, however.

Part of him wasn't surprised, especially after what happened the night prior. He texted Eric an apology before steeling himself to face the day. After grabbing everything he needed, he walked to the elevator and stepped in.

"Hold that, would you, please?"

He didn't have time to react as Clyde forced his way in. How had he not noticed the shadow following him?

"What do you want, Clyde?"

"Why do you always cast such a jaundiced eye at my every attempt at idle chat, Joseph? You and I never truly had an issue."

The door of the elevator-turned-prison closed, locking them inside. Joseph braced himself for the transport down.

It's going to be a long ride down. Joseph sighed. "You're the one who's butting heads with Eric. I always seem to get pulled into the middle of it."

"True," Clyde said, then changed the subject. "I can't help but wonder what you're doing here." He tilted his head. "Speaking of Eric, where *is* your loudmouthed sidekick?"

"None of your business."

"Come on, Joseph...it's all of my business. I'll make this easy for you to comprehend." Clyde hit the button for the next floor, causing the elevator to stop soon after. When the doors opened, he placed his hands on the frame to keep the door from closing. "I know all about your little... *involvement* on this island, because over here, it's invitation only. You two are hiding something, and I'll let you know, right here, right now, that I'm going to dig up that secret. I've been watching you both so you can either fess up or wait for me to discover it on my own. Trust me. I can, and I *will*."

A fire burned inside the pit of Joseph's stomach. Wherever this confrontation was leading into, he needed to prepare for the worst. "Go ahead, Clyde. You go figure it out." The manner of his voice was ominous, matching Clyde's threatening tone. "Dig as deep as you can, and when you do, you'll find nothing but a dead end." Joseph winked. "I *dare* you to try!"

He'd edged closer to his nemesis, ending up almost face to face with Clyde. A moment of tense silence followed, but then Clyde backed out of the elevator as his shaking hand slipped free of the door. "Enjoy your trip with the professor. I hope he delivers on his promises."

The door began to close, and Joseph got one last glimpse of Clyde's smirk before the door shut, severing their connection. He let out a long exhalation. His threat wasn't entirely toothless. Clyde would find the same wall they'd confronted. It was vacant, showing no clues or hints. That Clyde knew about Professor Ben worried him enough he muttered aloud. "How does *Clyde* know about all this?"

When he reached the base floor, his phone vibrated in his pocket. It was a text from Eric.

Eric: *Waiting outside*

He felt bad after last night, but once he arrived, the cheerful expression on Eric's face eased most of Joseph's misgivings.

"Feelin' better?" Eric asked.

"Yeah...I mean, a little bit." Joseph admitted. "Sorry about what I said. I was really out of it."

"Tch, don't worry about it." Eric assured. "Don't go getting all sappy on me, okay?"

He laughed as Eric gave him a short punch in the shoulder, then bounced in place as he jabbed the air with his fists. Eric was obviously excited for their meeting. Joseph could wait to tell him about his encounter with Clyde.

Eric threw a fist toward the sky. "Let's get this show on the road!"

When he stepped from the shade of the hotel, the bright morning sun quickly warmed his face. If getting up for school felt like this every morning, he'd never have a problem waking up. The image resembled a perfect painting hanging in a gallery even as the island breeze seemed to gently push them across the sand and stone toward the laboratory.

"There it is!" Eric pointed to the lab at the end of the city and scurried off. "Race ya!"

There was a new spring in Joseph's step. Maybe once they finished today, after Professor Ben explained more about the situation, he'd be more at rest.

Eric easily beat him to the door, which opened at his touch. "Huh, check it out. Door's unlocked."

Inside, Professor Ben sat slouched over a table. He clasped a wrench in one hand and a half-full mug of coffee in the other. Most of its contents slowly dripped onto the floor as the older man snored.

"Is he dead?"

"He's not dead. He's just sleeping." Joseph poked him in the shoulder. When he didn't get a response, Joseph pushed him with his full hand and gave Eric a puzzled expression. "Professor Ben, are you okay?"

"Looks like he passed out." Eric leaned over and gave him a hard push. "Man, he's a deep sleeper for someone who drinks so much coffee."

"He probably stayed up all night fixing the ship."

"Yeah, well, he has to get up now." Eric moved in front of the sleeping researcher, turned the volume up on his phone, and blasted a strong, energetic video game song.

The professor's eyes shot open as he dropped the mug to the floor, where it shattered into pieces. "Don't forget to—" When he saw them standing there, the professor jumped to his feet and wiped off his coat. Enthusiasm quickly returned to his face. "Oh, there you are! Yes, this is excellent, so very excellent!"

"Bright and early," Joseph said.

"Wonderful, as we have much to do." Professor Ben brought the wrench to his mouth, giving a curious look when he realized it wasn't his mug.

"Did you fix the ship?" asked Eric.

"It took a few tries, but the energy core should be stabilized." Professor Ben led them to the other room. "So, hopefully nothing will explode this time!"

Neither of the teenagers got a chance to express their concerns.

"Forgive me if I'm a little wired this morning." Professor Ben hummed through his office like a working bee at the hive. If he had wings, the man would have taken off.

"Four pots of coffee really get the mind processing on all levels. Past eight already? We need to get this show on the road! Come now, don't stand still—there is work to be done. Chop chop!"

He pushed them out the door and past the building, then along the cliffs and around the shore. They came at last to the resting body of the NM27. Everything had been repaired and cleaned up.

"Wow, the ship looks great," Joseph said.

"I wouldn't say great," Eric whispered.

"It looks great, it flies great, and everything is just great. Great, great, great!" Professor Ben slapped a rolled parchment into Joseph's hand.

"What's this?" Joseph unrolled it.

"I spent the remainder of my night researching Ryan's motives and could only come to one conclusion." The professor's words flew from his mouth faster than the spin of the ship's propellers. "There could be only one reason for him to take that elixir—one reason alone. Yes, indeed, one and only one! My missing files and tomes all point to a single artifact I had intended to add to my library years ago, but after much discouragement as to its purposes, I instead decided some things were best left untouched. It does not help that I was unable to find the darn thing due to the ruins being flooded. Fancy that! Ryan, however, sees fit to seek out this dangerous object. Oh, that fool is quite brave."

Joseph again opened his mouth to question the professor's statements, but he didn't get the chance.

"The Sunken Peninsula is where I believe he would have last landed. Quite the interesting name, is it not?" He quickly snatched the roll of paper back from Joseph in an eager effort to unfold the map within. "Far off the Australian continent lies a chain of islands to the south. There is an old structure that has long since collapsed inside of cliff sides. The sea eventually claimed most of the land and ruins, thus its name. Did I mention it had flooded? However, over the years, the water levels have dropped, causing a new opening to surface. I was only able to explore a few chambers before my research was diverted elsewhere by my employers. The rocky terrain and steep cliffs make it nearly impossible to land modern aircraft!"

"Which is why we have to use the flying paperweight?" asked Eric.

"Precisely!" Professor Ben snapped his fingers. "Treacherous landscapes edge every side. So many sunken ships rest deep around those shores. The Skyship's design may seem outdated, but it's far from useless. Land, sky, and even water prove no match!"

Joseph forced a smile, watching as one of Professor Ben's eyes twitched from the caffeine rush.

"I knew Ryan stole my other ship for a reason. Therefore, all evidence leads me to believe that he wishes to traverse to those chambers!"

"Why would Ryan go through all this effort?"

"There is much you and Eric still need to learn about our involvement in this chain of events. My own role seems severely limited. I don't know how much an older man such as myself can accomplish, anyway. That said, what Ryan seeks is an old tome said to show the locations of hidden Sanctuaries. I can only speculate as to his intentions. Because they hold wisdom beyond my ability, I'm unsure what resides in those texts. However, I fear not only for Ryan's safety, but for that of our world as well. Many efforts have been put into hiding these discoveries"—he raised an admonishing finger—"and for good reason! Freeing these energies simply can not come without consequence. Now you must be off. Off into the sky and beyond! Fly away! Hurry, now!"

"W-wait. What do you mean? You're not going with us?" Joseph's eye were wide with alarm.

"Oh, heavens, no. Someone of my age would do little more than slow down your quest. This is an adventure for your generation, not mine." Professor Ben pushed the rolled-up map back to Joseph.

Eric flashed a look of doubt. "Are you serious? I don't want to take care of your errands. What if that ship explodes again?"

"I'm not sure how you expect us to stop Ryan or convince him to come back with us." Joseph was growing more worried about the whole condition. "From what you've said, he—"

"I have the utmost confidence in your abilities to handle the situation properly." Professor Ben motioned Joseph to the ship. "Trust your senses, believe in the world around you, and never forget what I have shown you here. You fight not only for yourselves, but for everything we see around us."

"Being a bit dramatic right now, Ben." Eric boarded the ship, appearing like a passerby fleeing a caffeinated mentally ill man's energetic rambling.

Joseph couldn't believe how forcefully the older man was pushing them into this task.

The professor nudged Joseph toward the ladder before backing away, gleefully smiling. Joseph was about to confront him about the whole thing, but his words would likely be wasted. It seemed he had two options. They could run away from their situation and face Professor Ben's disappointment, despite the professor's reassurances they could do so at any time, or board the ship and risk what waited for them at the end of their journey.

He climbed the ladder.

"Joseph!" Professor Ben shouted once he reached the top.

Joseph leaned over the railing. "Yeah?"

"Don't forget to pull the ladder up before you take off!" he warned. "You don't want it to catch on anything while you are flying!"

"Okay, I got it. We're leaving now!"

The professor's constant jittery energy was giving him a headache. Joseph went back over to the ladder and pulled it up before the man could say anything else. When the task was complete, he moved to the deck's control center, where Eric waited.

"My sixth sense tells me that man is insane."

"We might be just as crazy for listening to him."

"Still beats going home. Actually, I just had the best idea. We should fly it back to Sethen County. Can you imagine the look on everyone's faces if we fly to school in this thing?"

"Let's not get carried away. My head is spinning. Does he really expect us to do all this on our own? He's had *years* of experience in...whatever this is. We have *none*."

"He did have a point. He's old and kinda weird, and we can probably handle this Ryan guy better than he can. Cause he's...you know...old. Or something; I don't know."

"Yeah, that's my point exactly."

Whatever Eric was trying to say, it did little to relieve Joseph's worries. Eric never appeared bothered by random events in his life. His friend took things in stride and acted with confidence. However, he couldn't help but feel like they'd been thrust into a shark tank with little more than swimmer's goggles.

"Let's figure it out once we're in the air." He strode to the steering wheel and opened the control panel. Professor Ben's rapid mental stream seemed to have thrown Joseph's own mind out of focus. He drew a blank when looking at the buttons and switches.

After a moment, Eric reached over and flipped a switch, causing the lower engines to rumble.

"You look lost." His friend laughed.

"Yeah, I need to get it together."

With Eric's help, and after the push of a few buttons and the pull of a few levers, they departed the ground below. The crunch of rock and sand beneath the body could hardly be heard over the bellowing engine. While the ship ascended, Eric ran to the side to watch their departure.

"Hey, there's Professor Ben!"

Joseph left the wheel to get a glimpse. From the top of a nearby cliff, the professor waved before he cupped his hands to his mouth and tried to shout something over the noise.

"What did he say?" Joseph asked.

Eric shrugged and tried to shout back to him. "What did you say?"

It was no use. Soon Professor Ben ran from sight.

Eric pushed away from the railing. "Eh, must not have been important."

Joseph returned to the wheel to keep it steady. He waited until they reached the ship's highest altitude, then cut the power to cease their climb. It was there they paused, floating aimlessly, the shrunken view of the islands below them.

"Wait a sec...do you know where we're going?" asked Eric.

"You're asking *me*?" Joseph looked at the map the professor had given them.

The only hint of instruction it held was a circled location near Australia and the words "go here" scribbled nearby. Splashes of coffee also stained the parchment.

"Yeah, I say we take this baby back home. We can seriously try taking it to school, you know? Screw getting a car!"

"Something tells me he didn't think this through." Joseph sighed. "I don't think he had any idea what he was doing sending us off like this."

"He was all caffeine and no brain."

Except for the hum of the engine, there was only awkwardness and anxious looks. Joseph rested his hand on the wheel as his mind wandered. The whole endeavor seemed ill-considered. Eric was right to speak up to the professor. The ship had already crashed once. What were they doing there? This was no place for someone of their experience, or even their age.

They were already lost, and they hadn't properly left yet.

An ear-wrenching ringing sound pierced the air, similar to that of a microphone's feedback.

"Gah, what is that?" Eric grunted.

Joseph recklessly searched the controls. "Where is that sound coming from?"

"I don't know, but it's driving me nuts!"

They scanned every surface within reach, but it was difficult to locate the sound over the pumping heart of the great mechanical beast.

"Shut up already!" Eric pounded and pushed a random selection of buttons.

The noise grew worse. Joseph feared the engines would blow at any moment, making their choice to go along with the professor's advice a potentially deadly one. With one angry slam of Eric's fist, the noise came to an abrupt halt.

CHAPTER EIGHT

JOURNEY THROUGH THE SKIES

Eric jumped back. "Crap, did I break it?"

A quiet voice arose from nearby, and a small device rose from the right side of the wheel as the words grew louder. A speaker, additional knobs, and a receiver comprised that particular section.

"—that—anyone—there?" a voice crackled.

"Looks like you might have fixed it." Joseph laughed as he picked up the corded attachment. "Professor Ben? That you? I can hardly hear what you're saying!"

"Turn—knob— to—speaker—"

He scanned the radio and messed with the dials. It got worse at first, but after a few adjustments the voice became clearer.

"Can you hear me better?" the professor asked in a perfectly audible sentence.

"Yeah, I think we got it."

"Wonderful. I'm sorry to have rushed you as I did! The lack of rest and the coffee—I may have had a cup or two too many." The man sighed. "I want you to know the ship is fully stocked with supplies. I may have forgotten to give out a few details in my haste."

"A *few* details?" Eric huffed.

Joseph frowned. "That's only *one* of our problems, professor. You gave us the map, but we have no idea where we are or how to get there."

"How could I have been so forgetful? Goodness me, I do not think you two would have gotten very far without seeing how the guidance system functions!" Professor Ben complained to himself. "Do you see that screen next to the speaker?"

"Yeah," Joseph said.

"Next to the screen there should be another switch. Flip it and it should activate the radar system, which will bring up the digital map."

Joseph did as instructed, and the monitor displayed a pixelated image of the ship's location next to the island. A compass in the corner indicated their direction.

"That's pretty cool."

"Is it up yet?"

"Yeah, it's up," Joseph confirmed.

"Excellent! You should not have to do much else as far as direction is concerned. I input the location of The Sunken Peninsula last night. If you run through the options on the screen, you will see a directional function to guide you there. It is pretty self-explanatory. As long as there are no malfunctions, the ship should be fine."

Eric rolled his eyes. "What are we supposed to do when we find Ryan? Ask him nicely to return? Knock him in the head and kidnap him? You didn't give us anything useful, Ben."

"Do whatever you feel is necessary, but by all means, don't risk your own safety in the process. Now...I do not mean to cut our conversation short, but fatigue is getting the best of me. When you arrive, let me know! Remember, all you require is your perseverance and inner trust." There was a crash, followed by a click and then silence.

Joseph set the receiver down and looked at Eric.

His friend laughed. "That's easy for him to say. He sits in his lab and lets us do all the work. Told you he was scamming us. I say we take this ship and—"

"Let's get this thing on track first. We can decide what else to do once it is, okay? Besides, I don't think the powers that be would just let us park this ship in the streets like an RV."

As per the professor's instructions, Joseph tapped directions into the navigation system. The green display of the world map adjusted position, setting the path to their destination. Surprisingly, helpful tips popped into place, voiced by a digital face of Professor Ben. Anyone who knew where to look could do it. With another button press, the auto-pilot was locked, and the propellers sent them onward.

"Everything seems to be working. Looks like we just need to wait."

"That's it? I could've sworn he said it could go faster." Eric had a mischievous look in his eye.

"Let's not mess with it. Last thing I want is to break something."

"So, we sit around and rely on autopilot? How does Ben know this Ryan guy is still there? He didn't even tell us where to look."

Joseph shrugged. "He didn't tell us much of anything. Look where we are. Look what we're doing. I'm pretty dead set on landing, looking around a little bit, maybe even camping out for the night, and then heading back. We'll tell Professor Ben we couldn't find Ryan, and that'll hopefully be the end of this crazy trip."

"Ugh...yeah, that's probably for the best. Not that we couldn't totally take Ryan down! It would be game over before he could blink." He shrugged. "Whatever, I'm gonna take a peek at the inside of this thing!" Eric vanished into the room below.

When Joseph glanced back to the digital map, the island of Murean already lay far behind them. The wind had picked up, and in no time they were floating high above the open blue vastness of the ocean. He stood at the edge of the vessel and looked over the sparkling waters. Each wave glimmered in the sunlight shining through the clouds overhead. A stunning sight to behold, it only served to make their quest seem more out of reach.

"Yeah...I really don't know what we're doing. Professor Ben is more than capable of handling this himself. Hell, I'm sure anyone else would be just as capable. What makes us so special?" Joseph's mind went blank as the question bounced around in his head, only to vanish without running into an answer.

He was growing tired of thinking about it.

He gazed absently at the water, and an unknown amount of time passed without his awareness of it. There was nothing else to do but kill time, so he decided to see what Eric was up to. When he left the controls, he also left his worries as he descended into the lower cabins. When he reached the bottom, he heard Eric shouting from one of the other rooms. What greeted Joseph upon entering didn't surprise him, though it did bring a smile to his face.

"What are you doing?"

"Testing...out...these...beds!" Eric bounced from one side to the other before finishing with a front flip onto the floor. "And he sticks the landing."

He laughed. "Sadly, the crowd goes mild. Just like our trip."

"Yeah, I have a feeling this trip won't be as exciting as I thought. At least not until we land." Eric sighed. "Still better than the plane ride!"

"Not much we can do until then. I'm gonna head back up. You coming?"

"Nah." Eric shook his head. "I'm gonna raid the fridge and see what kind of food Ben likes."

Joseph left his friend to his own devices and climbed back topside. Even the bright sun and invigorating wind did little to prevent his obsessive thoughts, which were beginning to wear on him.

Time passed slowly as he leaned against the railing. Eric appeared at one point to complain about how much of the food was freeze-dried, only to vanish once again. Each minute dragged.

Hours fell away, though he didn't bother to check how many. He drifted in and out of sleep for a while. Perched against the steering wheel, his eyes again closed as boredom shifted into something like a comfortable friend. He checked his phone—barely one bar of signal and useless as a source of occupation. As sleep was about to claim him again, the screen blinked, snapping him back to reality. Even before he looked at the map, the approaching landmass across the horizon caught his attention.

"About time." He looked at the radar, which showed they'd nearly arrived at their destination.

He gave a firm pull on the cord to his right after removing the auto-pilot. The ship slowed, but just as it did, a sudden gust of wind threw off its balance. He seized the wheel and steadied it as quickly as he could, just in time to keep the body from tilting fully to the side.

"Close call. Still not bad for a first-timer, I guess."

Eric staggered onto the deck, yawning as he rubbed his shoulder, and walked up to the side.

"The map shows we're almost there." Joseph cocked his eyebrow. "What happened?"

"Fell off the bed when the ship tilted, smacked my shoulder into the wall."

Joseph winced. "The wind was stronger than I thought. I'm still trying to get the hang of this."

"At least we can get back on the ground and do some exploring."

Joseph nodded.

"How much longer?"

"Let me check." Joseph pushed one of the buttons. The picture shifted to a perfect view of the Skyship and the nearby mark. A glowing line traveled from the NM27, extending in a dashed line to their target location. When it reached the other end, a number appeared in the middle of the screen.

They were roughly ten minutes from landing.

Eric perked up. "Oh, sweet. How'd you do that?"

"I was playing around with some things while you were down there. Professor Ben really put a lot of effort into this machine."

His friend struck a confident pose. "Think you could let the professional stick our landing?"

Joseph stepped to the side. "Please don't blow up the engine again."

"Very funny."

Eric proved himself better this time around, and Joseph watched as they neared the approaching cliffs.

"Let's land near the shore. It should be easier to aim for the open area." Joseph pointed out a smooth spot near the edge.

Eric nodded, but the ship remained on its steady course closer to the rocky terrain.

"Over there." Joseph pointed again. "We can explore the edge for a bit."

"Uh, yeah, I'm trying! See?" Eric spun the wheel, yet the ship gave little to no response at the command.

"What the—" Joseph ran back to the wheel and spun it again, but it wouldn't obey the direction.

"I swear I didn't do anything! This ship just hates me!"

"I know you didn't. It probably broke again!"

How could the Skyship be breaking at almost every given chance? Perhaps Professor Ben wasn't as thorough as Joseph previously thought.

"Get us up higher!" Joseph shifted his attention to the front, watching fearfully as the cliffs drew closer.

Eric yanked on the pulley and they waited.

"Come on...come on!"

"It's not gonna make it!"

They braced for the worst. The waves crashed below as if signaling the impending collision of the ship into the hard blockade. It almost looked like they would clear it, and a rush of hope came, like the rising ship. Until, alas, the bottom of the NM27 scraped firmly into the rocky surface, and their footing crumbled. Joseph rushed to get up, reaching for the power and cutting it. Once the propellers ground to a halt, the ship continued forward, raking the ravaged earth where its hull tore into rocks and soil. When it finally stopped, the momentum launched both him and Eric forward against the hard wooden floor before the NM27 settled with an uneasy creak.

"I think we need to work on our landing..." Eric groaned from where he had face-planted.

"I think we need a ship that doesn't fall apart every time we fly."

Joseph grunted as he stood, rubbing his head and taking a moment to examine the damage.

Eric walked to the controls and tried starting the ship. Though it took a few attempts, the engines rumbled and came back to life.

"What do you wanna bet Ben accidentally used coffee as fuel or something?" Eric kicked the controls before turning the ship off and stepping away.

They climbed down as soon as they tossed the rope ladder over the rail. They landed onto the rough, broken ground. The rugged stone jutting out at sharp angles made for little flat space on which to find their footing. Large boulders dotted the land as far as the eye could see, and all around the crashing of waves made gentle music as they sprayed the wind with salty mist.

Eric stretched, kicking his legs to wake them up. "Man, we were on that ship for nearly five hours? No wonder I'm so stiff."

"We'll get a good look of the area before we finish up."

"I love how Ben didn't even tell us what to look for." Eric cautiously jumped over a boulder. "There's *nothing* out here."

"Yeah, he forgot to fill in a lot of blanks. He seems eager to give directions without thinking them through."

"So, how do you wanna tackle this?"

Joseph gazed into the distance, away from the sea. "Keep an eye out for anything interesting." He picked up a small pebble and tossed it over the side of the cliff.

"Tch, talk about a rocky wasteland. This would be like the sewer level in a video game. You know, the kinda level no one likes."

Joseph ignored his friend's complaints. "Check around the edge, and I'll look further inland. We can meet back here in an hour."

Eric gave him a quick salute. "Yes, captain."

Joseph trekked into the peninsula and gave a closer look at the huge boulders. Some were decorated in odd patterns, yet that offered no aid. It would have helped them greatly had the professor given them more information about the location. Were they looking for a cave in the cliffs, a hidden temple, or something else entirely? There were no signs of Ryan or any life at all.

"This is pointless...there's nothing out here. If Ryan stole the professor's ship, where is it?"

Glancing at his feet, he noticed another odd-looking, discolored slab of rock on the ground. When he examined it closer, he saw its surface was covered with a strange writing encircling a central rune. He'd never seen anything like it before. He reached down to pull it from the earth, but the large disc remained firmly wedged in place.

The old man's words echoed in his mind.

"Mark on the cliff...jump three times. There's no way."

He didn't want to believe it, but out of curiosity he readied his stance, then jumped on the object as hard as he could.

When nothing happened, he jumped again. A third jump and stomp followed, and he stumbled when it sank into the ground. From nearby, the land rumbled, and the cliffs seemed to shift around them.

"Whoa!" Eric shouted.

CHAPTER NINE

THE SUNKEN RUINS

Joseph ran to where Eric stood near the ship. In the distance, massive chunks of stone broke from the cliff and plummeted into the sea. The breaking land slowly carved out an entirely new structure. Once all was calm, the result of the rumbling appeared in the form of a large opening near the bottom of the cliff.

"Huh." Eric scratched the side of his head. "You don't see that everyday. You do that?"

"He said to jump three times. Can't believe it worked."

"I'm glad Ben knew *something* for once. I was worried this entire trip would be a bust."

Joseph didn't want to reveal who had *actually* told him, so he let Eric's assumption slide. "I guess we found what Professor Ben was looking for."

They stood in silence, the waves below the only sound. Joseph tapped his foot, giving the occasional glance to his friend.

Eric suddenly snapped his fingers. "Treasure!"

Joseph raised an eyebrow. "Treasure?"

"Yeah, think about it. If there's some sort of hidden chamber here and Ryan was eager to search for it, there has to be something *amazing* hidden inside."

"You think we should go check it out?"

"I don't see why not, especially if we get to come out of this a little richer, right?" Eric smiled as he wiggled his eyebrows.

"I guess it wouldn't hurt to look around a little."

Joseph scanned the shape of the distant area. It was unclear from where they stood, but it appeared a decent path ran down to the entrance of the gaping hole that had appeared in the rock.

"We'll check down there. I think I see a way in."

He started off leading the way, but Eric soon overtook him, zooming off ahead. They found a section of cliff leading to the lower platform on the other side. It wasn't a secure situation, and Joseph tensed when he looked to the foamy white sea crashing in waves against the rocks.

A watery grave was the last thing he wanted.

"Have I ever mentioned I *really* don't like heights?" Eric gulped as he froze.

"Seriously? What's the difference between this and flying the NM27?" Joseph had to holler over the sound of the waves below.

"Yeah, there's a serious difference between standing on a secure platform and dangling over a cliff, where you could fall and die!"

Despite the fear of a short plunge to a watery death, their first attempt at amateur rock-climbing went better than he'd hoped. They jumped down to the lower ledge that led to the cavern's entryway. When he glanced inside the cave, an interesting detail caught his attention.

An impressive stairway led to a large doorway that had been set slightly ajar. It was hard to tell whether the quake or some previous event had caused it. What if Ryan waited inside?

"I knew it. This place has all the makings of hiding something really cool. Just look at that door!" said Eric.

Joseph studied the heavy metal and stone frame, which had rusted from the wear and tear of time and elements. Despite that, an ornate design was noticeable beneath the layer of copper aging. Joseph approached and shoved the door, but it barely budged. The opening was scarcely wide enough to let them enter.

A cold, stale draft blew over them from within.

Joseph frowned. "If Ryan's on this island, this seems like a good place to start."

"So what are we waiting for? Let's check it out!" Eric squeezed through the opening and vanished into the darkness.

"Hold on a second!" As Joseph followed, his voice echoed deep into the tunnel beyond before disappearing into the unknown void. It took a moment for his eyes to adjust.

Eric's silhouette appeared ahead. "Come on, dude."

Joseph shook his head. "Let's slow down. I don't trust ancient ruins hidden inside an isolated cliff."

"Yeah. You're right." Eric nodded. "This place is probably rigged with all sorts of crazy traps and dangerous things. One wrong move, and you could wind up with no head or flattened by a giant boulder." He grinned. "Good thing I'm an ace with quick-time events."

As Joseph's eyes further adjusted to the dark, they allowed him a better view of their damp surroundings.

Water dripped from nearby, and further down the stone hallway broken beams of light cracked through the structure.

"Careful. We don't know what else is hiding in here."

What should be their main concern—the old, crumbling cavern, or Ryan, who might be lurking nearby? Joseph drew a heavy breath as they moved forward.

Eric muttered. "You know, this would be a lot easier if we had a map or something. Most dungeons have one hidden in a chest somewhere...then we just need the compass."

"I'm surprised the professor didn't already have one." Joseph chuckled. "Just follow the light and we should be fine."

"Ooooooh, it's the light at the end of the tuuuuuuuunnel," Eric said in a spooky tone.

Joseph rolled his eyes at his friend's comment but smiled nonetheless. The ground beneath their shoes was broken and uneven, littered with chunks of stone and rubble. These details he picked up mainly by tripping over them.

"Look over there." Eric stole the lead, running to the illuminated section ahead. "There's some sort of weird writing on this wall."

Joseph followed, stopping where the illuminating rays from outside shone over the aged stone. Carved in the rock face were familiar shapes and lines of all kinds. Some of them he couldn't make out, while others seemed to fall into particular segments. They were like pictures telling a forgotten story.

"Kinda look like those symbols Ben had in that one room."

"A little bit, yeah." Joseph traced his fingers through the indentations.

He leaned closer, trying to make out what they meant, but some of the depictions faded away into the areas outside the light.

"Can you tell what it means?" asked Eric.

"I wish." Joseph looked away from the writing. "Professor Ben might be able to understand it."

"Oh, I know." Eric whipped out his phone and held it out in front of the rock. With a click, he took the picture. "Man, I love technology. Ben wants Magic? Watch"—he smiled impishly—"as I create light!"

Eric tapped the flashlight option on his phone and smirked.

"You're a genius, Eric." Joseph smiled and followed his friend's example.

"Hah, if only you knew."

Joseph made sure the few pictures he took showed off the markings before he held the light out. Most of the symbols appeared to be nothing more than strange shapes and other unfamiliar objects. He and Eric snapped a couple more photos, until one of the symbols caught his focus.

"Did you find something?" Eric asked.

"Only this one, an arrow that points to the right." Joseph moved his finger in the direction it revealed. "And if we follow it over here"—he walked, following the line—"we come across another wall?"

"Worst directions ever."

"Hold on. Something is wrong with this one," Joseph ran his finger over a raised indentation where the arrow-like object had pointed. The loose piece had distinguishing marks on it that resembled a flame.

He placed his hands on the wall and gave it a hard push, but it didn't move. He shoved harder, pressing his whole body into the effort. Giving a heavy sigh, he looked over to Eric and motioned for him to come. "A little help, here?"

"Oh, right; sure thing!" Eric walked over and got into position.

"On the count of three we push," Joseph said as he prepared. "Ready? One...two...three!"

They lunged forward, pushing the wall as hard as they could. Mid push, they crashed through as the rock collapsed into a pile of rubble beneath their bodies. Dust rose from their impact, turning their gasps of surprise into a choking cough. Once everything cleared, Joseph raised his head to look throughout the chamber.

"Dude, secret passages. This is awesome!" Eric hopped up and brushed off his pants. "I wonder what's next."

"Check it out, two passages...two of us." Joseph looked over at his friend.

Eric flashed a thumbs-up. "Great idea. We'll split up. That way one of us is *guaranteed* to take the wrong turn and end up impaled on a row of spikes or something. Splitting up is rule number one in Eric's survival handbook."

Joseph chuckled. "I can only wonder what the other rules are. We'll try this way first, then loop back if we don't find anything."

Their phones lighting the way, they pressed onward. Only the sound of shifting rocks or the occasional gust of wind blowing in from outside broke the eerie silence. The beams of sunlight penetrating the dark corridor were getting thinner and less frequent. The ancient smell grew stronger the deeper they descended, and in no time, the ancient earth and stone denied all hints of daylight.

"I never thought we'd end up doing something like this." Joseph shuffled along the damp hallways. "They really wanted to hide something down here."

"And we're crazy enough to go looking for it," Eric teased.

The wide pathway shrank, narrowing almost enough to force Joseph and Eric to walk shoulder to shoulder. The same etched drawings and patterns from before lined the gray stone on all sides. Their unknown meaning was enough to make Joseph uneasy.

Eric let out a sharp gasp. "Check it out! I knew we were on the right path."

His friend took off running. In the distance lay an open chamber. Mounted to the chamber's stone walls sat torches, the fresh embers of which danced in the air momentarily before floating into the darkness above. More picture-writings of times long past stretched across the room's stone walls.

"*Someone* was here recently. It must be Ryan." Joseph said. "Otherwise, how would the torches still be lit?"

Eric stood before one of two massive statues on either side of an open doorway. The sculptures looked like many different animals mixed into the body of a lion. It held its massive wings raised, as if ready to take flight.

Joseph joined his friend and looked up at them. "Those look like monsters from a video game."

Eric's eyes went wide, and he grinned. "I don't care where they're from. I care about what they're hiding." Eric pointed up at the stone beast's head.

The light of the room flickered in one statue's shimmering eyes, where two blue gemstones rested.

"Just like I said, man. This place was hiding some epic treasure." Eric rubbed his hands and started to ascend the sculpture.

"I don't think that's a good idea." Joseph took photos with his phone before putting it away. "Remember what happened with Aladdin in the cave of treasure?"

"That was fantasy. The treasure I'm *eyeing* has real written all over it." Eric smirked as he sat on the back of the stone head. He started to tug and pull at the embedded gem with his fingers. "We can't pass up a chance like this. Come on, you stupid thing!" Eric's fingers slipped off. "This would go a lot faster if you helped. We didn't get to play an exclusive video game, but we can still get rich."

Eric wouldn't give up. Joseph approached the statue and started to climb. Dirt fell onto his head, and he brushed it from his face.

The statue shifted, causing him to slip back to the ground. He stared as the rock paws curled and the body moved. "Eric?"

"Almost got it." Eric cracked his knuckles but froze in place as the lion's head shook. "The statue just moved, didn't it?"

Joseph nodded.

A deep growl filled the chamber as the stone body cracked. Its other heads came to life as the creature's massive wings spread to fill the air at its sides. It tossed Eric from the back of its head with a mighty roar, and he tumbled to the floor before scurrying to his feet. The second statue opened its ruby-red eyes, joining the first as they faced the duo.

Eric backed up until he was at Joseph's side. "Maybe that *was* a bad idea."

"This whole trip was a bad idea." Joseph took a cautious breath as the many different heads of the beasts snarled. "Any ideas?"

His friend laughed. "When have I ever been backed into a corner? Remember my joke about splitting up?"

"Yeah."

Eric flashed a thumbs-up before one of their enemies lunged. They dove to the side as it landed between them.

Joseph ran down one side of the room, while Eric took the other. He looked back as the red-eyed beast gave chase and gasped, weaving to the side as it leapt at him, crashing into the wall. Its claws tore into the rock, using momentum to run along the chamber's side to cut him off. The impact knocked him back, and he rolled as it pounced. A surprise came when the snake-headed tail snapped at him, just missing a direct hit but bitting through his hair instead.

"Meet me at the center!" Eric shouted during his own escape.

Joseph did his best to evade the swipes and bites, hurrying to the center of the chamber at the same time as Eric. The twin beasts began to circle them like sharks stalking their next meal.

Eric held out his hand. "Wait for it…wait for it…"

Both their attackers growled and went in for the kill.

"Move!"

Joseph followed Eric's command as they each leapt to the side. Their enemies smashed together, causing pieces of their rocky bodies to crumble, and they collapsed.

He gave Eric a high five. "Good one."

"Good thing they were dumb enough to attack at the same time. Turn-based combat has its perks after all."

The walls shifted around them, and a swift wind blew in their faces from the shadows. It was both somehow refreshing and menacing at the same time. Joseph took a cautious step back and held his breath. The room began to darken.

A low rumbling noise began. The sound of grinding gears churned within the walls behind the stone. The torches went out one pair at a time, as if each flame had been on a timer.

Joseph took in a deep breath. "We should get moving."

One of the stone beasts rose to its feet. The blue glow of its eyes intensified, and its mouth opened as a white mist formed within its maw. The door at their backs had begun to close.

Eric snapped his fingers. "Agreed."

They broke into a sprint through the closing chamber door and turned the sharp corner of the passage right as a beam of freezing ice cut into the wall behind them. It wasn't long before the remaining pursuer was hot on their heels.

The torches went out at a faster rate. Everything about the sequence seemed like that of a timed game, one they'd lose if they stopped to catch their breath for even a second. Their next obstacle—a wide pit—confronted them. They leapt and landed on the other side and hardly slowed as the race continued. Another ray of ice crackled along the floor as a thundering roar echoed through the hallway.

Eric grunted. "Sure is persistent, isn't it?"

"Focus on the lights!" Joseph called as they hurried down another turn.

Joseph's legs were going numb from exertion. The cavern was like an endless maze. They rounded one last corner, and the last lights went out next to an entryway. However, the stone above it started to close on the opening, like a colossal garage door.

"Death at our backs, and our only exit is closing?" Eric grinned. "We've got this!"

Joseph managed a short laugh between heavy breaths. The stone fiend leapt the pit and closed the gap. The two friends dove into the entry and crashed onto the dusty ground just as a beam of ice sliced the air. Joseph came to a rolling stop as the wall sealed itself behind them.

"They came to life...good for them." Eric panted heavily as he crouched. "No wonder Ben sent us to do his job."

A chilling pain broke Joseph's attention. His leg had been hit during the attack, and the lower half was encased in ice. All it took was a slam against the ground to shatter the icy prison, allowing him to stand.

"I don't like how he threw us into this. That was real, right?"

"You mean the stone statues coming to life and chasing us down a maze while shooting magical ice breath?"

A crash shook the sealed door, but the great slab of stone didn't budge, trapping the great beast no matter how many times it slammed against it.

"Sounds about right," Joseph said. "This isn't a video game...we're really doing this, aren't we?"

Eric nodded.

They'd emerged into a large, open cavern of damp cobalt rock. Each segment had been elegantly carved away, both by hand and by the twin waterfalls running to the darkness below. From openings came the calming daylight, bringing with it a gentle warmth to the air. Joseph's body was soggy from the efforts of their escape. He leaned up and reached into the flowing water to splash onto his face. Not only was it refreshing, but the water felt and tasted clean. "There must be a natural spring inside these caves."

"Water?" Eric grinned as he ran to the source. "Haha...water!"

Joseph moved over as Eric thrust his head into the rushing stream.

"Ahhhhhh, that feels good." Eric pulled his head away and fixed his hair. "There's nothing like a refreshing drink after a good escape. It's almost better than gold."

Once their thirst was quenched, Joseph looked back to where they'd entered. The door was firmly sealed shut.

"Looks like our way back is blocked."

"I wouldn't go back through that maze of death anyway."

Instead, they crossed the adjacent arch of stone over the emptiness below. It was a crude structure, but it served as an effective bridge to the other side. The sounds of water pattering against the stone was calming. They strolled deeper into the caverns, slowly, in contrast with their earlier, hectic race.

After a few yards along the arch, they entered another passage on the opposite side, which opened into a spiraling incline of roughly hewn steps. It was still bright enough they didn't need to use the flashlights on their phones.

"Man, this place must have taken forever to build," Eric said as they climbed.

At the top, they approached another doorway carved from wood. Placing his hand on the old iron handle, Joseph shoved with his shoulder. To both their surprise, it pushed open with only the slightest creak of protest from its hinges.

Eric moved in first, holding his hands like a gun. He jokingly scanned the area and waved for Joseph to follow.

Beyond the entry lay another new hollow, this one more intricate in its layout. Multiple platforms and steps comprised the design of the floor, where each stone had been carefully set in an ornate pattern. Shelves and cases lined the surface and walls, each filled with old, dusty books and papers. Desks sat near the openings of the room, where the fresh air of the shore battled with the old, musty atmosphere of the caverns.

"We might have found what we're looking for," Joseph said.

Eric ran from shelf to shelf. "This stuff has to be worth a fortune!"

"Don't touch anything. There could be more traps."

Eric dropped the clay pot he'd picked up, and it shattered. "Tch, fine."

147

There were no tracks in the dirt. If Ryan had been there, why was nothing disturbed? Had they somehow beaten him to the chase?

Something else caught Joseph's eye. "Over there."

Eric followed as they ascended a short set of steps in the center, where a stone pedestal stood. Though it presented nothing on its surface, it looked as though something had been there.

"That's disappointing." Eric gave a puzzled look.

"Look at the outline. Something used to be there." Joseph pointed to the smooth surface. "Let's keep looking."

They exchanged a nod before splitting up. Eric busied himself with eyeing the artifacts scattered around the chamber, while Joseph glanced over the writings on the shelves. He blew on the cover of a book, fanning away the cloud of dust disturbed by his breath. When he flipped through the pages, he frowned. The script was the same mysterious language the professor had shown them. Odd symbols and pictures accented the text, but none was legible. Each book he examined after that revealed the same thing. It linked Professor Ben's research to their current location.

"What if he's telling the truth?"

Joseph backtracked to the pedestal, looking for anything that stood out. The only things of note were the same pictographs lining the walls along the other chambers. Figures were depicted in all sorts of positions, holding a variety of objects. It was a story he didn't understand. Lacking new revelations, he trekked back to see if Eric had done any better.

"Getting bored now." Eric leaned against the wall. "Nothing but old books and pots without gems in them. Not even an empty bottle to store things in."

"Maybe there was nothing here to begin with."

One of the chamber doors opened, and a voice spoke. "Or maybe it's because you're clueless and can't think for yourselves."

Joseph jerked his head toward the open door. "Who's there? Show yourself!"

"Yeah, stop hiding, you coward!"

Giving one another a knowing glance, the two friends ran toward the source.

CHAPTER TEN

THE SHADOWS OF RYAN MORTER

"**W**ho are you?" Joseph confronted the shrouded figure in the doorway.

"You don't already know?" the figure asked in an ominous tone as he stepped from the shadows. "No surprise you're as dimwitted as you sound."

There was a fiery quality to the guy that made Joseph uneasy. The wild style of his black and red hair nearly matched the heated joy in the man's sharp, narrowed eyes.

"You must be Ryan," Joseph said as the mysterious figure approached the pedestal.

"You've heard of me?" Ryan moved with powerful steps as his imposing shadow obscured the light. "I should be flattered. I would be if I cared."

"What are you doing here?" asked Eric. "Waiting to give new adventurers their first sword?"

"I have the same questions about you." Ryan flashed them a wicked grin. "Odd that a couple of kids wandered onto a desolate island simply to play about in caves. I'm a touch surprised you found the back door."

"Who're you calling kids?" Eric practically snarled the question.

Ryan didn't answer Eric's question, instead keeping his vision locked on Joseph. When neither gave him an answer, he spoke up.

"You two got tangled up with that freak Ben, didn't you?"

They looked at one another before Joseph answered. "Why do you want to know?"

"I don't need to know, I can tell," Ryan replied. "You wouldn't have come here by accident."

"Then you know what we're here for," Eric said. "So why don't you just hand it over before I make you regret it?"

"You mean this?" Ryan pulled a small vial from the pocket of his dark gray coat. "Concentrated Magic in its purest form. Beautiful, isn't it? They say it can be made from a piece of Sealing Stone. I guess that moron found his fair share of interesting relics in his day."

"Dude, he didn't use it yet!" Eric whispered.

"I noticed."

"Give up, Ryan." Eric ordered as he took a step forward. "You're outnumbered, and there's no way you can get by me."

Eric blew past Joseph, charging up to Ryan with a raised fist. He swung, missed, and Ryan pushed him back to the ground.

"That all you got?" Ryan mocked. "Come on." He raised his arms, leaving his face and body unprotected. "I'll give you a free shot."

Eric growled and attacked. He threw his fist into Ryan's stomach, but the man didn't move.

Ryan smirked. "My turn." He swept Eric off his feet using his foot and then shoved him mid-air back to the rocky floor of the cave. "Better if you sit and stay, like a good dog."

Eric growled. "This dog is gonna chew you to pieces!"

Joseph grabbed his friend by the arm. "That's enough."

Eric snorted and looked away. "You're lucky Joe was here to hold me back, or else you'd be all sorts of messed up." Eric delivered the line in a low, menacing tone.

"Pathetic." Ryan shook his head.

Joseph let go of Eric and glared at the young man.

"What kind of person are you?" Ryan asked. "You're running around like a servant." He flipped the vial in the air while he spoke, as if taunting them with it. "Why are you listening to that idiot?"

Eric rolled his eyes. "That's a long story. It started with a video game demo and a..." He frowned. "Well, a lie. We—"

Ryan cut him off before he could finish. "Don't waste my time. I know why you're here."

The response caught Joseph off guard. "You do?"

He nodded. "You're just another one of his puppets. You're only here because someone pulled your strings and made you dance. That man could spew all the lies in the world, and you'd still be there cleaning up after him. Sorry, kids, but he doesn't pass out treats for the tricks you perform."

Joseph shook his head. "No, that's not true."

Ryan crossed his arms over his chest and tilted his head. "Prove me wrong."

Joseph fell silent, and his fingers curled into a fist. He had no reply.

Eric scoffed. "I bet he and Clyde would get along *real* well."

"I knew it," Ryan said. "You don't have any idea what's going on." He stepped away from the stand, and they backed up in response. "The lunatic professor deputized you into one of his errand runners, though that's better than a lab rat. You don't want to be on the end of *that* needle." Ryan scowled as he spoke those words. "He's an old, blind fool. Wants everyone else to handle the dirty work, while he sits back and collects the rewards."

Eric shrugged. "What rewards? There's nothing here."

"I bet he twisted the story to make me seem like the bad guy." Ryan chuckled in a deep tone. "I'm sure you've noticed the professor is great at fixing the truth to his benefit, though you're"—he shot them a derisive smile—"stupid for believing him."

"I'd believe him over you," Joseph said.

"Your choice. He's a broken man with broken dreams. He's weak but manipulative."

"He's got a few loose screws, but I doubt he's evil," Eric countered.

Ryan shook his head and gave them an impatient look. "Never said he was evil." He laughed. "Didn't you notice all the machines and equipment he has? Those are more than decorative light shows, not that you'd know what any of it does."

"Tch, he's a science nerd," Eric stated. "I bet he likes building things because he's bored. Doesn't have anything else to do."

"That's why I made my move!" Ryan bellowed in a voice that matched his impressive stature. "That moron wouldn't know what to do with any of it. I, on the other hand"—Ryan twirled the vial in front of his eyes—"know *exactly* how to handle it."

"Ryan, you can't drink that," Joseph pleaded in a low, slow tone. "You have no idea what it'll do."

"Drink it?" Ryan's look was one of disbelief. "Drinking this would probably kill me." He seemed to reconsider it. "Nevermind, it *would* kill me." He cast a glance at Eric. "Not a bad side effect if I wanted to silence loudmouth."

Eric folded his arms and glared.

"No, the solution in this vial has a much nobler purpose, but..." Ryan cocked his head, and the grin he gave them was the smuggest one yet—a tall order, considering smugness seemed the man's primary mode of expression. "I'm sure the good professor failed to mention it." He reached into a bag at his side and produced a deeply engraved black book. "You know what Seals are?"

"Pfft, what? I hardly see what sea mammals have to do with this." Eric laughed.

"Don't be stupid—if you can help it," Ryan groaned. "*Magic* Seals exist all over the world. They're arcane rituals used to lock away great abilities thought too powerful for any one person to control. Weaklings have kept these sources hidden and encoded their location inside books like this." He held up the locked object. "Imagine the possibilities were someone to gain command of that power."

"You're crazy." said Eric.

"Says a runt lost in the dark," Ryan taunted.

Joseph came up with a question of his own. "You obviously don't care why we're here, so why are *you*?"

Ryan stopped and looked down at him. "My motives are none of your concern. Find your own answers before questioning mine. You'll be better off in the long run. Regardless, this conversation has reached the end of its utility. I've got better things to do." Ryan turned. "Follow me and you may live to regret it." He nodded vaguely in a direction to his back. "See yourselves out." With a dismissive wave of his hand he left through the door.

"Guess we failed this fetch quest," Eric muttered.

Joseph waited only a few seconds—long enough for Ryan to get a far enough start so he wouldn't see them if they followed. "Come on, we need to go after him."

He'd already lost sight of their new nemesis, but the passageway was a straight shot. Even after they bolted down a descending stairway, Ryan was nowhere to be found. As they rounded a corner, he almost stumbled into Ryan's line of sight but skidded to a panicked halt behind a chunk of broken wall. A few seconds later Eric catapulted into the room. Joseph was quick to grab his friend.

"Hey, there he is! Come on, let's take him out."

"Hold on. There's someone else with him."

Eric gave a puzzled glance and cautiously peered over the rock. "Who's that guy?"

"Don't know. Maybe they planned this together," He sighed as he chanced a peek, too.

"Can you hear what's going on?"

Joseph shook his head. "They're too far away."

"Then what're we waiting for? Let's kick some ass."

Joseph motioned for his friend to stay back. Eric let out a disgruntled groan and slumped into the wall.

Ryan's voice was hardly audible but became louder as his tone grew more eager.

"This is a joke. I knew he wouldn't try to handle it on his own," Ryan said.

The rest of Ryan's words were lost in the expanse of the cave, as were those of the unknown accomplice.

Ryan's voice was suddenly louder again. "Come on. Let's get out of this crumbling heap. Time to claim our reward and show everyone what they're missing."

Joseph glanced at Eric. "Now's our chance." He sprang over the rock and darted toward them.

He crept along the chamber and stayed close to the outer wall, keeping a careful eye on the two as Eric trailed behind. When the next opportunity to move arose, the pair darted over to another busted segment of the ruins. As they did, a piece of stone slipped free and slid to the floor with a crack. They each pressed against the blockade and held their breath as the noise echoed throughout the chamber.

They now stood close enough to eavesdrop on the conversation.

"Problems?" the stranger asked.

"I thought I heard something. This place is so damn old." Ryan's reply was sharp.

"It makes sense. This Sanctuary has been buried for thousands of years, and it's on the verge of caving in," the other figure added. There was a slight Russian accent in his voice. "It's truly a fine testament to the architectural genius of the time. I wish we could have delved this far on our first excavation."

Ryan grunted and waved the stranger off. "Whatever. Not like it matters now."

Joseph held completely still before he leaned out for a look. Both men had continued walking. Joseph crept away from the wall to stay within listening distance. This time he made sure not to produce any noise.

"You think Ryan was right about Ben?" Eric whispered.

"I don't know, but that's the first thing we're going to find out when we get back. No more mind games."

Eric nodded then gasped as he shoved Joseph away. "Get back!"

He rolled away as a massive object flew between them, crashing against the wall with a thunderous impact.

Eric wiped his forehead and stood. "What *was* that?"

Chunks of stone rained down around them as Ryan emerged from the debris.

"Following simple instructions too complicated for you?" Ryan brushed his hands together to remove the dirt and dust from his gloves. An orange aura danced along the length of his arms like a flickering flame, but it was quickly extinguished. "For a couple of sneaky rats, you two sure are loud...and quick."

Joseph glanced at what had been thrown. The broken remnants of a stone pillar lay strewn on the ground. It had to have once stood at least ten feet in height.

"Didn't you *just* say we should stop taking orders? Jeez, make up your mind," Eric replied.

Joseph's body tensed, and he braced his feet as Ryan approached with a roll of his shoulders.

"I can tell we're going to endure a difference of opinion during our very short time together." Ryan cracked his knuckles. "Though I wouldn't expect anything less from two stubborn dumb-asses."

"You're the one that's going to be suffering!" Eric clenched his fists and got into a fighting stance.

"Forgive my lack of fear." Ryan smiled.

The unfamiliar man standing next to Ryan gave them a suspicious glance, then adjusted the round frame of his glasses. "These boys...are they the ones?"

"They're with the professor," Ryan said. "Other than that, I don't care who they are. They're an annoyance at this point."

"I'm Eric Superstar Castis." Eric threw out a fist. "And don't you forget it!"

"Joseph...Erift."

"I told you—I don't care. Come on, Boris. We've wasted enough time with these losers."

The man with greasy black and gray hair nodded and straightened his collar. His thick sideburns nearly ran to his jaw.

"Indeed. I'd rather not give my dear friend more time to gather his resources. Benjamin might be slow on the uptake, but I'd never discredit him entirely. He's the tortoise to our hare."

Ryan rolled his head back and laughed. "Didn't the tortoise win in the end?"

"Because the hare was foolish! Our path shall be one of victory."

The man spoke as if he knew Professor Ben. Yet that in itself drew them no closer to a positive answer.

"What are you planning?" Joseph tried to get closer. "What does any of this mean?"

"Told you they were oblivious." Ryan chuckled without stopping to look back.

"They are a rather poor choice of prospective allies, even for an old fool. Their minds are too dull to perceive great powers," Boris tossed in. "The weak will fall behind."

"Hey, we're talking to you." Eric scowled. "Stop ignoring us!"

The two halted, and Ryan gave his partner a nod. Boris glanced back before turning away to leave again.

"Call for me should you require assistance, Ryan— though I doubt that will be necessary."

Ryan shrugged before returning his attention to them. "You know, I have this terrible feeling you two will become a major cause of headaches in the future, and I'd rather not have to lecture you every single time. How about we take care of things? Right here, right now. You want to know what we're up to? Let me show you."

Ryan popped the cork from the vial with one hand, then pulled out the ancient tome with the other. Eric again tried to rush him, and this time Joseph also made the attempt. He didn't know what would happen if Ryan opened the sealed book, but something made him certain they needed to stop it. Ryan gave little effort in his defense. All it took was a simple spin and sweep of his leg under Joseph's own and they tumbled painfully to the ground.

"Try it again. I dare you!"

Ryan wasted no more time; he poured the glowing solution over the cover.

A previously unseen aura formed around the book's surface. It shimmered brightly in the dark chamber, only to shatter into tiny fragments of faded light. Ryan threw the empty vial to the ground and clasped the book in both hands. The lock snapped then the book was open.

"The details of thousands of years of work were recorded in these texts—history and locations meant to be forgotten. They say we're supposed to learn from the mistakes of our past so we never repeat them, but how can we do that if we leave them to waste and rot?" Ryan shook his head. "They were fools." He flipped through the book's pages. "So many possibilities lie at my fingertips. Soon, they'll all—"

Ryan froze in place, and his lips abruptly stopped moving. The book glowed a sinister black, and the very same kind of light hovered in the air before Ryan's face. The entity—for that's what the light was—forced itself through Ryan's unblinking eyes. Faint voices tickled the air around them, though whether they were real or imagined was impossible to tell. The pair of unseen whispers uttered words from every direction.

Ryan inhaled sharply and fell to his knees, clutching his throat and gazing at the ceiling. Joseph stepped back, unsure what was happening.

Eric also stepped back. "Dude, what's going on?"

"I-I don't know! Stay away from him!" Joseph's mind raced as the scene unfolded.

Ryan's eyes looked far away. "What are...who are you? No! You're lying! That's not what happened!" Ryan stood, punching the air around him. "You have no right! Get the hell out of here! I won't let—" Ryan grabbed his head, twisting in the most unnatural way before letting out a scream.

His eyes were wide with fear. Joseph stared as the light and heat in Ryan's eyes faded to a cold, dead black. At once, the young man's body went limp. Ryan Morter seemed to hang mid-air in front of them.

"Are we in a horror movie?" Eric gulped.

"For countless millennia...our souls have waited for this day, when a primed and tortured being would stagger into our prison and aid in our escape. Those chains are finally severed!"

Ryan's body slowly dropped to the ground and he— or whatever had taken residence within him—gazed at the ceiling. The lack of emotion on his face frightened Joseph the most. Released from those pages, something had found its home inside Ryan Morter's body. When the man's eyes met Joseph's, a twinge of recoil struck Ryan's features, and he turned away without another word. It was like he'd been yanked back.

Without thinking, Joseph pursued him. As quickly as possible, he frantically jumped into Ryan's path, his arms outstretched to block the man's exit. "You're not going anywhere!" Whatever power had been brought to life, he couldn't allow it to leave.

The voice in Ryan's body was cold. "Boy...you dare place your fragile body in our path? You are no obstacle to our release. Your bravery will go unnoticed, and you'll die, unsung, in this cave."

Thinking quickly, Joseph scanned the room for anything to serve as a weapon. Any sort of rock or sturdy item could help his situation. A body sat slumped against the nearby wall. Only its bones remained, swaddled in tattered cloth. At its side lay an old, rusted sword. Joseph snatched it up and held the weapon out before him. He gasped, shaking the sword until the boney arm still clutching the hilt fell away before he thrust the blade back out.

"I don't want to hurt you!" Joseph shouted, gripping the sword with both hands. "But you're leaving me no other option!"

"Yeah, what he said." Eric joined him, and together they faced their adversary. "It's a two for one special. Hope you're hungry!" Eric gave Ryan-who-wasn't-Ryan an absurd wink.

"*Hurt* us?" Ryan's smile was an uncanny rictus. You dare challenge us?"

A shift had occurred in Ryan's voice. It reeked of malice, each word delivered with a hollow echo, as if three voices spoke at once. Amoung the three, Ryan's was the least audible of them all.

Eric stepped back. "What's that about? Is he... possessed?"

"We can't let you leave." Joseph kept his voice level, though Ryan's stare had shaken his confidence. "Not until you tell us what's going on."

"You have a strange power...yet you know too little." A threatening laugh came from Ryan's throat. "It seems wrong of us. Yet what choice do we have? None, it would seem."

It was as if Ryan was conversing with himself.

"He's up to something." Eric warned. "Well, I say come on. Bring it!"

Joseph clenched his teeth and readied himself for the worst. Then, as he raised the sword, a golden light appeared around Ryan's hand. A dark blue swirling aura wrapped the man's entire body, all of which he then gathered into his palm.

"Gninthgila!" Ryan's eyes shot open in a blinding blaze.

The cobalt light in Ryan's palm gathered into a single ball of energy before it flew forward. The singular projectile broke into many arches of surging waves. The bolts pierced the air and sliced through their bodies as a strong electrical current. The force sent Joseph and Eric flying into the wall behind them. Even after the attack faded, jolting aftershocks danced along the stone floor like twitching worms.

Ryan lowered his hand and wordlessly turned to leave them.

"J-j-jeeze." Eric stuttered.

Joseph rolled his head to the side and opened his eyes. Had he been run over by a truck? He had trouble controlling his muscles. "I can't feel anything...my whole body is numb. It hurts." Joseph slouched to a stop and gasped for air.

"I...got this!"

Joseph shuddered in disbelief as Eric got back to his feet. "Don't...it's not worth it!"

"I can handle this!" Eric shouted.

Joseph fought to control his body, barely managing to get up as Eric picked up a rock from the chamber floor. His friend screamed, hurling it hard through the air, striking Ryan in the back, but it did little more than gain his attention.

"That was a warning shot. I'm not done with you yet!"

Ryan gazed at him and rolled his neck, cracking it in the process. "Do you not fear what lies in the deepest shadows of the past? It waits beyond the darkness. Do you know the future you face? It's a terrible...*terrible* fate. Our time has come, and you shall not stand in our way. The gate will open, yet you may not live to see that day."

Joseph staggered until he stood next to Eric. Though weakness plagued Joseph's body—as it seemed to plague Eric's— they each nodded to one another.

"That's not your choice to make," Joseph said.

"The only thing you're killing here is my patience," Eric replied.

"So be it. You'll find no warmth to guide you home. Let this be your first welcoming to the end of all things. Light? Darkness? Neither will find sanctuary here."

The friends needed no further encouragement; as a team they rushed at Ryan.

It was a mistake right from the start. Every punch Eric threw Ryan dodged, and every swing of Joseph's blade sliced only air. Each motion Ryan used to counter their efforts was fluid and effortless, even when he knocked them back with a wave of his arm.

"Krada!" He opened his hand, revealing a glowing orb that split apart and pursued them.

They couldn't move out of its path in time, and before they knew it, a massive fog of radiant darkness collided with them. It spun their bodies rapidly in the air before blowing them to the ground. The painful impact left Joseph's senses confused and broken as he dipped in and out of consciousness.

Ryan lowered his hand and strode to where they'd landed. He shook his head. "To think such weaklings would try to stop us. What a disappointment."

Joseph fought to keep his eyes open. He even attempted to raise the sword he still held, but the strength simply wasn't there. What came next frightened him. It was only for a split second, but two shadows stood at Ryan's sides. Within the single blink of an eye they vanished.

"Soon, the Seal will break, and this age will relive terrors long forgotten. Those of your blood shall kneel before its greatness. Pity you don't know what you truly are. Journey further into the forest of the unknown, if you're curious. The trees have many stories of your lineage. What waits there is beyond imagining."

"W-what...?" Joseph fought to stand, using the sword to keep from falling over. "What did you say?"

Ryan—or whatever entities resided within him— seemed uninterested in his questions. The man that had been Ryan Morter turned away, leaving Joseph with the mental echo of those last words.

Ryan's erstwhile companion Boris had been watching from the back of the chamber. The man cautiously approached, but Joseph couldn't hear the man's words. A sharp, painful ringing had colonized his hearing. He watched, helpless as the man left with Ryan.

He fell back against the wall. Everything in him ached. He looked down. A large gash had been opened on his leg beneath his torn jeans. "We need to get out of here..."

They couldn't stay. He didn't know the effects of the Magic Ryan had unleashed on them. It was real. Magic had come to life around them; they'd felt its power firsthand.

It was like the Magic he experienced in his dreams.

Eric groaned. "Is it finally...game over? Ugh, it feels like it." He let out a sarcastic laugh. "Y'know, I'm starting to think we're not very good at this..."

"We're not done yet. Come on."

The pain was unbearable, but he did his best to help Eric to his feet. Together they limped to the exit, using the wall as support.

"Wait until I get my hands—ouch—on him!" Eric grunted through each agonizing step. "He's gonna be...sorry!"

"Let's worry about getting out of here first. We need to get back to Professor Ben."

"You're probably right..."

Helping one another up the stairs, they climbed until the light from outside glowed warmly into the dark ruins. The fresh sea air drove away the damp, murky chill. Following the path, they emerged outside the raised cliff.

"Hey, look." Eric pointed at the sky, where an engine roared above them.

Joseph raised his head. The ship was almost identical to the one Professor Ben had made. The only differences were the sleek body, extended wings at the back, and the darker red balloon at its top, which rose off the ground while its front end was redirected toward the open ocean. Its propellers spun, and once it got moving, the craft quickly shot away through the sky.

"They stole our ship." Eric pounded a fist into the wall, only to shake it after. "Those thieves! How are we going to get out of here?"

Joseph let out a heavy, painful sigh and shook his head. "That must be the other ship, the one he stole from the professor. That other guy must have helped him." Joseph leaned down to check his leg, and the sight of his own blood made him cringe. He stopped when he noticed Eric was constantly blinking. "You okay?"

Eric rubbed his eyes. "Huh? Yeah, my eyes are just a bit blurry from when I got hit. Got dust in them or something. Think you could look out for me? I'm feeling a bit woozy."

Joseph shook his head. Eric was facing the wrong direction while talking to him.

He tugged his friend's shirt to guide him. "At least we made it out."

"Hardly." Eric joked as they limped onward. A second later, he nearly face-planted from lack of balance.

"You going to be okay?"

"Tch. Don't worry about me." Eric rubbed his shoulder. "I've had injuries ten times as bad as this puny thing. Remember that accident on my bike?"

Joseph laughed quietly. "You were in the hospital a week."

"Yeah." Eric smiled proudly. "Good times."

It took over an hour to reach the other side of the cliff where they'd crashed the NM27, but the battered vessel served as a comfortable sight. When they were close enough, Eric hobbled faster, wasting no time climbing the rope ladder. He almost fell due to his excessive eagerness.

Joseph's leg had gone numb during the walk, but it was an improvement from the throbbing pain from before. He tucked the sword through his belt loop and climbed to the top. When he got there, he pulled up the ladder and tossed it to the side. Oddly, Eric lay face down on the deck near the opening to the lower cabins.

"Too tired and weak to open the hatch," Eric mumbled. "Gonna rest now…" He closed his eyes, and his head flopped to the side.

He didn't move another limb.

Joseph staggered to the controls and drooped against the panel. His ability to focus was leaving him; he could only hope his strength held on long enough. He pulled levers and hit switches, bringing the systems to life. Everything was still functional after their landing. Fighting fatigue, he brought the radio receiver to his mouth.

"Professor Ben...you there? Professor Ben? Damn it, professor—answer. Hello? Are you there? Hello?

It took a moment, but through the speaker came the sound of someone fumbling with something on the other line.

"Joseph, is that you?" came Professor Ben's voice.

"Yeah, it's me."

"What's wrong? Are you and Eric all right?"

"Not really. We had a run-in with Ryan. He was here, and—"

"You found him?" Professor Ben interrupted. "Oh, thank goodness! How did it go?"

"We found him, but we had some—"

"Did you get the solution from him? Did you stop him?"

"Let me finish," Joseph shouted through the throbbing of his head. "We couldn't stop him. Something weird happened to him. He opened this crazy book, and we couldn't get through to him after that."

"This is not good." Professor Ben's tone sounded fearful. "I should have acted sooner. If only I'd been more vigilant, I could have—" He cleared his throat. "But never mind that. There's no point in dwelling on what could have been. Are you and Eric okay?"

"Eric is asleep, I think. We're both pretty beat up. Ryan used some kind of Magic on both of us...my body is starting to feel weird. You were right—Magic is real."

"Oh, goodness. Are you able to fly?"

"The ship is running. Haven't tried to *fly* it yet." Joseph's voice began to fade. The world was growing dark.

"Don't force it. As long as you can initiate the autopilot, I can guide you back safely from here. Are the systems running?"

"Yeah...everything's working."

"Excellent! Press the black button to the left of the screen, and a full map should appear. We can set your course after that."

He pushed the button, bringing the digital display to life. "Got it."

"Do you see the small dot blinking on the map?" Professor Ben asked.

"Found it."

"That is the current location of the NM27. Above it should be a dot that's *not* blinking. Can you tap it?"

Joseph was growing weaker, but he did as Professor Ben asked. "Okay, now what?"

"Give me a moment. I'll enter the coordinates from my labs. Once I am done, I need you to activate the auto-functions, then everything should be set!"

Joseph's head bobbled up and down as he struggled to keep steady. Everything was getting blurry, and the feeling in his fingers faded. Something was humming, though it wasn't clear if it came from the ship's engines or the blood rushing in his ears.

"You're all set!"

Joseph struck the black button with his hand, and the ship began to adjust its direction.

"I still wish I knew how Ryan planned all this out," Professor Ben mused.

"He was with someone else—another man. Look, Professor Ben—"

"Someone else? It could not have been..."

"...Ryan...said you...you were..."

The world went black. Joseph dropped the radio and fell forward. The professor's voice rattled on through the receiver, but Joseph was powerless to respond. His head struck the side of the panel and slid down the controls before he came to a stop on the floor.

He was dragged into a world of dreams.

CHAPTER ELEVEN

HIDDEN PASSAGES

Joseph opened his eyes, but little more than darkness greeted them. It hardly came as a shock that he was back at home. *This dream again?*

The words—his own internal thoughts—became external, spoken aloud in his voice. They reverberated around his room, echoing and repeating.

He shifted to his feet. The cut on his leg was no longer there. He shook his head and stood.

Where is this place? It can't just be a dream, can it? Those thoughts echoed aloud and faded like the ones prior. *I don't get it. What does all this mean? Are you trying to tell me something?*

Again his words would trail into the void, where they called to him from the nothingness and whatever lay beyond.

A female voice interrupted the strange noise of his externalized thoughts. "Are you really that stupid? They could have killed you. You need to think before you act! I can't do this alone. None of us can."

Even though the sound of the voice was soft and understanding, it carried a firm tone, a secondary connotation behind the gentle delivery. Her words had slapped him across the cheek. The door to his bedroom creaked open slightly.

"What if the path I choose is wrong? What happens then?"

This time there was no answer, and he could do little more than follow the guidance. As before, the moment he approached and opened the door, his world shattered like glass. All around him the pieces tumbled, and he fell with them. Yet strangely, during the familiar plummet, it was as if he hardly moved before he landed gently on the invisible ground below.

The voice followed him. "When I was little, someone told me all adventures start with a dream, and we determine who we are when we awaken. At the same time, how can one choose if they don't understand the weight of their decisions? It's not easy to believe, but sometimes when we accept what we don't understand, it helps us find those answers. I can't force you to do that, and I can't do it for you. It's something you'll have to discover for yourself."

The mysterious girl's vague details annoyed him. "Who are you? Why are you telling me all of this?"

There was a pause, then a reluctant sigh. "We both seek the same thing. You have to believe me."

The whispers came again as they had before, but for the first time, these unseen voices were familiar. They were his own words, the words of Eric, the words of Professor Ben and everyone he knew. Questions about everything happening and influences of all sorts floated in all directions. He turned to run, unsure whether he could face the answer, only to come face to face with an image of himself. It stared back at him, as if it were nothing more than a reflection. He raised his hand, and so did the reflection, though a surface of invisible glass kept them from touching.

"You aren't ready, or are you trying to fight it?"

"I don't understand..."

His likeness shook its head and stepped forward. The smooth surface that had been the invisible barrier rippled as the mimic came to life and shrugged.

"Hard to answer, isn't it? If you can't believe yourself, who *can* you believe? Every choice you make has an impact, but how you feel also matters. If you don't feel confident, you won't *be* confident."

"How can I be confident when I don't have any idea what the hell is going on?"

"Forever lost in a dream. Forever lost in a dream. Forever lost in a dream..." it repeated, taunting him.

"Stop, I don't know what to do! Or what to think!" he shouted into the darkness. He covered his ears and fell to his knees. "Why am I here? What do I have to do with any of this? What if I don't want to be a part of it?"

An object struck the ground, causing him to look up. A wave of white light spread from its point of impact.

The hooded figure stood before him, adorned in the same robes of sapphire and white as she had been before.

She extended her hand, helping him to his feet before smacking him in the head with the top of her staff.

"What was that for?"

"You're overthinking this. If you keep this up, you'll be a lost cause. Talking to you doesn't seem likely to get you on the right path."

Her tone had grown frustrated now that she was visible.

"It's not like I can control these dreams. I haven't had control of anything since we got here."

"You could have said no and walked away at any time. If this is so terrible, why didn't you?"

He sighed and folded his arms. An answer evaded him.

"Maybe I felt bad for Professor Ben. Maybe I just didn't want to go home. I don't know..."

The figure gave a short laugh. "Good thing I'm here, then. You need all the help you can get."

"I'm glad this is funny for you." He looked around in the dark. "Is any of this real? Are *you* real?"

"One thing at a time. Let's stay in the moment. Yes, this is real, but also a dream. It's the only way I can communicate with you. Look, I don't want you to screw up and hurt yourself—more than you already have. That's why I'm here. You found a sword, right?"

He nodded. "Back at the caves. It was—" Joseph gasped. The rusty blade had appeared in his hands. "How did—"

"I told you, it's a dream. Don't worry about the details. Do you know how to use it?"

He swung it back and forth in front of him.

The young woman sighed. "That would be a no."

"The only swords I've ever swung before were in video games, and you just press buttons for that. Except for the motion control ones. Eric broke his TV the first time he tried that."

Before he knew it, the hooded figure had swung the bottom of her staff into the sword, knocking it from Joseph's hand. She caught it midair and drew both sword and staff in his direction.

"This isn't a game you're playing with friends. This is real, got it?"

She offered the sword back to him, hilt-first. He took it, frowning as she raised her staff in an offensive stance, causing the crystalline top to glimmer in the dark. The metal staff seemed to extend and retract at her command.

"Let's see what you can do."

"Isn't it a little late for a tutorial? We already lost our first fight."

"That's exactly *why* we're doing this." She sighed. "If you won't start, I will!"

She was on him before he could react. She feinted an attack to make him raise the blade, then swung the staff the other way, knocking him off his feet with a sharp strike to the back of his legs.

He groaned as she loomed over him. Even so close, the details of her face remained hidden under her hood.

"You won't last long like that. Show me how you stand with it. Your stance is important."

Joseph frowned and thought about the games he and Eric had played. He extended the sword, spaced his legs out, and clenched his other hand into a fist.

The young woman put a hand to her head and groaned. "Never do that again. Your intent should be to defend yourself, not pose for a portrait."

"Then what should I be doing?"

"Relax and keep your sword arm ready. Your reflexes are the most important aspect. You want to be able to defend against a strike *and* counter with your own when an opening arises. That's the best an amateur can hope for. Actually, you might want to hold the sword with both hands for now."

Joseph changed to a two-handed gripe. "Like this?"

She gave no warning when she charged again.

Joseph eyed her movements, watching carefully when she slid to his side, dipped down, and swung her staff toward his back.

He raised his arms, blocking the hit with his blade. He stood immobile with shock as her next attacks served as quick rebuttals to his success, hitting him in the stomach and finishing with a smack to the head.

"Stop thinking about what you're going to do. Your enemy won't wait for you to decide!"

Joseph rubbed his head. "Not a turn-based system. Got it."

She gestured with two fingers shaped like a "V," first pointing at him, then at her own face. "Eyes on me. Block my hits without letting me through, then I'll guide you from there."

He nodded, readying himself once again.

She swung her staff. Joseph guided the blade to her strike, causing a small flash of light when their weapons collided. She dipped back, then swung to his side, where he met her again.

The speed of her attacks gradually increased. Struggling to keep up, his nerves on edge, he kept his focus on her. Sparks and light flashed each time her staff met his sword. He fell into the motions of moving and blocking, shifting his feet as together they danced between one another's attacks in the darkness of his dream.

He wasn't sure, but had she smirked before she shoved him back that last time? Another strike of her staff caused a flash of light to stick into the ground. The upright bolt of light remained stuck in place, letting her swing her body around and kick him firmly in the chest, knocking him down.

She landed from her gymnast-like maneuver, and her weapon vanished as she knelt. "Not bad, but not good either. You're not totally defenseless. I think I see what he was hinting at now."

He accepted her offer to help him up. "What's that mean?"

"I'm complimenting you. Just go with it."

He raised an eyebrow but didn't argue. "You're right. Thank you. Can you at least tell me who you are?"

She smiled and shook her head. "Let's see what happens next, okay? My connection with you is fading, and my head is starting to hurt. We each have things to do, but I'll try to visit you again." She approached, placing a hand on his chest and shoving him back. "Good luck out there."

Joseph flailed his arms and gasped as he dropped the sword and tumbled into the nothingness that lay behind him.

He opened his eyes, this time to a different darkness and a more true reality. The dream was gone, and the NM27 was nowhere to be found. The soft sound of crashing waves rose above the peaceful night winds outside as they weaved through the palm trees.

This time he'd awakened back at Professor Ben's lab, or so it seemed. He tried to get up, but the stinging pain in his leg had returned, and he fell back.

"That stupid dream again," he mumbled. "Why always that same one? Am I going crazy? Who's that girl?"

He leaned on the couch on which he lay, one near the back of the room, then felt around his wound. It had been bandaged, and that calmed him some.

"Where's Eric? Where's the ship?"

He glanced around while his eyes adjusted. The heavy sound of Eric's snoring rose and fell from the other end of the room. He sighed in relief and flopped back down to try for more sleep. Joseph turned on one side, then the other; even then, when he began to drift off, a trigger, like the snapping of a tense rubber band in his mind, jolted him awake. His restless thoughts refused to go away. "This is pointless."

A loud crash rang out from the other room, followed by the sound of someone grumbling and papers shuffling. It started as a one time occurrence, but it repeated, then became almost constant. Joseph sighed, then got up to investigate the source. The pulsing sting from the wound on his leg made him limp, but it was bearable. Carefully hobbling to the other room, he found Professor Ben sitting at a desk with a small light in the corner as he fumbled through books and documents.

"Professor?" Joseph staggered into the room.

"Oh, thank goodness." The professor jumped from his chair and approached. "I'm relieved to see you alive and well, my boy!"

"What happened? How long have we been here?"

"You don't remember? You programmed the ship, and it brought you here. However, I'm still in the dark as to what occurred between you and Ryan." He walked back to his desk. "I'm so relieved you two survived. I do not know what I would have said to your parents, had you..." Professor Ben stopped and cleared his throat before he sat on the edge of the table. "That is a thought we need not think about. It was foolish to send you out as I did. I sincerely hope you can forgive me."

"At least we made it back."

"Indeed. I did what I could to pilot you back by remote. You and Eric were passed out on the deck, so I had you both brought in. Of course, I needed to enlist the help of James Carnella to get you back to the labs. You must tell me...what happened over there?"

"After we found Ryan, he told us about how he wanted to use your research to find even greater power. It was something about wanting to get back at someone."

Professor Ben gave a simple nod, as if he already knew. "Ryan seeks revenge? I wish he could learn to control his anger. It seems to be reaching a boiling point. Did he find what he sought?"

Joseph nodded. "There was a book, some sort of information about Magic Seals. He needed the solution you created to open it, but after he did—"

"The Sacred Atlas," Professor Ben said. "That means he found it. Now he wants to unlock each of the Seals. I thought it was nothing more than legend. If he successfully breaks those barriers..."

"Wait, slow down." Joseph waved for his patience. "What are these barriers protecting?"

"Long ago..." Professor Ben strolled to the window. "When Magic was almost a daily pattern of life on this planet, there existed a great and wonderful power, and it was all balanced by the guidance of Light and Dark. A single body for each side held supremacy over those forces. I am not sure of the details, but the holder of darkness became corrupted, and people came to fear what they referred to as Obsidian Magic. Those spells and the beings who wielded them were ordered locked away. The spells were forbidden from further use. While Ryan seeks the power behind these locks, I fear he might find much more than the Magic held within them."

The full weight of the situation hit in the most realistic way. It was hard to deny all the things he'd witnessed.

"That explains what happened to Ryan. After he opened the book, it was like he became possessed by whatever had been locked inside it. He referred to himself as more than one person and seemed to lose control."

"I have no doubt Ryan has unwittingly released one, if not more, of the ones buried behind those barriers. However, I am unable to know for certain." The professor's expression softened. "Thank you, Joseph. You should get some rest. I will do what I can tonight and research this information."

Joseph started to walk away, but paused. "Professor Ben, I want to ask you something."

The man lifted his head. "Yes?"

"Ryan said...he thought..." Joseph struggled to say it.

"Go on," the professor encouraged.

Joseph took in a deep breath as he gathered the words. "He said you were only using us, that you were hiding secrets. Is that true?"

Professor Ben looked at the floor.

He pressed further into the question. "You've already lied to us about a few things, so is what he said true?"

A wan smile graced the professor's face. "Joseph, there are many things in my life of which I am not...proud. My research has taken me down paths I wish I'd traveled differently. A fine example would be my poor choice in sending you and Eric alone on such a dangerous task, though I had no idea what Ryan was planning." He looked up. "This is about more than helping me recover lost research, but I will not unveil the full story tonight."

It wasn't the answer Joseph wanted to hear. "What do you mean?"

"Years ago, I worked with a small team of researchers within a growing organization. We investigated and uncovered many wondrous aspects of the lost world." Professor Ben withdrew a photo from his desk and placed it on the table. The photo depicted three men. One of them Joseph didn't recognize, but two looked oddly familiar. "Nicolas Kerna and Boris Scaylec were part of this growing function. I worked alongside them."

"Wait." Joseph now recognized the second man in the photo. "Did you say Boris Scaylec?"

"Indeed. Why?"

"Yeah, that's him. He was at The Sunken Peninsula with Ryan."

The professor nodded slowly. "So he *is* still out there. Now I know how Ryan knew exactly where to find everything. That must be how he—" the man stopped and shook his head. "I guess I shouldn't be surprised, though I am shocked Ryan would accept his help. Boris and I never saw eye to eye on much. Nicolas and I believed we needed to take our time and properly catalog our findings to the research team in order to predict Magic's stability. But Boris, seemed all too eager to take our field work to the next level. He's an impatient individual. That impatience usually resulted in quite a few injuries to the poor man, but he always persisted." Professor Ben laughed. "We'd research all sorts of things, though Magic was always our top priority. We scoured the globe in pursuit of our passion, from scorching desert ruins to frigid valleys hidden in the mist. Those were the days." An eager smile returned to the professor's lips. "Back then, there was no location we couldn't conquer! It was with their help I was able to forge the solution Ryan stole. I suppose I should be thankful he had the guidance to use it properly, but it doesn't excuse such reckless behavior."

"So, Boris helped Ryan with everything, including the ship he stole?"

The professor nodded. "Boris and Nicolas helped me construct it. We took the prints we dug up during excavations and with them were able to rebuild a fully operational model. I must sadly admit my second attempt to recreate the same vessel wasn't as successful. I had fewer knowledgeable associates, so there was more coffee than funding that time around."

Joseph laughed. "We can tell."

"I came to realize that maybe the dream I sought was a false hope. Boris abandoned our research, and Nicolas found work in another position to continue with his own methods. He and I parted on good terms. I isolated myself from society and simplified my research to studies and paperwork. I continued to work with Magic, but only on a learning basis." The professor took a deep breath. "Yet a fire still burns in my heart to seek answers. The initial discovery of Magic was the first stepping stone, and curiosity sent us to deeper excavations. These events are happening for a reason, and were it not for my aid in these discoveries, I'm positive these ancient works would still be buried and hidden."

"I feel like we've only made things worse."

Professor Ben paced around the room. "No, Joseph. This is the fault of *many*. Magic was not meant to find its way back into the modern world, but that chain of events has already come to pass. Otherwise, that solution would never have been developed, Ryan never would have had a reason to steal it, and none of us would be in this position. There are many things that would be different, but that cannot be altered now."

Joseph crossed his arms. "So, you just want to fix everything?"

"I suppose you could call it my true purpose. While Magic is an amazing force, it comes with great sacrifice. I fear this is only the beginning. You must trust me and help me solve this conundrum." The professor's expression turned hopeful. "In doing so, perhaps you might also learn something."

Joseph sat quietly. The whole story was much deeper than he wanted to admit, but it still made little sense. For all he knew, he was only involved in all this because of Professor Ben and his reluctance to tell the truth from the start.

Looking back at the photograph, Joseph couldn't believe what he saw. A familiar figure that wasn't there before now stood behind Professor Ben and his teammates. The old man with the white beard—the same he'd first met at school—had returned, dressed in the same lab coat as the others. He winked, causing Joseph to gasp.

"Something wrong?"

"The man behind you in the picture, who is he?"

Professor Ben leaned in to look. "I've already informally introduced you to Nicolas and Boris. I'm not sure who else you are referring to."

Joseph looked again, but the man had disappeared. He didn't want Professor Ben to think he was losing his mind, but that reminded him of another topic.

"That brings up something else. I keep having these weird dreams where I hear voices and see this girl who looks about my age, I think. She talks to me directly, and I can't tell if I'm going crazy or if it's something more than that."

"Hmm, that *is* quite interesting. It could mean something, although it could also be caused by stress— little more than your mind attempting to work out an inner issue. I can tell just by speaking with you that you're fighting with your own choices. A worn brain is quite good at overworking itself. That would be my opinion from a psychological viewpoint."

Joseph frowned. "I guess you're right. Thanks, Professor Ben." He started to leave.

"One moment, Joseph."

When Joseph turned, the man tossed something in his direction. Reflexively, Joseph caught it with a quick spin to steady the item at his side.

"Good catch," Professor Ben commented as if the results fascinated him. "A very good catch, indeed."

Joseph's eyes widened. "It's the sword I found in the caverns. Are you trying to kill me?"

"I simply thought you might want it back. You should get some sleep now. Morning will be here before you know it, and we shall have much to consider."

He sighed and walked back to the other room. Clutching the sword, he shook his head and laid the weapon to rest next to the couch. He was tired from the rush of information Professor Ben had fed him, and so, exhausted, he crashed into the pillow. Sleep came quickly, carrying him into a deep slumber.

***

Daybreak arrived, and the warmth of the morning sunbeams warmed his face. The loud yet soothing commotion of avian life outside the windows brought him back his senses. It took a moment, but he shook away his drowsiness and got up with a long stretch. Professor Ben's furniture wasn't the most comfortable. When he placed his foot on the ground and his leg no longer stung, he looked down and moved the bandage to the side. The wound was almost completely gone, as if it had healed over night.

The professor wandered into the room half asleep.

"Did you stay up all night again?" Joseph asked.

"I uh...huh? Oh, why yes. Took me the entire night." He stopped to let out a lazy yawn. "If my studies prove correct, I may have finally narrowed down where they're going, because I surely know they *are* going somewhere."

"Professor Ben, what happened with my leg?" Joseph removed the bandage. "I've never seen anything heal this fast before."

182

The older man gave him a knowing smile as he leaned against the wall. "The wonders of modern medicine are made all the more powerful by Magic. With it, the simplest first aid application becomes an astonishing healing agent. I'm going to get another round of coffee brewing. When you are ready, could you please wake Eric? I have something to show both of you. I believe it is time for us to take another step forward."

Joseph nodded and watched as Professor Ben walked into the side of the wall on his way out. He couldn't help but stifle a laugh when the man finally made it out of the room.

"Sure thing." Joseph took his time getting up before he went to where Eric slept. "Eric. Time to get up."

Eric remained where he was, half-slumped over the edge of his makeshift bed. The situation felt all too familiar.

It took another shake before Eric's body slid forward until his head smacked against the hard floor. Even then, his friend was slow to wake, as if the impact hadn't fazed him in the slightest.

"Did...the ship crash again?" Eric lifted his head, yet his eyes remained closed. "Jeez, what a stupid piece of junk."

"We're back at the island."

"Ugh, I didn't think we—" Eric opened his eyes and snapped to full attention. "Wait, how did we get back here?"

"I contacted the professor on the radio after you passed out, and he told me how to get the ship back. I guess it worked. I don't remember much after that."

Eric stumbled upright and rolled his shoulders, then maneuvered into a few other stretches. "Awesome. So, uh, what's up, then? Breakfast?"

"He said he had something to show us. He's in the other room, waiting." Joseph caught the smell of coffee filling the air.

"I hope it's bacon and eggs. Maybe he'll even have waffles!" Eric stood and abruptly left.

Joseph caught up with them in the next room, where Eric was shaking his head in disappointment. Professor Ben poured a fresh brew into his mug.

Eric frowned. "There's no food. Worst meeting ever."

"Right, then; I'd say we are just about ready." The professor took a long sip of his coffee.

"Ready for what?" Eric asked.

"Ready for our next step in this mission, of course!" Professor Ben pulled the lever behind him.

They stepped back as a nearby shelf shifted away from the wall, revealing yet another hidden passageway.

"This guy is all about caffeine and secret doorways. He really needs a new hobby," Eric whispered.

Joseph smiled. It was true.

"Quick, get on!" Professor Ben waved them onward. "We have much to do."

Eric stepped onto the platform, but Joseph hesitated. He wasn't sure why, but his first steps were reluctant. Maybe it was all the cloak and dagger to the whole situation, but the confined nature of the room he was about to enter didn't sit right with him. Regardless, Professor Ben's insistence and the promise of further explanations pushed him to overcome his reticence.

"Now then, shall we get this show on the road?" The older man pulled the lever, and the platform began to descend. Once it dropped beneath the level of the floor, the area above was sealed off. Railings shot up around them.

Joseph grabbed the border as the podium inched forward, guided by the track system underneath. Once it had moved a few feet, it stalled. The two teens looked over the sides.

It was nothing more than a dark tunnel.

"Why did we stop?" asked Joseph.

"Just wait," Professor Ben replied. "This is the most exhilarating part. Tell me, do either of you enjoy roller coasters?"

"Roller coasters? What does—"

"Hold on tight!"

Lights shot forward, illuminating a long plummet trailing beneath. Joseph held his breath. Something was released from under their stage before it plunged. His scream joined Eric's as the platform fell into the pit. The acceleration was so swift it nearly threw him off balance and his stomach felt ready to come out through his mouth.

The stand hit a curve and swooped as it straightened out and rocketed even faster.

"Wooooohoooooo! This is amazing! Joe, put your arms in the air!" Eric shouted.

Joseph clung to the railing, worried he'd be flung from the safe confinement at any moment. The professor seemed unconcerned as he stood like a mounted statue, taking the occasional sip from his coffee.

The floor took several brief stops before it shifted in direction. The air rushed by their faces as lights from the supporting tunnel raced overhead to guide their way. They sped by every corner and flew in every possible direction, as if in some sort of wild race.

Then, anticlimactically, it was over.

The platform came to a rolling stop near a door, and the rails lowered. Joseph remained still as his brain tried to catch up with his body. Eric tumbled to the floor with an exhausted sigh.

185

"Haha...aw, man. That was the best! I think I'm gonna be sick." He tried to stand up, only to topple back over.

"That is a *perfect* reaction, Eric." The professor put in a code for the door. "Life is not worth living if we don't take a few risks!" He faced Joseph. "Would you not agree?"

"Yeah, sure—just let my stomach catch up." Joseph tried to take a few steps onto the floor presented to them.

The whole world seemed to roll beneath his feet.

"How did you build all this?" Eric stood.

"I had plenty of free time when my expeditions came to an end. Though my research kept me occupied, I missed the rush of discovery. That led to one or two interesting projects, simply to keep myself entertained, you understand. This ride was one of those."

The older gentleman opened the door and led them into the next room. Sunlight coming through the large glass ceiling above illuminated the brightly accented area, yet ripples of water overhead obscured the details of those sunbeams. The sparkling ocean washed over them, and tropical sea life floated through a watery sky.

Eric's jaw dropped. "How in the world did you build all this?"

The professor closed the entrance and led them to the back of the room, where he stopped next to the wall. The chamber was nearly vacant, featuring only a few metal shelves, containers, and one or two strange machines.

"Where are we now?" Joseph asked.

"This is my private lab at the other end of the island. I come here to get away from the racket of the city." Professor Ben danced, moving his arms in the air to show off the space. "It's also perfect for testing more personal experiments away from prying eyes."

Eric gazed at the ceiling. "Is it safe down here? It's pretty sweet, but I don't want a shark to crash through the roof."

"I assure you it's all perfectly secured. That glass is an unbreakable compound similar to what they use for space exploration. You've no need to worry."

It was impressive to think one man had considered and constructed these features. All the trapdoors and secret locations truly made the professor's home a fully operational fortress.

"Now then, down to business. I promised you an explanation and I intend to deliver just that!"

He gave the wall behind him a quick punch with the bottom of his fist. As it rotated, the section revealed a display containing many small objects on the other side. Among them was a remote control. With the push of a button, the room sprang to life.

All around, the walls turned to uncover more inventions and hidden compartments. The floor in the center of the room slid open as the metal surface of a large contraption rose. A crude-looking device, it had been fitted with a seat in the center as many other parts hovered in a close orbit. A spark of electricity made Joseph cringe and step back. When it all finished, the once empty location had been transformed into a living workshop bursting from floor to ceiling with strange inventions and experiments.

Eric took out his phone, snapped a picture, and looked at the professor. "Have I mentioned before you have *way* too much free time?"

A state of shock gripped Joseph; each new invention left him more and more amazed. What most caught his focus was the strange chair-like device in the center of the room. "I think too much free time is the least of his worries." He chuckled before redirecting his attention to the professor. "What *is* all this stuff?"

Professor Ben tried to pluck Eric's phone from his hands, but Eric hid it. "Various knickknacks and creations of mine I've been testing these past few years, but I would like to skip right to our point of interest." He approached the object at the heart. "I must be truthful." His expression became somber as he addressed them both. "It was foolish of me to send you after Ryan with only a flight and a dream. However, I won't deny I had reasons for that action. I hoped a stressful situation within a magically driven atmosphere would help your dormant powers to the surface. The experiment was partially successful. However, I fear I undertook this method without enough precaution, given its dangerous nature. The task of waking your abilities now rests upon my shoulders."

"Wait, you sent us after Ryan without enough information because you thought it..." Joseph sighed. "I don't even know."

"I guess he thought it would give us some sort of special powers. News flash, Ben—it didn't work."

The older man sighed. "Once again, my explanations are lacking. Showing an example of my reasoning would better suit the situation." He pointed to the seat. "Joseph, if you could have a seat right over here."

"Do I have to?"

The contraption looked like something out of a science fiction movie mixed with a carnival ride.

The professor looked to Eric, who jumped back.

"No way; I'm not getting anywhere near that thing. I've seen what your inventions do, dude."

The professor frowned. "What will it take to get you to trust me?"

Joseph could accept the theories. and Magic had proven more than real. However, he wasn't willing to trust the man's skill as an inventor. Between multiple crashes of the NM27 and the other exploding objects in his lab, the last thing he wanted was to lose a limb or end up dead. "I'll try it on one condition."

"Anything. Name your terms."

"You go first."

The professor frowned, but then a fire of assurance flashed in the man's eyes.

"While I doubt this machine will awaken anything inside myself, I'll demonstrate, if that's what it will take." Professor Ben gulped as he moved to the awkward chair. "Could you lock these straps into place for me?" He pushed his wrists and ankles into the gyroscope portion of the mechanism. "Once secured, you need to press the blue button to start it up. As soon as the green button flashes, press that to release the core. The red button will stop it. By all means, if I request you to stop it, *please* do so!"

The teens fastened the professor into place. then approached the panel near the contraption's side.

Joseph pressed the blue button and the machine began to spin. "I really hope this works."

Eric rubbed his hands together. "This'll be fun. About time he got a taste of his own medicine."

"I have a feeling he's tasted that already—more than once."

Bit by bit, the speed increased. The wheels turned faster, spinning Professor Ben within the hub's center. Electricity built up at the top pillars as the rotation formed an aqua-hued barrier of light. Joseph smiled. He could only hope everything went smoothly.

The green button blinked, and Eric jabbed it.

The machine's pumps sped up, as did the spinning wheels. The professor's calls were barely audible from inside the pulsing base.

"What did he say?"

"Huh? I couldn't tell. Sounds like he said give it an hour." Eric squinted his eyes from the light. "I wonder how long before he throws up."

"Maybe we should stop it."

"Cut...the...power!" Professor Ben shouted.

Joseph smacked the button on the panel, but nothing happened. He beat on the red indentation. The machine gave no response.

Eric sighed. "Great, I think it broke."

Joseph slumped his shoulders. "What else is new?" He pounded on the controls. "It won't stop!"

"It...I...can't..." Professor Ben's voice careened wildly about the room. "...sick!"

"Why does he suck at inventing things?" Eric pushed his friend to the side and beat his fists on the malfunctioning controls.

Joseph ran to where the professor was trapped. Sparks flew in the air, and he backed away from the out of control device. It shifted into higher gear as bolts and parts began to break free from their bindings.

"Aw, crap." Eric stopped beating on the buttons and shot a panicked look at Joseph. "It's gonna blow!"

"Quick, get behind something!"

Together, they ducked behind a nearby desk. Smoke rose to the ceiling as a painfully loud humming filled the room. The floor and the entire chamber quaked until everything gave out, almost all at once. The machine shattered, throwing Professor Ben into the far corner, where he crashed into a shelf and slumped to the floor. Small pieces of his broken creation rained down on him.

CHAPTER TWELVE

REVEALING THE MAGIC WITHIN

"**W**ow, he went flying!"

"Professor Ben!" Joseph ran to where the man had landed.

Eric slid on his knees along the smooth floor to join Joseph next to the collapsed professor. "Whew! That flight was easily worth a double score." He licked his fingers and used them to put out a flame on the professor's head.

Joseph lightly slapped the side of Professor Ben's face a few times before the delirious researcher opened his eyes.

He coughed, and small puffs of black smoke drifted from his singed hair. "Might be a few...a few bugs left to work out on that device."

"You think?" Joseph and his friend helped the older man up. "Now you know why we're concerned over you trying to jam us into these odd inventions of yours."

"Your point might...I just need a moment." The professor hobbled on his feet, then collapsed into a nearby stool. He reached for his coffee mug, but in trying to drink it, he got more of the dark liquid on his face and coat than in his mouth. It was so careless, it seemed intentional. "Ahem. Perhaps we should skip to Plan C."

"Oh wonderful. Can't wait to see what *that's* gonna be." Eric rolled his eyes.

"Rest assured, this method of awakening will prove much less risky." Professor Ben staggered to the shelf, coughing up the remaining smoke from his lungs. "Confidence is key!"

"I wish I knew what you were talking about, but since you almost killed yourself, I guess we can afford to give you a chance," Joseph said.

Eric shrugged but didn't smile, as if he'd finally reached a level of risk that concerned him. "Sure, bring it on, I guess."

The researcher shook his right leg as he hobbled forward. "Right then. If you two could just follow me."

Joseph stayed close, as every few steps the professor stumbled and swayed. A few times he nearly toppled to the floor. They approached another device near the back of the room. The thought of what might happen next made him cringe. This contraption appeared to be an electric ball of light. It sparked and shimmered on its pedestal.

He was still worried.

"Should I just get back behind the desk now?" asked Eric.

"I promise this method is as simple and safe as humanly possible."

"You've been saying that about pretty much everything." Joseph leaned in to examine the object, but from a safe distance.

As if to settle their fears, Professor Ben reached out, and without hesitation placed his hand on the orb. Nothing happened, aside from his hair standing upright from the static. He gave them a confident smile. "Satisfied?"

Joseph glanced at Eric, who appeared more than interested in the mechanism.

"So, what do we have to do this time?"

"I'd like for Eric and you to place your hands on the orb. I'll guide you from there."

Eric was first to do as instructed as he gave a toss of his head in response to the static in his hair. "Shocking." He flashed a wink at his friend.

Joseph chuckled as his palms touched the surface. A warm tingling rushed through his brain and the rest of his nerves. He looked back to their instructor.

"I'm sure you feel the current. That's a pure magical charge. A crystal in the core keeps the radiating energy in a constant pulse. Think of it like a battery." The professor walked around them. "Now then, I wish for you to simply close your eyes and focus as deeply as you can. Think of absolutely nothing in this world or beyond, so you might allow outside influences to come forth."

"There goes my excitement," Eric muttered.

Professor Ben continued talking, but the voice grew less prominent in Joseph's mind as his closed eyelids blacked all visual input. He did as told, focusing on nothing. Bit by bit, the mental images and thoughts slipped away. Only the older man's slow mumbling remained. Silence and serenity had taken over, but as this wave of calm was building, a shout from Eric shattered it.

"Jeez...what the hell?" Eric complained.

Joseph opened his eyes, but it was too late.

The sharp pinch of an injection needle pierced his skin. Though he jerked away and swatted Professor Ben's arm, the deed was finished. The professor had already shot whatever was in the needle deep into Joseph's body.

"What did you do?" Joseph raised a fist, ready to strike the older man, but a rush of energy made his legs buckle. Had Professor Ben drugged them? "What's happening?"

"I promise my intentions are not sinister!" The researcher remained close. "Give it a moment, and the side effects will dwindle. Pushing so much arcane energy into a body all at once can cause a head rush."

Joseph's vision faded in and out, and the colors of the room were changing around him. Ripples ran through his vision, distorting everything as the world shifted in and out of slow motion.

"This is it...this is the end! I'm a goner!" Eric groaned from nearby while recording the event with his phone. "A mad scientist is going to use me as an experiment. If anyone finds this, post it online for the world to see."

Joseph's breathing grew rapid. His vision dimmed until only the bright, fiery outlines of the room were visible. Was Ryan right? Had they unwittingly become one of Professor Ben's experiments?

"I can't believe it!" The professor said in a shocked tone. "This is truly fascinating. I knew the effects would be potent, but I never dreamed the results would be so *forceful*. The combination is astounding."

Rage built inside of Joseph. It was like a flame had appeared all around him. Then his vision returned. Something else had been set ablaze.

Joseph flailed his arms, extinguishing the small hot flickers that had appeared along his hands. After he'd extinguished them, there was no trace of a single burn.

He stood to confront the mad scientist. "Enough with the games and the secrets! I'm tired of it!" He stepped forward, pushing the man back against the wall. Not only was he infuriated, but the literal flames he'd seen frightened him. "What did you do to us?!"

Eric stood as well, then raised his fists in an offensive stance. "Start talking before I punch the Magic out of you!"

The professor quickly raised his hands and calmly approached them. "Please, calm down. I am well aware of the trust I just lost, yet what I did was akin to jumpstarting an engine. Had I asked, would you have permitted me to inject you? I doubt you currently trust me enough to allow it."

Joseph rubbed the point of injection on his neck as his breathing settled, too flustered to reply.

"Of *course* not!" Eric said. "That's crazy, and so are you!"

"What did you do to us?" Joseph asked in a more collected tone.

"I have infused your bodies with a powerful Magic concentrate. In time, I'm hopeful it'll aid you in recovering the dormant energy that rests inside your souls." The professor stepped forward once they let him move. "It has just shown me a definitive result. Everyone has some Magic lingering inside them, but not everyone can awaken that power on their own."

"You've gotta be kidding me," Eric tapped his shoe on the floor. "First you yank out my hair, then you jab a needle in my neck?"

Joseph couldn't think of anything to say. The odd images inside his head distracted him and made his brain itchy.

"I truly wish there were another way. However, if we're intended to follow through with our course, this was a path I had to take."

"*Our* actions? Like we have a choice in the matter? Every time we trust you, it backfires."

"This vacation keeps getting worse," Eric added. "The only *treasure* we found in that dungeon tried to kill us. Our parents are going to ground us for eternity because of you!"

"You have been doing a lot more choosing than you believe." Professor Ben chuckled. "I could not force you here, nor could I force you to remain here. You made those choices on your own, did you not?"

"Curiosity," Joseph shrugged. He truly wanted to believe his words. "You keep telling us one thing and doing another."

"This is the last time I listen to a strange man in a lab coat who bribes me with cool stuff." Eric shook his head.

"Destiny has a way of guiding us down our chosen path. However, since we're here at precisely *this* moment as well as this choice, I feel it best to continue onward." He turned to Eric. "If you look, you'll find that, unlike Joseph, there is no mark on your neck."

Professor Ben presented Eric with a mirror.

"Hey there, handsome." Eric smiled and blew a kiss to his reflection.

"Look closer at where the needle pierced your skin," the professor instructed.

Joseph's eyes widened. Even from where he stood, it was obvious Eric had no mark.

The man pivoted to face Joseph. "I'm sure those flames you saw were all your imagination, right?"

He wasn't sure how to respond. That the professor mentioned them meant Joseph wasn't the only one who'd seen them.

"You might think my methods on the strange side, that you have little reason to believe me. Yet what you've seen is by no means false. Since words alone have not fully convinced you, and I knew they wouldn't, I have done what I can to show you this new world. That way you may come to your own conclusions. The Magic you've seen in this very room came not from me. It's always been a part of *you*. I am simply helping you awaken them."

Joseph couldn't argue with his own experience. The Magic from his dreams, Ryan's attacks, and now their own bodies were hard to deny.

"You mean we've always been able to do this?" asked Eric.

The professor shook his head. "I'm afraid that is not the case. While this odd fate has set you and many others on a remarkable journey, the trials down that road remain rather diverse. You share an *inner* knowledge of Magic. That doesn't mean you can acquire it at the snap of a finger. Yes, it is there, but it was inactive."

"Hmm. So, we totally *do* have the Magic in us?" Eric's face lit up. "Sweet." Eric turned to face his friend. "You're a wizard, Joseph." He smirked. "The powers of the universe are ours to control! Prepare to face my infinite cosmic power, Ryan Morter!"

Eric's amusing reaction helped lighten Joseph's sour mood.

"I'm afraid you still don't understand, Eric. You each have the *ability* to manipulate the forces of Magic, but that doesn't automatically give you the knowledge and skill to do so."

"I don't get it. Can we do stuff with Magic or not? You're confusing me," Eric grunted.

197

"If you permit me to finish, I would be more than happy to explain." Professor Ben crossed his arms.

Joseph nudged his friend in the side to keep him quiet. Eric's interruptions were keeping the professor from explaining what had happened.

Eric sighed. "Fine, but make it quick!"

"As I was saying. You have the gift of Magic, and I'm"—the professor exaggerated his slow speech with hand motions for emphasis, as if explaining something to someone hard of hearing—"going to teach you how to use it. This is an intense road, so don't expect much at first. Everyone starts somewhere."

"Do we have the time for this? You said we need to go after Ryan as soon as possible, but you want us to study Magic?" Joseph asked.

The man let out a quick burst of air, seeming to acknowledge the truth of Joseph's words. "Time really is our worst enemy, and while I can't fully prepare you in the small window we have in which to act, I can place you on the correct road. Before we start, however, you will both need a Channeling Device!"

Joseph flashed his friend a confused look as Professor Ben strode to one of the shelves and pulled open the display drawers. He blew away the dust inside, then quickly waved them over. Inside lay many different wand-like objects of all sizes and colors. They ranged from simple-looking sticks to more radiant specimens adorned with crystals and elegant patterns on their hilts. The whole thing seemed rather hokey.

"Your Channeling Device will be what you use to draw forth the Magic inside you. While the appearances mean very little in terms of function, I always felt personalization was an important factor. I've read some Magic casters didn't even require such devices. Sadly, as novices, you'll need one to fully operate your casting preparations."

"Novices? You clearly haven't seen me in action." Eric struck a confident pose. "They don't call me Quick-Draw Castis for nothing!"

"When has anyone ever called you Quick-Draw Castis?" Joseph chuckled. "I thought you were set on 'Eric Superstar Castis'?"

Eric made a few mock punches at Joseph's face, grinning when his friend jerked in response. "See? You barely saw it coming."

The professor ignored him as he moved to the side. "Select whichever one you want, and we shall proceed from there."

Joseph stepped back when Eric jumped in and began rummaging through the selections.

"Nope. Nope. Not this one." He picked up something shiny. "Too flashy." He selected a black mat doodad. "Not flashy enough."

Eric's shuffling occasionally required Professor Ben to reach out to grab a stray item carelessly tossed in his direction.

"Aha! This one is perfect." Eric held up a rather fancy item, a stick with a twisting handle and a round orange gemstone at the top. "It's the perfect magic wand for the most skilled Magic user."

Professor Ben cleared his throat. "It is a Channeling Device, Eric, not a magic wand. A wand doesn't—"

"Yeah, yeah. Tomatoes are potatoes or whatever. Let's get to the good stuff."

The older man motioned for Joseph. He stepped closer to the box and scanned the different devices, but none particularly caught his eye. What felt right? Did he care? He reached in, grabbing the first item he touched and pulling it out. It had a straight base and a jagged green stone perched on its peak. He was satisfied enough with the choice. "Yeah, I guess this one will do. So how does this work?"

"Seriously. I want to get to the part where I blow things up with my mind."

Professor Ben made a gesture that demanded patience. "We will get to that, but we must—" He cast Eric a bemused expression. "Blow things up with your mind?" The man blinked vacantly before shaking his head. "We must first delve deeper into the powers of your mind. Magic is a method of focus and concentration, especially at beginner levels."

Eric again rolled his eyes at the mention of their inexperience.

The professor ignored it. "Now, Joseph. I want you to clear your mind of everything. Rest assured, I'll not be jamming any more needles into you!" He laughed in an exaggerated way at his own joke.

Joseph cocked an eyebrow but did as he was told. "No more surprises this time."

"Let your thoughts drift away. Act as if you're swimming through your dreams, seeking out a hidden power. You know it's there, buried in your subconscious." Professor Ben spoke gently. "Float through the nothingness, and wait for it to find you."

Eric snickered, but Joseph ignored him. He had to admit he found the process silly, but he followed along. The professor went completely silent, and the room seemed to float away.

"That's...there's no way." Eric gasped quietly.

"What is...?" Joseph paused as he opened his eyes again, this time catching sight of the same fire from before. Dancing arcs of red and orange had gathered atop the crystal on his wand, though they faded into the air when his concentration broke. He looked at Professor Ben with wide eyes.

"You know more than you think, Joseph." The professor gave him a reassuring pat on the shoulder before he wrote down a few notes in a nearby book. "I feel by the end of this we'll all have learned great things." He turned his attention to Eric. "If you would please follow your friend's example."

Eric's eyes had already closed as he stood with fists raised in an eager stance. "Come on, baby. Give me something good."

"You need to concentrate for this to work," Professor Ben admonished.

"I know. I'm doing that." Eric squinted tighter. "I hope it's something amazing. I wonder if I can fly. Oh, man, that would be so cool!"

"Eric!" The older man shouted.

"Oh, right. The focusing thing. Got it!"

Still in awe, Joseph couldn't keep from smiling at Eric's attempts. For once, his friend seemed to find something that calmed his bountiful energy. Professor Ben's whispering words guided him through, and soon enough a strange light formed around Eric's chosen device. It faded when his friend opened his eyes at Professor Ben's command. While Joseph didn't know what it meant, it made for an impressive display.

"Hah! I *knew* we weren't amateurs. How's *that* for a first try?" Eric stuck a victory pose.

"Excellent. Now give me a moment." The professor returned to his notes, then grabbed a nearby book from the shelf. He searched the pages, nodding to himself and humming enthusiastically before slamming it shut. "Right, then." He looked up at them. "These are a bit basic, but they're not a bad start. They should be more than suited to your current objectives."

"Come on, tell us!" Eric was at risk of nearly chewing through his own lip.

"Joseph, the power you unveiled was that of Fire." He shifted to the other teen. "Eric has revealed a talent in the healing arts known as Cure. This makes for an excellent balance."

"Excuse me?" Eric's smile faded. "Healing...arts?"

"Healing is a vital talent, Mr. Castis. The ability to aid yourself and others is not to be underestimated, especially in a dire moment."

"Oh, come on!" Eric groaned. "You're telling me Joe gets the cool setting-things-on-fire spell, and I'm stuck playing doctor? From everything we've seen so far, I thought Magic is all about shooting lightning bolts from a stick, not administering modern first aid." Eric pranced around the room, twirling the item in his hand. "Look at me. I'm a fairy, and I'll make all your troubles go away with a wave of my wand."

"It kind of fits when you do it like that," Joseph teased.

Eric grunted. "Do shut up. Right now."

"There is much more to it than that, Eric. These are only the first steps in uncovering the latent powers dwelling within you. Over time you will learn more, but you must be tolerant. Patience and practice will help, but they must be given a proper chance."

Eric lowered the wand and walked back over to them. "Yeah, fine. You better not be lying again."

"Before I start, do either of you have any questions?"

Joseph glanced at Eric, who shrugged in response.

"Then we'll move on to our first lesson. Now that you've taken the first steps in learning Magic, you need to learn how to cast the spells. To do this, you'll need complete concentration." Eric opened his mouth to speak, but the professor cut him off. "No exceptions. Even in chaotic situations, you must remain focused on the spell of your choice and think about nothing else. Envision it so thoroughly you bring it to life. You need to *feel* the heat of fire, the *chill* of ice, and even the soothing effects of a healing moment. While doing this, the power will move from your body and soul to the Channeling Device, where it will gather in the gem. Once the spell has built enough strength, you release it by calling its name. Of course, those already trained in these arts can obtain more powerful effects, gaining greater knowledge of far stronger spells. Does that make sense?"

Joseph nodded. "Sounds simple enough."

Eric smiled. "Finally. Something easy to understand."

"At its core it is very basic, but don't let your guard down. Casting spells requires more than speaking their name. It comes from a deeper understanding of the balance in this world, or in this case the balance of Light and Darkness. Spells of an offensive nature are often referred to as Obsidian Spells, as they cause harm to others." The professor raised a lecturing finger. "Including the caster if they're inexperienced. Then you have Magic that heals and protects. Those spells are called Ivory Spells. Years of study were often required to learn a single enchantment, and that was back when Magic was at its prime and casters displayed natural talent. In this day and age, that energy has faded from people's minds, and Magic sources are few and far between. Its knowledge and effects can still be found. These pools are scarce, but our research shows that works of Magic can still be performed. Perhaps our minds have become lazy in this era." The professor shot Eric a menacing look as the teen pulled out his phone.

Eric put the phone back in his pocket. "Why can't we learn from those books?"

"I am afraid the books act only as guides toward the lost knowledge. They have no magical properties left within them. You must master how to focus, so your mind is always open to learn." Professor Ben brought over another book and opened it. "You never know when you might cross paths with an object or location that still clings to the Magic it once bore witness to."

Joseph thought over the information the professor had given them. What he understood of it made sense, and he understood quite a bit; it was the first time Professor Ben's rambling hadn't sprained his brain. "You said we need to declare the name of our spells to summon them?"

"Precisely, and the process is rather simple. You should already know the name of your spell is Fire," the professor clarified.

"So after the spell's complete, I raise the Channeling Device and shout Fire?"

"Not *precisely*. Sadly, this is the only step that requires a part of the caster's memory." Professor Ben shook his head. "Nothing would happen if you only said the word fire."

"But you said that's what it was called." Joseph raised an eyebrow to the conflicting statement.

"It is, but for it to work, you must say the name of the spell in its *original* form. That's how it works for some reason. I never fully learned how this came about." The professor scratched his head. "From what I've read, the spells were altered slightly from their original intent in order to mask their effects from enemies in battle. I suppose, in comparison to how Magic functions in fictional writing, it's still a rather simplistic method. Whatever works, I suppose."

"What's its original name?"

"The spell's original name is the name of the spell in reverse." He took a book from the table and flipped through the pages before setting it down. "The name of your spell is Erif." He shrugged. "A simple fire spell."

"Erif. Easy enough, I guess."

"It should be. You say your last name often enough. It's like it was meant to be." Eric playfully punched his friend in the shoulder.

The connection made it easy to remember.

"Now then, Eric; the name of your spell would be Eruc, which is a basic cure spell."

"Ugh, they always stick the healer in the back, too. I never asked for this."

"Now then; let's see these spells in action." The researcher smacked a button on the wall, and an object that looked like a large punching bag on a stick rose from the ground and maneuvered until it was in front of them. He nudged Joseph forward. "Try to hit that target with the spell you just learned. Give it a good, hard burn."

"Wait, right now?" Joseph scrunched his face at the thought. "Are you sure?"

Eric goaded him on. "Go on, dude, let's see some action."

He sighed, looking at the item in his hand. Despite whatever fancy term Professor Ben gave it, the thing looked like a magic wand from a fantasy game or movie. He gave the object a skeptical look, then faced the target. "I'll try my best."

"I have the utmost confidence in you. Focus on the spell, imagine the energy, and bring it to life. It'll be like painting a picture in your brain and"—the man pantomimed the act of pulling a rope—"pulling it into reality."

Eric whistled and stepped farther away, smirking.

Joseph carefully gripped the wand and focused. Images of fire flooded his mind as he tried to picture the thing he wished to create. Images of burning buildings, a campfire, and matches helped fuel him. He felt strange, as if a surge of energy welled up inside him. Then the energy faded as the gem at the end of the wand pulsed an intense red and small sparkling embers swirled around the stone. The gemstone flashed, and he felt the distinct physical presence as the energy peaked, crackling in the air around him.

The professor's smile was pure. "Now is the moment of truth. Cast the spell!"

Joseph thrust out the wand. "Erif!"

Something within him, perhaps his soul, rattled to life, and the device trembled in his grasp. There was a powerful force pushing back, akin to a handgun's recoil, when the wand released a powerful burst of fire. It blasted out in the form of a small orb, then smashed into the target. A blazing eruption burst outward as the crackling flames spread along the bag until the fire reduced it to nothing more than a sizzling pile on the ground. He surveyed what he'd done, still as a scarecrow and with the same astonished, unblinking stare.

"I just..." He turned to the professor, his mouth agape. "Did you see..." He glanced at Eric. "Can you believe it?"

Eric lowered his phone and slowly nodded. "Caught it all on video!"

"Congratulations!" Professor Ben slapped him a few times on the back. "For your first attempt, I'd say you handled it incredibly well."

"Hah." He shook his head, trying to dispel his awe. "Thanks. I can't believe it worked."

"Tch, how am I gonna compete with that?" Eric gave his wand an annoyed look. "Cure isn't as cool as Fire."

"Don't underestimate your abilities, Eric. You have great power inside you. All it requires is for you to reach out and take it. This is our first step of *many* into the task of uncovering it."

"But I want to set stuff on fire, too. Aren't there any healing spells that can blow things up?"

"Would you *please* stop worrying about blowing things up and looking cool."

Eric cringed. "Okay okay."

"Now, come here." The man beckoned Eric closer. He quickly and unexpectedly produced a small knife from his coat and cut Eric across the arm in one swipe.

Joseph cringed at the sight, but the cut wasn't deep. His face took on an anxious expression. *I hope Professor Ben knows what he's doing.* He forced himself to relax. Joseph had produced a fireball, just like the professor had promised. He had more trust in the man than ever.

"Ow!" Eric jerked his arm away and cradled it. "What do you think you're doing, you crazy psycho!"

"Quickly, use the spell," Professor Ben demanded.

"Screw the spell. Call an ambulance instead! My arm is gushing like a river. I didn't come here to donate blood, man." He held his arm out, keeping the dripping wound away from his clothes. "Somebody get me a towel."

"You have to be able to focus in *any* situation. Danger could arise at any time, and you *must* be prepared to act. Now," the professor pointed to Eric's wand. "Use the spell."

Eric's dramatic display made Joseph smile. His friend was great at putting on an act, but he was intrigued.

His friend held the wand in his other hand, pointing it at his cut as his face took on an expression of focus. His wand glowed a bright white as if something sparked within him. "Eruc!"

The teen's wand released two small sparkling orbs that shot out and surrounded his arm. They swirled in a delicate orbit around the open wound and drifted closer before disappearing into it with a soft flash. The cut shined, as if filled with light, then both the cut and healing light faded away. The blood dried before flaking away into dust at Eric's touch.

The astonished young man moved his arm around, a dazed look on his face. "I think I just found my calling. I"—he stared at them—"am a god."

"I think he's over not being able to blow things up." Joseph flashed a smirk to Professor Ben, who nodded.

"This is all a step in the correct direction. Each victory brings you closer to a new beginning and more advanced spells. Do you feel comfortable with what you have learned here today?"

Joseph nodded. "I'm glad you finally explained something. It still feels like we've stepped into a weird corner of reality."

"Hah, a corner? This is insanely awesome." Eric admired his wand. "Ryan Morter, you're about to feel my fury." He flashed a condescending smile. "Dude, we went easy on him last time. Wait until he sees this."

"Excellent." The professor nodded. "Now that we've got the basics covered, we can discuss our next step." He slowly walked to the room's exit.

Joseph and Eric followed, and they rode the hectic platform back to the main lab.

The researcher closed the passage behind them before he led them to the front. Next, he pulled a pile of papers off the shelf, took one, and spread it open on the table.

The professor moved a finger around it. "Ah yes, *this* is where I believe Ryan has gone."

"I hope your directions are better than your inventions," Eric teased.

Professor Ben ignored the cocky teen. "This is a map of a Sanctuary called The Forbidden Sands. It's located somewhere among the ruins of ancient Egypt. If Ryan is after power, he may very well find it there." He tilted his head. "If the myths are true and the location exists."

Joseph remembered something. "Oh, I forgot to mention. Right before Ryan left, he said he can't let us interfere with *our* plans, and he mumbled about breaking some sort of seal, no matter what it took. He talked about the trees knowing the location or something. Any idea what that means?"

Eric looked confused. "Did he say that before, during, or after he beat us senseless?"

The professor thought for a moment before he crumpled the map and tossed it aside. "Well, that's worthless." He searched the pile of papers again before pulling out another and setting it down. "Let's try this one."

Eric sighed. "We're gonna get lost again."

"Joseph has revealed a very important clue. Were it not for him, you'd have been wandering the scorching desert for absolutely no reason." He chuckled as he flattened the paper.

Joseph folded his arms. "Okay, where does this lead?"

"This is the Sealed Forest. It is rumored to be somewhere in an isolated area said to hold sacred powers. If Ryan is looking for a seal to break, this is where he's heading. It is rumored to lie somewhere near the southern region of the Pacific Ocean. I think it's an immense chunk of land covered in a vast forest." The professor hummed after the last sentence. "That's what the legends say, though it is not an easy landmark to pinpoint. This is the last *known* location."

"I'm starting to feel like his personal assistant, only without the pay," Eric groaned. "Run here, grab this, do that, stop someone. This sounds like the work of an intern, not a hero, Ben."

"Hmm. Perhaps you're not familiar with The Twelve Labors of Hercules. Remind me to find something on the subject for you at another time." Professor Ben smiled before continuing, "According to what I have read, the location is home to the Protection Seal, a spell that prevents corrupted entities from gaining access to our world. They were defeated and ultimately locked away. Suffice it to say, it's a doorway to another realm, one we would never want to open. There are many labyrinths outside our known reality."

"Why does Ryan want to break it?"

"Perhaps he's not the one hoping to open it. Something about his actions makes me fear there is more going on. Our only course of action is to locate and stop him. It's a stretched effort, but one we must attempt nonetheless." Professor Ben handed Joseph the folded map as he walked by, then paced the room.

Joseph stuffed it in his pocket. "What if we can't stop him?"

"We won't know until we try. I'll give you the location details before you depart. That should—"

A knock at the door interrupted the discussion, so the professor excused himself to answer it.

"Oh, good morning, James," Professor Ben said from the other room. "Please, come in."

Professor Ben appeared with Jam Carnella behind him.

"Hey, Jam," Joseph said.

"What's up?" Eric bumped fists with the islander.

"Hey, what's going on?" Jam smiled.

"Eh, same old thing. Magic, evil things, and *lots* of explanations," Eric replied.

Joseph nudged Eric with his elbow.

Jam chuckled and pulled a book from the bag he carried. "Hey, it's all good. Nice to see you two are awake this time, you know? Anyway, I wanted to return the guide to you, Professor. My aunt said it was a great help with her mixtures."

"By all means, it was no problem at all. Tell her she's welcome to it any time she might need it. I hope you are ready as well, James. We've a long road ahead."

"Jam's coming with us?" Joseph squinted.

"I am sure you'll find James' particular talent rather useful."

"I don't get it. I thought we were, like, the chosen ones or something." Eric frowned.

Jam smiled. "Hey, looks can be deceiving, you know?"

"He's been helping me for a year or two now. I was amazed to see James has a rather special talent in the workings of Magic. A profound and deep understanding of how the world's energy flows together with the life around it."

Eric folded his arms. "I don't recall ever being told we'd share the spotlight."

"As always, demonstrations work better in these cases. James, would you show us the power behind your melody?"

"Hey, no problem. It can be like a send-off, you know?" Jam waved for them to head outside.

They followed him out the door, and it didn't take long for Jam to prepare as he pulled out a small piece of aged parchment from one pocket and a flute from the other. The instrument extended with a twist. After quickly licking his lips, he raised the instrument and played.

It was a low melody, but it held a familiar upbeat tone that reminded Joseph of the evening he and Eric watched Jam play with the island band. It was then he recalled the other event he'd seen as the effects of the song took hold. A steady wind picked up, one far warmer than the cool breeze from the nearby ocean shores. The other strange thing was that the winds Jam summoned were visible, appearing as faintly colored aqua and white-hued swirls gathered around his body. The intensity was strong enough that they wrapped his body completely, then lifted him from the ground. It lasted only a moment, but it was a powerful display.

"Phew!" Jam took off his hat, wiped his forehead, and smiled. "It's still a work in progress, but the more practice, the better, you know?"

Joseph was speechless. It seemed they weren't the only ones who had the gift of Magic.

CHAPTER THIRTEEN

SURVIVING THE STORM

"As you might have noticed, James possesses a unique gift. He has the ability to gather the life of our very world through his music. Over the course of the past year or so, I've noticed he is quite the talented Channeler. Just as you and Eric hold your own gifts, James also has an awakened sense of his own." Professor Ben smiled. "In fact, almost every person has an inactive connection to Magic resting within them. It's all a matter of how it is circulated."

"Hey, you might say I have the music in me. It's all about the melodies of life!" Jam closed his flute, gave it a twirl, and tucked it away. "So, it looks like I'll be sailing off with you two!" Jam grinned. "More the merrier, you know?"

"That's impressive," Joseph said. "We'd be glad to have you along. Right?" He glanced at his friend.

"Oh that is *so* not fair," Eric mumbled. "They might as well be handing out tickets at this point. Free Magic for everyone."

Professor Ben laughed. "Right, then, I believe we have our course, and our goals are set. I do not ask you three to place yourself in harm's way to prevent Ryan's errors, but something must be done to make sure he doesn't break that seal. Nothing good can come from disturbing the slumber of ancient Magic in such a reckless manner. But I also fear for his life."

"I guess we'll wing it. Not like we haven't done it before," Joseph replied.

He wasn't comfortable with being rushed from place to place all the time, though Professor Ben musn't have planned for any of this in the slightest. They weren't the ones winging it; *he* was.

Once inside the building, the researcher hurried around his lab, gathering things for their journey before ushering them onward.

"I think he's had too much coffee and not enough sleep again. He's more wired than an electrified cat," Eric said.

As they walked down a familiar passage, Professor Ben turned on the lights and hurried them to the dock, as that's where the NM27 had been moved.

"Don't just stand there, get on. We might already be too late in this mission."

"Then maybe you should let up on these lectures. I feel like I'm back in school," Eric complained.

Jam went up first, followed by Eric.

After Joseph started to go, he stopped and turned around. A curious thought had come. "Professor, I have something I've been meaning to ask."

The older man raised his eyebrows. "What might that be?"

"If Eric and I didn't agree to go along with everything, what would you have done?"

The professor shot him a rare smirk, and his tone grew menacing. "I have *many* connections, Joseph. It would be easy for me to make you and Eric disappear without a trace."

Joseph let out an insincere laugh. "Really?"

The professor chuckled. "It's a joke, my boy. Though I admit I can be rather persuasive when the situation calls for it. But I must insist we continue."

Joseph was about to climb when the man halted his progress.

"Have you forgotten?" The scientist handed him the sword and a piece of paper.

"Why do I need that when I have this?" Joseph asked, producing his wand.

"You never know what could happen. Plan for the future, or you may regret the past. As for the paper, it contains the instructions on how to get information into the ship for its autopilot. And please, watch yourselves out there. I'd hate to admit it, but the dark powers surrounding Ryan might not be the only threat you encounter. I am sure the forest won't be happy to be awoken from its slumber."

Joseph nodded and continued climbing, though he had an uneasy feeling about the professor's warning. When he got to the top, he put the ladder away and approached the controls. After a few flipped switches, the engine started and he yanked the lever to get the propellers going.

"Hope everyone's ready!"

The ship rose to the crest of the room, and he rotated the craft toward their exit. The ceiling overhead parted, allowing the sun's afternoon rays to welcome them into the sky. After Joseph set the controls, the engines thrust forward, carrying them into the blue wilderness.

The familiar feeling of the wind rushing by was refreshing, and Joseph glanced back as they departed the professor's labs. Soon, they'd left the entire island behind once again. It wasn't long until the radio at his side alerted him, and he looked to where Eric and Jam were talking.

"Eric, could you grab that?"

"Huh? Oh yeah, sure." Eric ran over and snatched up the receiver. "You've reached second commander Eric. S'up?"

"Ah, yes, Eric. I wanted to be sure you were able to enter the location of your destination into the ship's internal database through the system controls."

"Uhhhh..." Eric looked to Joseph. "Did we do that yet?"

Joseph pulled the paper from his pocket and handed it to Eric.

"Okay, got it." Eric unfolded the instructions, and after a few taps, beeps, and clicks on the panel, the screen lit up. "Looks good on our end!"

"One moment. I can check the information from the data here." There was a moment of silence on the other end of the radio before the professor's voice returned. "Excellent. Everything's in perfect order! As long as we don't stray from our goals, we have a decent shot at this. There is just one last thing you all need to know. When you arrive at your destination, don't be discouraged by the contradictory appearance of the area. These sanctuaries are protected from the view of our kind. The Sealed Forest will more than likely be hidden from view. Magic is extraordinary in that it's unseen until it's in the presence of other Magic. That is very much true for these locations, so it should be the key you require."

"What does he mean by 'our kind'?" Eric tilted his head away as the voice continued from the other end.

Joseph shrugged, keeping his eyes on the sky until they were a safe distance from the island. The last thing he wanted was to encounter another aircraft in midair.

"The presence of other Magic should be sufficient to remove the protection spell. Put a good casting in that direction and you should be good to go. I'll be in touch the entire route should you encounter any issues. The best I can do for you now is wish you the best of luck. I have faith you'll pull through."

Professor Ben signed off, and Eric set the receiver back down.

"Hey, it sounds like everything is all set." Jam gave the panel a good pat with his hand. "I've always been impressed with the professor's research. It's amazing the kind of things he's created, you know?"

"You've known all about this from the beginning?" Joseph set the ship's autopilot.

"And you never told us about any of it?"

"Hey, sorry, guys. The professor asked me to keep it all under the sand. He wanted to make sure his tests were accurate. He also didn't want me scaring you off with crazy talk about Magic. Have to admit, you were both really jumpy when you got here, you know?" Jam laughed.

"Eh, whatever. Not like it matters now. When Ryan gets a load of us, he's going to beg for mercy. He won't know what hit him."

"I don't think it's Ryan we should worry about. I don't want whatever happened to him happening to us."

"Tch, yeah, right. Those shadows couldn't handle this much awesome." Eric raised and lowered his eyebrows a few times. "All right, captain, how long before we get there?" He tossed his arm out to the sky beyond.

"The location he gave us means we might not reach it until nightfall. Good thing he stocked the ship with supplies."

217

"Great. More of that weird dried food. Good thing Ben installed electric outlets on this ship." Eric took out his phone and wandered off.

"I'm glad to have some down time. Having that man rush us all over the place gets…tiring." Joseph let out a long sigh and stretched.

"Hey, you get used to it after a while. He's like a hurricane at times when it comes to his passions. I remember the first time I met him and he saw what I could do. The man actually fainted." Jam chuckled. "It keeps his drive moving, you know?"

"I'm not surprised. I'm sure all the coffee doesn't help. How long have you been able to do that?" Joseph felt strange talking about Magic powers like it was a normal occurrence. It made it sound like a hobby people shared with one another.

"It happened one day when I was practicing my music. I was with a group of friends playing when I noticed the ground beneath us shifting. I thought it was because of how loud the melody was, but later that night, when I played on my own, the same thing happened. It was strange to see. Water on the beach would do it, too, and even the wind seemed to like it. Talk about moving the earth, you know? The professor calls it Channeling. Ever since I told him, he's helped me develop it further. Who would have thought, you know?"

Joseph nodded. "This trip's had lots of surprises, that's for sure."

"Hey, I'm going to check our situation on the ship. Keep things moving." Jam raised his fist, and Joseph gave it a bump with his own before he walked away.

Left on his own, Joseph looked to the sword on the deck and the wand already in his hand. "So much for a summer of gaming and junk food. Who'd have thought?"

Eric's voice caught his attention from the other side of the ship, where he was playing a game on his phone. Jam's music soon rose from the lower cabins, even if it couldn't fully exceed the hum of the engines. It was unnatural having everything so calm, especially without Professor Ben's chaotic energy spiraling around them.

The day progressed slowly. At one point the three of them raided the pantry and sat down for a makeshift meal. The discussions were light, consisting mainly of things unrelated to their destination. It was a nice break from all the talk about Magic.

By the time evening rolled around, the ocean below had become entirely still. All wildlife had vanished, and the golden fire of the sun at dusk cast its shadow over the water. Despite the quiet atmosphere, it was an eerie combination. He strode to the controls, where the map still failed to show any marks on their destination.

"I would have thought we'd at least be close by now."

He strolled where Eric and Jam sat messing with some stones on the deck. It looked like they were playing an improvised version of checkers.

"Anything yet?" Eric slid one of his pieces forward.

"Nothing. Screen's still blank."

"Good, 'cause I love the sight of the ocean everywhere." Eric's sarcastic tone rose as Jam claimed one of his pieces. "Oh, come on. You cheated."

"Hey, you gotta watch where you step on these waters." Jam taunted.

After another hour, there was still no indication of the location or even any land. Boredom had proven their biggest enemy. At this rate, would they find Ryan in time, or at all?

Joseph's gaze wandered from the digital map after a low rumble from the distance drew his focus. From the south—in the direction they were heading—clouds had begun to weave into the sky. "Now what?"

The billowing cloak grew larger and darker the closer they got, and a troubling wind blew across his face and through his hair. It was a warm gust that greatly contrasted the cool ocean air. It wasn't long before arcs of lightning flashed over the reddening canvas of the sky. The sparks seemed to come from a living shadow, as he'd never seen a storm form out of nowhere so quickly before.

"Guys, I think you should check this out." Joseph kept his vision on the tempest ahead.

The event was unnatural.

"Hold on. I'm about to make a comeback," Eric said.

"Yeah. I really think you should see this."

Jam left the game to join Joseph by the side of the ship.

"Hey, you can't run away from a boss battle like that," Eric called after him.

"I don't like the way that looks. This wind feels disturbed, you know?" said Jam.

Eric gave in and joined them.

"Now what's the big—whoa..." Eric's jaw froze at the sight of the atmospheric wall forming over the horizon.

There they stood, silent. The sound of the howling wind was increasing in strength to match the crashing lightshow.

"Hey, is there any way around it?" asked Jam.

Joseph gazed into the horizon, where the clouds formed a ring around the ship. Every angle was being swallowed. "I don't think we have a choice in the matter."

He slowly approached and placed a shaking hand on the ship's wheel to brace not only the ship, but his own body as well.

Eric's gaze never left the atmospheric phenomenon. "Anyone else getting a strange feeling of impending doom?"

A large bolt of azure lightning raced across the sky, followed by a loud cracking rumble as it faded.

The radio hissed as Professor Ben's voice came through in a distorted tone. "Is anyone there? Can any of you hear me?"

Joseph grabbed the receiver. "Professor, what's happening out there?"

"Joseph, I've just picked up an *incredibly* strong gale developing close to your proximity. It's something I have never encountered before. It might be dangerous for you to continue, given the circumstances!"

"*Might* be dangerous?" Joseph replied. "You should see it from here."

"It's like staring down that last piece of pizza after trying to eat an entire large by yourself." Eric had broken away from his fascination with the oncoming storm.

"You need to get the ship above the clouds or it'll be torn to shreds," Professor Ben urged. "The systems aren't primed to handle higher elevations, but it's a lesser risk than facing this squall head on. The protective field from the magic core of the engine should be enough to keep you safe at such an altitude."

"I thought you said this ship could withstand anything!" Joseph shouted over a roar of thunder.

"Well, yes, I believed it could, but when I picked up this low front, I realized it might be better to play it safe over sorry. The winds I am picking up could send you right into an electric storm and fry you to a crisp! You *must* find a way through. I've never tested the NM27's resistance to external electrical interference."

"Once again, this is information we could have used *before* we left! I just learned how to fly this thing a few days ago."

The radio static grew more intense as the dark sky closed in on them until, slowly, everything was encased by the crimson billows.

"You can—just try—just—" Professor Ben's voice was lost to the sea of static, and the white noise claimed him completely.

"Professor Ben? Professor, you there? Can you hear me?" Joseph tried desperately to regain contact. "Damn it!"

He slammed the receiver.

"I'm guessing this would be a bad time to use the bathroom," Eric said as he watched the glitches on the map.

"Hey, did he know what's causing this?" asked Jam.

"The radio went out before he could finish." Joseph rushed to the front of the ship to watch the storm.

The clouds swirled as if ready to burst into something more dangerous.

"Ben really needs to learn to get to the point," Eric added.

The deck below their feet tilted as the ship listed from the rocking gushes of air. The low creak of stretched and twisting boards filled the air each time it adjusted. In a desperate rush, Joseph darted back to the wheel. All the systems had started to shut down, forcing them to default to manual operation. Every button he tried malfunctioned.

"Have I ever mentioned I hate this piece of crap ship?" Eric kicked the control panel.

Joseph's whole body trembled. While the blood-red clouds unleashed no rain over the scene, the whipping winds and electric strikes rocked the very sky. The ocean below also swayed in an uneasy series of undulations, as if beckoning the ship into its watery clutches.

"Hey, it looks like we're flying right under it. Is there any way we can get above the storm? Try to ride it out, you know?"

"The professor said the same thing, and I've been trying, but the controls aren't responding." Joseph yanked on the levers, but nothing happened.

"I hope he installed some airbags," Eric groaned.

"We're not going to crash. We've just—"

Joseph couldn't finish his sentence when the storm shook the ship. Lightning crashed near the side of the vessel as the wind kicked up. He lost his grip on the controls, and all three of them plummeted to the deck. The platform turned again, buffeted by the wind.

Eric was the first to leap up and regain charge of the wheel. "Anyone have a kite? Bet we could set a new world record."

Joseph staggered back to his feet, but the ship hadn't stopped rocking. Lightning split the heavens again, splitting the blackness around them. The rain came next, pelting the ship like a battalion of machine guns.

"I'm starting to miss our boring summer!" Eric shouted over the noise.

Joseph and Jam ran to join him, and together they fought to regain mastery over the ship. Their rocking and drifting became constant, driving them off course. Sheets of rain quickly made puddles on the ship's deck and slickened the surface.

"Hey, of all times to leave the umbrella at home, you know?" Jam joked.

Joseph appreciated the musician's attempt, but there was no time to enjoy it. They twisted downward as funnels of wind and water snagged them from all directions. The ship was cracking under the weight of pressure.

"Eric, turn the wheel left. We need to try and level things out!"

"I'm trying."

Before they realized it, the body of the NM27 had crashed into the water's surface. They'd descended right into the ocean, only to be raised back into the air by the rising currents. Everything around them was tossed back and forth. Joseph grasped the wheel as his screams joined Eric's and Jam's as they all rode the waves. The storm jolted them from one side to the other; up and then back down again.

"I think I'm gonna be sick!" Eric called out.

"You're not the only one." Joseph slammed his foot against the deck, trying to keep his balance.

He spotted the lever beneath the wheel when he fell. Professor Ben's warning echoed in his head, but it was the perfect moment to ignore the man's advice.

"Jam...hit that lever!"

Jam darted over and shoved it.

The fires at the back of the ship roared to life, sending the entire frame into convulsions.

"Everyone, hold on!"

They gripped wherever they could as the force from the rocket's fire drove the ship to the very limits of its ability to hold together. After a swift nosedive into the water below, they shot off into the sky, slicing through the wind's lashing current. The direction of their flight was unsteady, and it took a moment for it to realign before their ride gained full speed. The shaking of the sudden blast bordered on painful. The fatigue of steadying themselves against the ship's momentum mixed with the constant assault of the falling rain, which acted like needles on their skin.

"I don't know if the ship can survive these speeds... you know?" Jam struggled to speak through the rushing gusts.

Joseph couldn't reply; the forces pressing against them were too strong. They rose, the ship carrying them higher as they all fought to keep from falling off. The vessel ascended so rapidly, their breathing became harder to maintain until with a final burst the bow of the NM27 pierced the black and red clouds like a great cresting whale on the cloud ocean's surface. They'd broken free of the chaos.

Their acquired altitude was frightening. There were no clouds to obscure their vision, which allowed a full view of the approaching night. A smooth, cold wind blew around them, while the serene sparkle of stars and the bright glow of the half-moon contrasted against the angry flashes of the storm below.

"We are literally...on top of the world. Selfie time," Eric whispered before snapping a picture with his phone.

However, even with the protection of the vessel's core, the oxygen was overwhelmingly thin, and Joseph began to feel lightheaded. The momentum they'd gained from their breach slowed. The ship creaked as its front tilted forward before it gradually plummeted back down through the clouds. Arcing flashes of purple and blue still tore through the sky, but they were growing less frequent.

On their return, a break in the storm had shown itself. All around them the clouds had started to drift apart. The gushing storm calmed, and a crispness in the air became apparent once again. The threatening gale had ventured off and given up the chase. Despite the reprieve, it took all three to keep the ship steady until the controls returned to normal.

Stumbling away from the wheel, Joseph stared in the direction from which they'd come. The spirals of crimson shade dispersed, as with a last rumble and flash of light the storm was gone.

Eric let go of the wheel and hurried to the starboard side of the ship to look at the sky. "Man, we really breezed by that one. Take that, lousy weather."

"This can't be the eye of the storm if there's no storm to have an eye, you know?" Jam retrieved his hat from where it had snagged on a wire. He shook off the water before placing it back on his head.

Joseph couldn't believe the circumstances. A freak tempest had materialized out of nowhere, encircled their location, and nearly sunk them. Then in the blink of an eye it had faded back into oblivion.

"Did Ryan cause that, or something else?" Joseph sighed. "I can't believe we're alive. We're alive." A sense of joy came from saying those words.

"Hey, we even got a free shower, you know?" Jam said with a grin.

The sky had changed from the golden glow of dusk to the purple hues of evening. The sun faded and the stars appeared overhead, twinkling through the clouds in the shifting canvas. Joseph looked at the map to see it had come back on, but the radio wasn't functioning. The map showed the ship was now flying right next to the Sealed Forest's location. Yet when Joseph looked over the ocean, there was nothing. He reached over and turned off the engines, causing them to drift until they hovered, dead still.

"We're here, but I don't see anything." Joseph stepped to the side to show them the map.

"That doesn't make sense. How can we be right over it and not see anything, you know?" Jam gave them a perplexed look.

Joseph recalled what the professor had mentioned before they left. "The barrier."

He wiped the water from his eyes. It looked like the sky ahead was moving. It wasn't caused by the movement of clouds in the soft breeze but something else entirely.

Ripples appeared in the air as if it were a body of water, and everything around the area appeared distorted. Even the glowing moon was a strange, rippled version of itself.

"Hey, did you see that?" asked Jam.

The odd formation soon became more visible. It was as if the ship had bumped into an undetectable presence.

"It must be the barrier Professor Ben talked about."

"Did he tell you how to get rid of it?" asked Eric.

"Magic requires the presence of Magic to be seen." Joseph took out his wand and approached the edge of the ship to face their obstacle. The veil seemed close enough for him to touch, though it wasn't. He began to focus, but this time was different—Professor Ben wasn't there to guide him. Eric yawned as time seemed to stop. The gem of Joseph's wand flickered, flashing with small flames as he envisioned the spell. Before long, the energy rose, ready to be let free.

"Erif!"

The flames gathered before they flew from his wand in a fiery orb that cast a glowing light into the dark. It raced into the distance before it caused a massive disruption across the surface of the invisible obstacle. As the shock wave passed, its light enveloped the area, blinding them with its flare. Then the illumination shattered, fading into the night as their sight slowly returned.

The view of an island materialized as the rippling wall broke into fragments of glowing white. The image was blurred at first, but once the magical veil broke up completely, a new vision greeted them. An enormous mass of land covered from one end to the other by immense trees now floated in the vast ocean below.

They'd found the illusive island of the Sealed Forest.

CHAPTER FOURTEEN

SECRETS OF THE SEALED FOREST

"**W**here in the world did *that* come from?!" Eric leaned over the side to gawk at the remarkable view.

Joseph would have happily gazed over it longer, but a lightheaded feeling swept over him, causing him to stagger.

"Hey, you okay there?" Jam steadied him.

"Yeah, I just...felt a little weak. Casting spells takes a lot out of me."

He shook it off, making sure his legs didn't go out from under him. His stamina had never drained so swiftly before.

"Check that out!" Eric pointed to the shore of the island. "Isn't that the ship Ryan took off in?"

"Maybe we're not too late." Joseph piloted the craft to the clearing and hovered over the sand until he had the right mark. It was difficult to find a location, as the beach was littered with large roots that snaked through the sand and extended far out into the dark, blue ocean. Once they landed, he shifted the gears off and grabbed what he needed. It felt good to land the ship *without* crashing.

Joseph tossed the rope ladder over the side. "Make sure you have everything, and keep an eye out for Ryan and Boris."

"Yeah, let's go kick some ass!" Eric said.

Once they had their things, they descended the ladder. Joseph pulled a flashlight from his bag. Eric and Jam did the same.

"I don't see anything over there. They must already be inside, you know?" Jam flicked his light in the direction of the silent vessel.

Joseph frowned. "I doubt they'd waste any time, but if they're still inside, we don't want to—"

"It's the perfect time for a surprise attack." Eric dashed down the beach, making a line straight for the docked ship.

"Eric!"

Joseph and Jam took off after him, but Eric had already made it inside the second Skyship before they could reach him. Facing no other choice, they rushed up the same path. By the time they'd scaled the top, Eric was already returning from the lower cabins.

"Figures. There's no one here. We were too slow. And look at this thing!" Eric spread his arms wide to indicate the entire ship. "It makes our ship look like garbage. You should *see* the rooms down there."

By now, the only light they had was that of their flashlights and the moon watching over the island with its army of twinkling companions.

Joseph sighed. "I think at this point we should wait until morning to go after them. I don't want to go in there at night. We can rest up, get everything set, and be prepared bright and early."

"Hey, sounds like a good plan."

They performed a quick sweep of the ship before they left but found nothing out of the ordinary. After pilfering some food supplies, they headed back down. They gathered a large stack of driftwood from the shore before Joseph summoned another Fire spell to ignite the logs. This time, his vision went blurry from casting the flames. It worried him; would it be permanent? Perhaps it was because he was a novice. He had no shame admitting that's exactly what he was.

Gathered around the fire, they cooked the canned meats and other foods they'd taken with them. Without the noise of a city, the only sounds remaining were the crackling of burning timber and the gentle wash of waves against the shore. It made for a peaceful setting and mixed well with the upbeat melody Jam practiced on his flute.

"You know, this stuff isn't that bad." Eric took a bite of his meal.

"Hey, you'd be surprised what you could make with that canned stuff. It's a delicacy back in Hawaii."

"Just don't try to feed me any more fish guts." Eric cringed.

Jam let out a lighthearted laugh and returned to his music.

Eric shoved Joseph in the shoulder. "Everything okay over there? You haven't said much since we landed."

Joseph snapped free of his thoughts. "Huh? Oh, it's nothing. I'm just...thinking."

"What's there to think about? We find Ryan, and we knock him senseless. He doesn't break this seal thing, and we finally get to enjoy our trip. *Bam*. We're heroes."

Joseph shook his head as he stirred his food with a finger. "Something worries me. Ryan had a full day ahead of us to reach this island. Right now he's in that forest looking for the seal."

He cast his eyes to the looming jungle. Everything about the location seemed unusual.

Eric shrugged. "Maybe he got lost."

"Why would it take him this long? Why hasn't he already finished it? What if something in that forest stopped him? It seems…"

"Weird…" his friend said. "Now that you mention it, that does sort of freak me out." Eric paused before stuffing his face with more food and continuing on in a mumbled tone. "Guess we'll find out when we get there."

"Yeah, I guess so." Joseph set his plate to the side before lying against the log so he could look at the sky. Out there above the island, away from city lights, the stars sparkled in the celestial canvas over their heads.

***

Night passed into its uneasy slumber, but it slipped nonetheless. The light of day too quickly came and chased away their sleep. The fire had gone out. They packed their supplies, and shortly after, they set off for the forest. Sandy beach transitioned into tangled grass. Trees as high as skyscrapers blotted out their view of the sky. A problem arose.

"Anyone know how to get inside?" Eric gazed at the towering walls of living wood.

His friend was right. There was no way into the core of the woodlands. The trees grew in such a way around the outer rim that it was impossible to see beyond their massive trunks. It was a true fortress of nature, unless it had been aided by a lost magical force.

"Whatever's inside obviously doesn't want to be found."

"We could always try burning it down." Eric smirked.

Joseph shook his head. "I'm not burning down the forest. I doubt it would work anyway."

Jam pointed out footprints between the massive roots in the sand. "Hey, what about those? They can't be ours, you know? They must have found a way in."

It made sense. Whatever passage Ryan and Boris discovered could serve as theirs as well.

The trio followed the imprints, which led them back out the way they'd come to the other edge of the thicket. The tracks took them through the sand, into the mud, and wrapped back toward another clearing. There, the trees formed a path that led them to a formation of old, broken stones; the ruins of a decaying structure.

"Oh, man, just look at this place. I'm telling you, guys, there has to be something valuable in there." Eric was nearly overcome with energy.

"Hey, the tracks just sort of disappear." Jam followed the footprints to where they ended at the wall of trunks.

Joseph knelt, looking where the steps had stopped. "There must be a way in." Something caught his attention when he glanced up. "Look, there's something on the trees."

An intricate pattern formed from many different lines and pictures had been carved into the bark of the trees. Though the pattern was brilliantly designed, none of it made any sense.

Joseph sighed and stood up. "Guess we need to find another way inside."

"Hey, wait a moment. I recognize those incantations." Jam jostled the two friends as he stepped between them to get a closer look. Running his fingers

down the carvings, he nodded. "Just as I thought. These are keys."

"I don't see any locks." Eric gave him a confused stare.

"Sort of, but they're written in a different language, you know?" Jam pulled a small booklet from his bag. After glancing back and forth between them, he put it away and retrieved his flute. "The professor taught me a lot about how the ancient users of Magic often hide messages in song. A little movin' and groovin' might do the trick, you know?"

"Yeah, because trees totally love to dance," Eric teased.

Joseph shushed his friend and stepped to the side. "Can't hurt to try. This seems to be right up your alley."

He and Eric went silent, allowing Jam to focus. The air around them fell still before the first deep note emerged and rolled into a soft, earthy tone. Bass notes melded into an enduring melody that seemed to rise from the earth.

Eric playfully snapped his fingers to the beat.

The carvings in the trees began to react. Not one tree but many displayed the same carvings. Glowing green marks spiraled up to the canopy where the wind further guided the mystical song. The ground vibrated, and as Jam finished, the notes echoed through the currents as if an unseen orchestra from afar desired to join in. From the soil came an eruption of roots, and in a strange, whipping dance, the trees stirred and roamed, astonishingly free from the ground. The group backed away to avoid getting crushed in the movement until the quaking of the earth died off. When the performance ceased and the resonant music faded into unheard whispers, the pathway revealed itself to them.

"I guess trees like music too?" Amused by the results, Joseph stood still as if dazed at the same time.

Eric also stood with his mouth open. He seemed to be trying to form words, but they never came.

Amazed at his own results, Jam watched as the same green glow left his flute, which he then tucked away. "Like parting the seas of earth."

"Let's get going." Joseph patted Eric on the shoulder to snap him from his trance as he walked around him.

They left the sun behind, tramping into the dark unknown. The forest was one of the creepiest yet most amazing places Joseph had ever seen, even in video games. Tense emotions surfaced within him, giving him the strong feeling they'd crossed a veil on the way in. The lush trees loomed overhead, as if watching every move the trio made beneath their winding limbs. The thick branches and leaves formed a woven sheet that prevented most of the light from reaching the ground, producing a dull, pulsing effect like that of a verdant disco ball. The few rays that did tunnel in were weakened by the journey, though they provided enough illumination to highlight the mystic details of the bizarre environment.

Joseph breathed in the damp, hazy air, teemed with hints of the flourishing life around them. Bending roots crawled along the thick foliage, worming down the paths into the distance. Butterflies of all colors hopped and floated around the growing flora. The artistry of nature was made even more miraculous by the glowing luminescence of the insects' radiant wings.

"It's like a living fantasy, you know?" Jam touched one of the nearby trunks.

The tree shifted in response to the contact as the canopy swayed softly. It could have been a simple breeze, but it left Joseph with the sense that the forest held much more than they understood.

After their first few steps, a sickening, crackling noise played into the scene from behind them. Each turned his head as the trees slid back into place with a loud groan, once again assuming their duty as the guardians to the gate.

Their exit had disappeared.

"There goes our way out," Eric sighed. "I hope no one forgot anything back on the ship. I doubt there's an elf with an item shop here."

"I don't think it wants us to leave," Joseph said, breathing in the mist.

"Yeah, you're not helping with all the spooky talk," Eric muttered.

"It's hard to describe, Eric. The feeling in this place is just *off*. I think it can feel our presence."

"It feels like it's alive, like it has a soul of its own, you know?"

"Raging storms and dancing trees. This keeps getting better." Eric reached for his wand and kept it at his side.

"Keep your eyes open. Professor Ben said something about disturbing its slumber."

"We should have asked Ben to pack some coffee for us. Maybe after a cup of Joe, not you"—Eric smirked and nudged his friend in the side—"it wouldn't be so cranky."

That *was* exactly how it felt—as if they'd awakened a sleeping giant, as if *they* were the annoying alarm it wished to turn off. Yet behind the anger there was also a strange sense of acceptance, as if it welcomed them with open arms like an old friend.

"Hey, let's just hope we end up watching them before they start watching us, you know?" Jam chuckled.

As they continued deeper, a cool, musty breeze blew down each of their necks, sending a chill down their spines. All around the sounds of motion rustled, groaned and scraped. The earth beneath their feet made hardly a sound, as if there wasn't a single remnant of decay or broken life along the forest floor. Instead, the lively moss and tender soil embraced their every step.

"I wish Ben had given us a flamethrower or something." Eric swatted at an insect.

"Whatever happened to charging into danger head first?" Joseph asked.

"Look, I'm not scared. I just don't want *you* two to get worried." Eric tilted his head to look at the lost sky. "You uh, never know what might happen."

"No worries," Jam interjected. "If we run into something, it'll have to get by all of us, and that won't be easy, you know?"

It was the most bizarre thing. It sounded like every time they spoke, something in the far distance mimicked their voices. It wasn't an echo, but something akin to having their words whispered back to them by many unknown sources. A deep, throaty croak followed, and Eric slashed at the air with his weapon as if on reflex.

"Even if it can swallow us whole?" Eric gulped as he spun in circles to try and locate the source of the noise.

"Hang on, look over there." Joseph pointed to something near the trail in the distance.

Something ahead was glowing as its dry light refused to mix with the hazy air.

He took off, with Eric and Jam in tow. When he got to the location, what was there revealed itself to be an old wooden board on a post once the shining light had faded.

"What is it?" asked Eric.

Joseph wiped the dirt and small vines from the wood, revealing script. "It's hard to make out."

Joseph placed his finger on the indents and read it aloud.

The path ahead and back to day,
By these marks may you find your way.

He shrugged. "That's all it says."

"Hey, it sounds like some form of instructions, you know?" Jam leaned in to look for himself.

"I wonder who wrote it," Joseph said.

"Maybe Ryan?" Eric wore a skeptical expression.

"No, it's too old. Ryan couldn't have made that."

"Hey, it looks like whoever wrote this was in a hurry." Jam examined the engravings. "The letters may have been carved in with a knife of some sort. See how the letters are etched into the wood?" He moved his hand around the timber, scraping off a chunk of mud that had been stuck to it. "Hey, I think I found something!"

The teens crouched as Jam pointed to another carving on the sign.

"Looks like a compass." Joseph shifted his gaze around it. "It's pointing north-east. Maybe that's where we have to go."

"This feels like a trap. I don't trust it for a second." Eric grumbled.

It was odd how even in the dense forest there was a breeze. It flowed through the air, pushing against dust and grass at their feet. Then, before their eyes, the straight path they'd been walking on shifted. Roots adjusted, the earth skipped, and the flow changed their course so it ran in the direction of the compass.

They stared at one another, unsure what to make of the event.

"We need to go that way." Joseph's voice was faint. "Keep your guard up. We're not alone here."

Joseph mustered his bravery as they stepped onto the new path.

The gentle wind faded, leaving them on their own again. As they passed a larger tree, an owl burst from a hole in the trunk and flew past before it vanished into the forest canopy. Joseph grabbed his sword as Eric and Jam clutched their weapons as well, pointing them in different directions with their backs turned to one another.

"Hah. *Okay*...just an owl. Jeez, calm down, everyone." Eric tried to shrug off his reaction.

"I think we're all a little jumpy." Joseph sighed. "We need to stay calm."

It was easier said than done. The ancient forest made it difficult to keep himself calm.

The moment they moved, the sound of a twig snapping from nearby echoed in the damp air. Joseph stopped and spun around.

"What's the matter?" asked Jam.

"I don't know." Joseph gazed into the fog. "I thought I heard something."

"Heard what?" asked Eric.

Joseph sighed and shrugged. "Guess it was nothing."

"Hey, we're all nervous. We need to keep an open mind to the earth, you know?"

The sound returned again, and this time, Eric and Jam acknowledged it, too.

"See? I told you I heard something."

"Hah, so much for staying calm, right?" Eric held out his wand with a trembling hand.

"Maybe we're being followed." Jam took off his hat as he looked around.

The sound of a whispering laughter encircled their stance and carried through the forest.

Eric shuffled in a circle and kept his wand ready. "What was that?"

Joseph gazed into the maze, gasping when a looming figure moved in the fog. "See, someone *is* following us!"

"Where? I don't see anything," replied Jam.

"Right there." Joseph pointed to one of the outside paths. "It just went behind the trees."

"He who sights it, fights it! So, uh, have at it, man!" Eric said.

Joseph watched as the figure emerged again, walking along the shadows of the tree trunks. This time he didn't wait, and before he knew what was happening, his legs carried him after it.

"Hey, I wasn't being serious!" Eric shouted after him.

Joseph kept his focus on the target and leapt over a large rock as the fog surrounded him. He landed and slid down a hill, scanning his surroundings once he stopped. The figure stalked nearby in the mist. Joseph swiped his hand into the vapor, only for the shadow to vanish again.

"I know you're here," he called. "Show yourself!"

He caught it again and charged, only to have it disperse with the haze once more. Whatever it was, it seemed greatly amused as he searched blindly for it. Running out of breath, he gave in and lowered his sword to the side as he stopped to regain his energy.

"You are searching for answers that require no questions," a voice said from somewhere around him.

Joseph looked up as the form of an individual materialized. The details were hard to make out, but through the obstruction he recognized the manifestation. The shadow was the elderly man he'd seen back home and on the island. This time he wore robes of green and gold that covered most of his body. The mist swirled and gathered near his covered feet.

"You've got to be kidding me." Joseph gazed at him, unsure if the woodlands were playing tricks on his mind. "First you're at my school, then you follow me all over the island, and now this? Who are you?"

The old man made a slight bow. "Forgive my recent absence. This form is quite difficult to maintain at such vast distances. After all, we're truly worlds apart from one another. That said..." The man glanced around. "The magical forces of this Sanctuary make the connection much easier on the mind. Now then, I believe the question is not *who* I am, but who *you* are." His tone was kindly as he stroked the fancy braids of his white beard. "Do you know why it is you're here?"

Joseph opened his mouth to answer, but the words seemed stuck in his throat. Unable to speak, he shook his head. He hated the mind games but didn't know what else to do but play along.

"I see, though I knew as much. Do you know what it is you're doing?"

Relief flooded Joseph's mind as he regained the ability to talk. "I...I'm not sure. I feel like I do, but it's hard to tell. This isn't exactly a normal situation. I feel like I'm losing my mind whenever I see you. Are you real?"

The old man chuckled in a reassuring manner and waved his hand. "Why, yes, from what I've seen, *normal* would be...*insufficient* to describe what you have encountered thus far, wouldn't you agree? You have much to learn and a long path to walk. Nonetheless, the trials we face often sculpt us into stronger souls."

"That's good to know, but...could you answer my question? Who are you? Do you know what's going on? Why do I keep having those weird dreams? Please, just tell me something—anything!"

The fog rose around the old man, draping him in a thick cloak. "I'm someone who wants to guide you all down the right path." The old man bowed slightly again. "Call me Kilgan. I know of the girl you see in your dreams and her attempts to reach out to you and the others. One's soul is a powerful essence that binds us together. She wishes to help, but like you, she doesn't have a full understanding of her abilities. An ominous force looms in the ashes behind us, and it grows restless in its slumber. Never forget—you're never alone in your struggles." The man faded into the fog as his voice trailed in the air until, finally, no remnants of his existence remained.

He blinked and looked around, but there were no signs of the apparition. It was hard to tell if what he'd seen had been real, but he couldn't blame it on the forest. The man had been trailing his steps from the beginning.

"Kilgan..." The girl in his dreams kept mentioning that name.

Other voices called for him from within the fog, and he made out two figures as they approached.

"Joe!" Eric yelled from nearby.

"Hey, are you there?" Jam's voice joined.

Both his friends gasped when they slid down the hill and came to a stop in front of him, trailing a small avalanche of tumbling soil and rocks.

Eric was first to speak. "What happened to you, dude?"

"I don't know." Joseph looked again for the old man. "I was just..." He let his voice trail off. "Nevermind. I think this place is playing tricks on us."

It seemed prudent not to tell his friends what he'd seen, though seeing strange entities was no stranger, for better or worse, than casting spells.

"Did you find out who was following us?" Jam asked.

"No." He shook his head. "Thought I did, but it must've been a tree or something." He sighed. "Forget about it. We should keep going before we stray too far from the path."

"A tree? A tree can't mo—" Eric cut himself off and nodded. "Yeah. Never mind, you're right."

Eric and Jam exchanged nervous looks. Eric shrugged.

They returned to the path—Joseph hoped it was the right one. In the ominous forest, it was hard to tell. At times, it was comforting to see other life forms seeking a home in this world, but they were scarce, and their existence was hardly enough to settle Joseph's mind. The beautiful landscape appeared to travel forever into the distance, forming an eternal spiral for them to navigate. Were they simply walking in circles? It was a persistent question in Joseph's mind, at least until things around them started to change.

Clumps of mushrooms sprouted to life, arranged in the forms of various staircases on the sides of trees in a matter of seconds. Single ones rose up from the ground as they walked by. When Joseph touched one, it wobbled in the air and gave off a faint blue light along its pearled surface.

"Where did these weirdos come from?" Eric kicked one of the large fungi.

After he did, it bounced back, bumping firmly into Eric, sending him tumbling before it resumed its post.

Faint, playful giggles chimed around them, as if coming from the very trees and plant life. Joseph would have found it funny if it weren't so disturbing.

The gathering of mushrooms stirred. One of the smaller heads lifted as the rooted body popped free of the ground. Arms separated from the stubby stalk as it waddled forward, and previously unseen eyes, tiny and slitted, opened to gaze at them.

Joseph stared back, unsure what to say.

Eric gulped and patted the mushroom creature on its cap. "Uh, sorry about that, I guess?" He grinned, but his eyes betrayed his anxiety. "Hey, I bet you have lots of friends, because you seem like a real *fun-guy*. I bet you know a lot about one another too, because there isn't *mushroom* over here."

Silence greeted Eric's lame jokes, and the fungus being suddenly leaned forward and charged. It rammed its head into Eric's legs, achieving nothing but knocking itself over.

"Did it just attack me?"

The gathering of mushrooms shifted as many of the knee-high beings sprouted from the earth and ran at them.

The group readied their weapons as the mushrooms piled forward, attempting to headbutt and attack with small hits of their tiny limbs.

"I don't think they liked your jokes."

A few of them stacked atop one another to smack Eric in the head. The blow was enough to knock him back.

"Fine, no more joking. It's game time, you fungal freaks." Eric hit the top of the pile with his wand before kicking the mini tower over.

Joseph sliced at the few charging him, chopping off a top and cutting another in half. The creatures perished with a high-pitched laugh. A melody from Jam's flute froze some of them in place, allowing him and Eric to stomp or knock them away.

Joseph withdrew his wand, preparing his spell between attacks. The flames began to form, but before he could cast it, the assault abruptly stopped. They giggled and turned from the encounter, fleeing back into the forest. He lowered his wand, and the flames faded. "They must not like fire."

Eric chased after them. "Yeah, that's right. You better run!"

The ground rumbled, and the laughter grew louder. One massive mushroom began to rise, tearing through the earth and soil until it towered over them. It opened its eyes and stared them down.

Eric rolled his shoulders and got into position. "I've got this one." He charged forward, raising his fist before he jumped atop one of the blue mushroom heads, using it as a trampoline. He bounced off and punched the torso of the giant creature. His fist sank into its body. It stared down at him as the smaller mushrooms laughed.

Eric pulled his hand free and carefully walked backwards to join his friends. He smacked his lips and shrugged his shoulders. "That's uh...that's a big mushroom."

The imposing fungus reared its head back, and its cry echoed through the forest. It ran towards them, its stubby legs carrying it at an impressive speed.

"Time to go!"

They fled from the path, tearing through the foliage of the forest. Joseph hopped over a small stream, though Eric soon took the lead, with Jam beside him. The thundering steps of their pursuer were never distant. A tree toppled at their rear, nearly hitting them. The entire forest seemed a riot of laughter, and they were the butt of the joke.

"There's a jump coming up!" Eric warned before he leapt over a short divide.

Joseph and Jam followed, leaping the fissure and rolling to the ground as they landed. The mushroom tried to stop, but it fell forward, hit the opposite side, and tumbled into the crack. The mini versions that followed all stopped, then retreated, still giggling as they returned to the forest behind them.

Joseph gasped, trying to catch his breath. He then led them up the nearby hill. "I think I see another path."

"So, mushrooms don't appreciate comedy. Tough crowd." Eric took in a deep breath as they came to an opening. "Wait a second—isn't this the same place we just came from?"

The trail was exactly the same as the one they'd just left. As they realized this, the giggling returned, echoing through the trees above.

"The life in this forest sure is energetic." Jam turned to examine their location. "Maybe it's messing with us, you know?"

"Everything keeps changing." Joseph lowered his guard. "Things are there one minute and gone the next."

The mushrooms shifted aggressively, so the trio didn't linger.

They continued onward. The trees stretched higher above them. The path wound around bends and up hills before seeming to carry them back the way they'd come. It felt like a game against an omniscient opponent. They rolled loaded dice, so everything they did put them further from their supposed goal.

The forest was forever playing with them. When they reached a pond, the group took a break to reassess their situation.

Joseph pulled a candy bar from his bag and munched. Water poured from a fallen log and followed along its body, where it trickled into the hollowed stump abutting the water. The pool was pristine, its bottom easily visible through the transparent water. Along the stoney bottom, twisted roots drank their fill. The gentle croak of frogs gave the setting an atmosphere of calm, and lavish flowers poked out from the surrounding soil where Jam was busy examining them.

"I've never seen plants like these before. I wonder if they're a new species, you know?" Jam plucked a few from the ground, then wrapped them and placed them into his bag.

Once again the forest stirred at the interruption of its life, and Jam stopped taking samples.

"Man, this water is super clear. You can see to the bottom and everything." Eric bent and took a handful of the fresh spring liquid to sip.

"I don't think that's a good idea," Joseph said.

Eric finished his drink and wiped his chin. "What do you want me to do, drink from yours? I forgot my bottle back on the ship, and—" Eric cupped his mouth as the croak of a frog cut off his words. However, the sound had come from Eric's lips, not from those of the aquatic choir.

Joseph shook his head. "What was that?"

Eric waited and then opened his mouth again, only this time no words followed. Another vibrating croak came from Eric's attempt to speak. He clenched his mouth shut and mumbled.

Joseph sighed. "Stop messing around."

Eric shook his head, opening his mouth as he pointed to his throat. His effort to speak resulted in yet another frog-like response.

"Hey, he has a frog in his throat." Jam chuckled.

Eric flashed him an aggravated expression and tapped his foot on the ground.

Joseph couldn't believe it, and he leapt up to look over the crystalline surface of the pond. Many frogs called the sanctuary their home. He stepped back from the water and pulled Eric with him. He didn't know what was in the water, but something wasn't right.

"Hold on, I have something!" Jam set his shoulder pack down and rummaged through it, retrieving a small vial. He hurried to Eric, popped the top, and handed it to him.

Eric croaked in response, rolling his eyes to the sound he'd made.

"Try this. It's a mixture my aunt made. It's supposed to help with a sore throat and loss of voice, you know?"

Eric grabbed the concoction and downed the small volume of brown solution. His face contorted, as if it had a foul taste. He looked like someone had shoved a lemon into his mouth.

Joseph waited until Eric finished before speaking up. "Did it work?"

Eric didn't reply at first, as if frightened to find out. "I think so?" He paused. His words had returned, but his voice came out in a much deeper, baritone manner. "Oh, come on, this isn't funny!"

Joseph couldn't help but snicker, but he was glad Eric's voice had returned. "I told you it wasn't a good idea. Maybe try out for the school choir if we make it back."

"Hey, it's an experiment, you know? You should be good to go once the side effects wear off. It's better than turning into a frog." Jam smiled as he picked up his bags.

Eric narrowed his eyes at them before he grabbed his things and pointed to the path.

Joseph nodded as he joined them. "Yeah, we'd better keep moving. I don't trust being in one place for too long."

The shape of the trees surrounding them gradually changed once they restarted their journey. Whereas they'd started out straight, green, and full of life, the further the trio walked, the more twisted and darker in color they became. The previously active mushrooms also went into hiding, taking their azure light with them. The further they went, the colder the air became. The leaves of the trees changed colors. One by one they turned orange and brown, littering the path with dried and wrinkled versions of their former selves. It was as if the seasons advanced the further they walked.

"Didn't think I'd need a jacket for this place," Eric said in his deep voice, tucking his hands into his pockets.

Jam looked back behind them. "It looks like the whole forest is changing, you know?"

Between the trees arose another dull, lifeless glow. Joseph pointed to the source and motioned for his friends to move. "Up ahead."

Weaving through the trees, he arrived at the light. It faded away into another broken wooden sign beneath a pile of dead leaves. After pushing them aside, he knelt to read the carvings in the wood.

The lives it takes, the power it makes,
Do not lose our way in the illusions it fakes.

"More fun warnings. Thanks for nothing, sign," Eric muttered.

"Hey, I don't see a compass, like there was on the last one." Jam squinted as he looked it over. "Where do we go from here?"

"I'm beginning to wonder if it matters at this point what direction we go." Joseph looked at the ground to get his mind off the subject. When he shifted his foot, something buried under the leaves moved. Curious, he reached into the decaying mound and pulled out a blue book. Its cover was worn, its spine tattered, yet it showed no signs of wear caused by the forest.

"Where'd you get that?" Eric peeked over Joseph's shoulder.

"It was next to the post under the leaves. He flipped through its pages. None of the words were legible, but they were oddly familiar. He felt strange holding the book, as it gave off a slight chill.

"Weird. What do you think it's for?"

"It might have been dropped by the same person who wrote those warnings, you know?" Jam concluded.

Joseph nodded and placed it in his bag. It seemed important; he hoped Professor Ben knew something about it.

From the corner of his eye, he caught a glimpse of the sign tilting. Another compass appeared, pointing them north. Again the pathway changed to match this direction as leaves danced and swirled on the forest floor. The trees also shifted, as if beckoning them deeper into the forest.

"That's not creepy at all." Eric shook his head. "What if it's a trap?"

"Won't know until we find out."

The slow rain of falling leaves continued, acting like a cleanser to remove most of the life from the forest. Yet even without the thick ceiling of leaves, light still barely breached the barrier of woody branches on its way to the ground. The air grew colder until a light cloud accompanied each of their breaths. The movements around them died off until there was only silence, everything still but for the cracking of leaves and branches under each step.

None of them knew what to think about the constantly altering environment. It felt as if the very land had perished or gone into a deep slumber. The chill grew ever more intense, and from above something cold touched Joseph's neck. He stopped, reaching to feel where it had landed.

"What's up?" Eric turned while rubbing at his arms in response to the freezing air. His tone had finally returned to normal, and he let out a relieved sigh. "Phew, finally! I thought I was going to be one lonely frog without a single princess to smooch me back to health!"

Looking up, they watched as small flakes of snow descended from the darkening sky. The sunlight had vanished entirely, replaced by ominous clouds that would have been appropriate for winter.

"Seriously?" Eric held out his hand and let the white flakes fall into his palm, where they melted into tiny droplets.

"I'm not used to this back on the islands, you know? It's not like we get snow flurries in the tropics." Jam pulled off his hat to blow away the gathering of snow nestled on the brim.

It didn't take long for the light dusting to turn into a heavier blanket. As the snow became denser, their view of the trail ahead grew more blurred by the heavy snowfall.

Eric grunted as he brushed the ivory mounds off his shoulders. "Anyone have some of that anti-dandruff shampoo?"

The snow didn't only cover his friend. In only a few minutes, the weather had gotten so intense that snow coated every inch of ground and all remaining plants. The falling flecks felt unnatural, as if they hadn't come from the murky sky. Instead, it seemed the wind itself had delivered them. Each step became hazardous, with slippery roots hidden under the snow. The wind whipped their faces, stinging their skin with a bitter chill.

"It's too dangerous to keep going, you know?" Jam shouted over the intensifying storm.

"We'll turn into popsicles if we stay in one spot," Eric complained.

"I don't understand this." Joseph stopped. "Where is this coming from?"

Soon they were trudging through ankle-high mounds. The weather never let up for a moment. Joseph's body was beginning to go numb, making him feel like he'd freeze at any second. Ahead, the trees began to open up, revealing a break in the frosty foliage. Barely visible through the silhouettes of gray and white lay a cave.

"Eric, Jam!" called Joseph.

They bumped into one another when Joseph stopped.

He pointed to the opening. "We can get out of the snow up ahead!"

Joseph trudged toward it, dragging his feet across the chunky snow and ice that dragged him down with every step. The trail may as well have been made of glue. The opening appeared to him more clear now. The moment he ripped apart the dead plants and set foot into the cave, relief washed over him. The wind didn't reach inside the cave.

Eric shook his entire body like a dog before trying to fix his hair. "Gah, I feel like a snowman."

Joseph peered outside and pulled a large piece of broken branch into the cave. After setting down his bag and sword, he pulled out the wand and focused. Drawing on the images of fire in his mind, the gemstone flashed as the fiery spell charged.

"E-erif!"

The cold air stabbed his lungs, but the spell was cast. Fire raced out, striking the log with its intense heat. When the spell ended, the flame had been successfully set. Gradually, its warmth enveloped them. Casting had also left him with a slight headache.

"All right! Hah, and Ben said we can't solve problems by setting them on fire." Eric rushed outside to grab more of the fallen branches to throw on the pile.

Joseph did his best to hide the discomfort from the dizzying pain in his head as he joined Eric and Jam around the fire. They kept their hands and bodies close to the flames, away from the howling cold outside.

"I wonder how long this could possibly go. Talk about a crazy thing happening, you know?" Jam shivered as he rubbed his hands together.

"I hope we're not trapped in here. We'll run out of food." Eric rustled through his bag and frowned.

After only a few moments, Joseph raised his head. The sounds from outside had grown quieter, as if the environment had become less ferociously set on killing them. He walked to the mouth of the cave. Ice had formed around the perimeter, but already it had begun to melt.

Eric got up to check as well. "It stopped?" He glanced up to where the dark clouds had hovered like a gloomy roof above them. Now only a blue sky peeked through the thick tangle of branches. "Man, and I thought the weather back at home changed a lot."

"Hey, at least it seems to be warming up." Jam smiled.

"It's just like that storm we hit on the way here. One second it's there, the next it's gone." Joseph looked at the ground. The snow had already begun to separate and dissolve. He traversed to the deeper parts of a nearby clearing and stared over a frozen lake. "This place must be overflowing with so much Magic, it's unstable."

"I suppose it's pointless to try to find where to go from here, you know?" asked Jam.

Joseph glanced around the field but found no sign of the path. The blowing snow had erased everything.

"How about over there?" Eric pointed to a portion of forest on the other side of the lake.

Across the thawing body of water lay a tunnel of trees. Their dark colors and twisted trunks seemed to bend inward. The branches on their lower halves looked like beckoning arms.

Joseph nodded. "It's worth a shot."

They marched from the clearing and to the new trail across the lake. Leaves were nowhere to be found by this point. However, the melting snow revealed their pathway.

Another season seemed to have passed, leaving them in a new limbo.

The ground on which they walked abruptly slid, and Joseph stopped.

"Whoa, what's the hold-up?" Eric asked.

The dark path of dirt twisted and rolled with the wiggling feet of the trees. Ahead, the single choice they'd been following divided into two separate ways.

"Haha. Split paths. That's hilarious!" Eric threw his arms up in disgust, then let them fall back to his sides. "This place has a sick sense of humor."

That their way forward had twirled and wound down different directions was one thing, but having multiple paths appear out of nowhere made the mind-bending voyage even more confusing.

"We just have to see where one goes. Not much we can do about it, you know?"

A soft, familiar light pulsated before them, dead in the center between the two trails. Once they reached the location, its guiding glow faded. Joseph knelt by the damaged carving and removed its debris.

Our chance to make a choice we couldn't trust,
Now our friends who chose wrong have faded to dust.

"Makes me wonder what happened here." Joseph looked over the carefully sculpted letters.

The indentations were deep, but what worried him the most were the ashen remnants of a dark substance embedded in the wood.

"Does that mean if we take the wrong path we'll die?" asked Eric.

"Could mean anything at this point. Almost like it's the lesser of two evils, you know?" Jam added.

Joseph stood and peered down each branch of the path at the fork in the road. Nothing indicated what the warning meant. There were no other signs, no directions, and not a single living creature. How were they supposed to tell what was even real at this point?

Something called to him, something that could have been a whisper or simply the wind.

"You know where to go. Take the left path."

Drawing a deep breath, he sprinted forward.

"Dude, what are you doing?" Eric's expression was one of alarm.

Joseph didn't stop until he stepped foot on the left fork of the path. Once there, he turned to see what, if anything, happened.

Eric and Jam came running up the path when they saw it was safe.

"The hell? What if this is the wrong path?" Eric wore a panicked look, which was rare for him.

The soft creaks of the shifting wood offered no surprise. The other path they hadn't taken was claimed by the forest. Roots ate the soil, devouring it entirely, as if it had never been there.

"How did you...What did...How did you know?" Eric sputtered.

"Not sure. Something told me it was right." Joseph sighed deeply.

"Man, talk about a lucky guess." Eric seemed to be recovering, and his ever-present smile threatened to recolonize his face.

"Hey, looks like you flipped a coin and called it right." Jam's voice was chipper as he looked back to where they'd been. "I'm happy we aren't dust in the wind, you know?"

Their long journey into the forest continued without any signs they were nearing an objective. Going up felt like going down, left felt no different than right, and Eric mentioned he kept seeing the same tree over and over. He paused only long enough to place a rock near the twisted trunk to mark their position. When they'd made a return trip, he looked at the tree, but the rock was gone.

It felt like the same area, but it never was.

Hours passed, but for all Joseph knew, the whole forest could experience time differently than normal.

"Hey, anyone know what time it is?" Jam sat on a rock.

Eric pulled out his phone to check but gave a troubled expression when he did. "That isn't right."

"Something wrong?" asked Joseph.

Eric turned over his phone. The clock on his display was constantly changing. The time shifted forward by a couple minutes, only to reset and run backwards in a chaotic manner.

Joseph checked his own. The same unnatural scene played out as the displayed time skipped forward, then back. Hours changed, the day of the week jumped, and everything always reset. "It has to be the forest. Magic doesn't only mess with *us*, but with anything in its range."

When Eric tapped the screen, the phone gave out a crackling static noise. "It better not be broken! I just upgraded this thing!"

"That explains the shifting seasons too, you know?" Jam added.

"Looks like the only thing we can rely on is each other." An idea struck him, and he jumped off the rock. It all made perfect sense now, and he could only hope his crazy idea worked.

"Where are you going? I'm not done resting yet," Eric protested.

"Nowhere." Joseph walked away. As he did, he made sure to believe exactly, and only exactly, what he'd said.

Eric looked confused as he stood up. "Then why are you leaving?"

"Because we have to get going."

Eric followed but continued his questioning. "But you just said you weren't going anywhere."

"That's right, I'm not." Joseph kept his voice calm as he walked.

"Hey, I'm not sure I follow, you know?" Jam joined.

"*Exactly*," Joseph whispered when he turned to them. "As long as we're here, this place will continue messing with us. I'm not sure if it's trying to keep us lost or what, but something's definitely going on. Maybe if we stop trying to find our way and just wander around, it won't know which way to make us go. If it's playing tricks, maybe we can play our own."

"That doesn't make sense, but in a place like this it might make perfect sense, you know?" Jam nodded slowly.

"Um, okay?" Eric sighed. "Whatever. Not like we have anything else to do." He cleared his throat and looked to the trees. "Hear that? We're *totally* not onto your little game, and we're not going anywhere. We don't know what's not going on here...or there. Maybe it's over"—he pointed in another direction—"that way." Eric raised his eyebrows for emphasis.

They continued their search, but this time they purposely walked in circles and retraced their steps. At one point they even walked backwards to see what would happen. After a few minutes using this method, something slowly began to stir around them. The soft giggling from before rose, but its tone was different, seeming to signify approval instead of mockery.

They wandered for what felt like only a few minutes before the forest slowly took on a whole new manifestation. The trees and ground rumbled, and the roots of the living arboreal towers retreated back into the ground. The entire area was quaking with uncertainty.

"Eric, Jam—stop walking." Joseph put out both his arms. They stopped and waited.

The air around them grew clouded, something thicker, something more than the fog that had pervaded the air prior to their change of strategy. It was as if a dense smoke had moved in, and it was getting bad enough they could no longer see the trees or one another.

Joseph tried to remain relaxed until the mist faded, but when he looked around, his friends had gone missing.

"Guys?" He turned in circles. "Hello?"

Mid-search, he was forced to back up when the old entity he'd met previously materialized in the smoke, his form partially hidden in the thick shroud.

"Strange, is it not?" Kilgan laughed, pacing slowly before Joseph. "It's amazing how Magic can affect so many things. This ancient Sanctuary is no exception. It's slept for quite some time, and now it's taken its first breaths of the new world."

"You're still following me." Joseph cocked his head. "Why?"

The robed man hummed softly. "Allow me to ask again. What is it you seek?"

"How should I know?" Joseph folded his arms but stayed alert. When Kilgan didn't answer, he gave a straight answer of his own. "A man by the name of Professor Benjamin Thessit sent us here to stop someone named Ryan Morter, who's attempting to break open some sort of barrier. I don't know why he wants to do it, or why I'm supposed to stop him."

Kilgan waved his finger in a taunting, playful fashion. "Ah, I must say that is quite a fair statement. One more question." The man gazed at the tree, then brought his attention back to Joseph. "Does this forest seem familiar to you?"

The teen shook his head slowly. "I've never been here before."

"I thought as much, but perhaps you're not as lost as you feel. You must, however, keep your wits about you. Many dangers lurk near and far. You're the only one who decides what path you'll walk. Trust in yourself and you'll prevail against these growing entities. Your journey started with a dream." The old man winked. "Who knows what else you'll find there. One step at a time, one foot in front of the other, and onward you'll go! You're on the right path. We shall meet again when the time is right. Remember. Every adventure starts with a dream, and yours is only beginning."

The elderly man waved his hand and vanished.

The thicket dwindled, and a heavy smell of smoke rose, burning his nostrils. When the haze cleared, Joseph gasped.

The sight of burning vegetation confronted him, and the flames had already claimed the colorful wooden soldiers and marsh grass that had previously covered the forest. Most of the smaller trees had been reduced to ash or were blackened and burnt stumps dotting the ground. Dark soot covered everything. He was unsure whether to flee or stand against the fire.

Joseph located Eric and Jam as they came running from two different directions, and he sighed in relief. "There you are!"

"What are you talking about?" Eric asked. "I was trying to find you guys when you ran off into that fog! I thought you were trying to ditch me."

"Hey, what are you talking about?" Jam retorted. "I thought I had been chasing you two the whole time when you took off, you know?"

"I doubt any of us saw what we thought we did. It must be trying to separate us."

There was a brief moment of tense silence before Eric seemed to notice their surroundings. He coughed from the smoke. "You know, when I suggested burning down the forest, I didn't mean while we were in it."

The sizzling inferno had faded altogether. The marks of searing flames now scarred the trunks of the trees, and the sky, partly hidden through the haze, had shifted in color to a deep red. Was what they were seeing visible from the outside world? The waking forest appeared to maintain a realm of its own.

Joseph scanned the ground and trees, trying to get his bearings. Far in the distance, a massive outline was visible beyond the smoke. "Let's try over there."

"Hey, look at this!" Jam said as he knelt. "Those two must have taken the same path. So if we follow these tracks, we should eventually find them, you know?"

Footprints led forward in the ashen soil.

"How do we know they're his?" asked Eric.

"We don't, but we know *someone* else was here," Joseph said. Part of him wondered if they belonged to the elderly Kilgan.

In its new form, the forest hardly stirred. A gentle wind drifted by at times to blow away the ash along sections of the path, frustrating any attempt to keep their sense of direction. It was as if the wooden spirits were impeding their advance at every turn. The object in the distance was closer now. It was a structure built by hands, not one produced by nature. Was this what they were searching for? What waited for them once they arrived?

Would it be Ryan or a mere empty illusion?

Would there be more twists and turns brought on by the ever-changing forest?

Perhaps the trees hid a much darker, more sinister shadow in the mysterious clutches of their roots.

CHAPTER FIFTEEN

BEYOND THE ROOTED SEAL

"No way." Eric shook his head. "How are we going to get across *that*?"

Their path had dropped completely from sight, replaced by a deep, dark abyss. From where they stood, the land appeared as if it had been stretched downward. The trees sprouted and grew sideways within the cavernous ravine. The footprints they'd seen prior had long since vanished. Joseph shifted to lean closer, causing a small chunk of dirt and rock to separate. It tumbled into the unknown, and though he listened, there was no sign it made contact with the bottom.

Down one side and up the other, there appeared to be no passage across.

"There has to be a way. We just need to find it."

Their search dragged onward. Traveling along the edge of the vast oblivion, they found no point to cross. The gap was far too wide to consider jumping. With every step, Joseph's hope diminished, until he wondered whether they might need to turn back. What made that thought worse was not knowing how to escape.

"Ugh, screw this stupid forest and its dumb trees." Eric gave one of the large trees a swift kick.

The tree screeched. Despite its size, it swayed from the impact. Even in their decaying state, the rest of the trees shifted, but Eric didn't seem to care.

"Yeah, you like that, don't you? I use the corpses of your cousins as chairs on a daily basis."

Joseph rushed over, trying to calm his friend. "Come on. We—" He stopped, looking at how the giant moved from Eric's strike. Their path forward suddenly became clear. "Eric, you're a genius!"

Eric smirked. "You just now figured that out?"

Joseph ran to the back of the tree, planting his hands on the trunk. With a hard shove, the pillar of charred wood moved. The fire had rotted away most of the roots. When he tapped the base, it sounded hollow. "We could probably push it over."

"Hey, it might be long enough to get us across, you know?" Jam said.

"We're probably gonna piss off the forest again, but whatever." Eric grumbled. "It owes me after what those mushrooms did."

They got into position and braced their hands on the opposite side of the tree so it would tilt toward the gap.

"Ready? One...two...three...push!"

They each threw their weight into the trunk at the same time, rocking it, only to have it slide back into place.

"Again! One...two...three!" They slammed into the wood, this time harder, timing their second push to match the slight rocking left over from their last hit, using its own momentum to send it farther.

Joseph panted and readied again. "Almost there. One last time. One...two...three!"

The final strike succeeded. All around them the roots at the base snapped free of their earthy anchor.

"She's coming down!" Eric shouted as they bolted out of range.

With a slow, extended cracking sound, the tree went over, its bottom splintered by the force of the impact that vibrated down the trunk. When the dust cleared, the broken timber had settled, serving as an uneven bridge to the other side.

"And with that, we just made the best bridge ever." Eric cheered.

Even if the fall had caused numerous cracks and splints to the trunk of the broken tree, it seemed sturdy enough to hold them.

To test his hopes, Joseph leaned over and pressed his foot on the top of it. "It seems safe."

"Hey, so who's going first?" Jam asked.

Eric's adrenaline seemed to get the best of him; with a few jabs in the air and a cocky smile, he took off running. "Just try and stop me."

Once at the other end, Eric leapt from the log and rolled to the ground before hopping back to his feet. "Score another point for team Eric against the evil forest."

"I guess we should get going, too, you know? It doesn't seem like it'll be much of a problem!" Jam made the next trip across their handmade bridge. He crossed inch by inch, one foot in front of the other. The islander kept his arms out, keeping his balance steady until he reached the other side and landed safely.

Lastly, Joseph hopped onto the timber. Halfway across the divide he glanced down. The looming darkness below seemed as though it were alive, ready to swallow him whole. The broken trunk on which he stood shifted, its center snapping piece by piece as chunks of its bark tumbled into the pit.

"Hurry up, man. It's falling apart!" Eric warned.

Joseph's balance slipped, and he rocked back and forth. The trunk was falling and about to take him with it. He sprinted up the slippery surface at full speed and jumped as quickly as he could. As he landed on the other side, the improvised bridge gave in, tumbling in two halves into the shadows. The sounds of the massive trunk hitting the side of the pit never stopped, they simply grew more faint until no longer audible.

"Awesome. We're on a roll! You better watch yourself, Ryan. We're in it to win it!" Eric smiled.

Before Joseph could regain his stability, Eric bolted, gone from sight within a matter of seconds. Joseph didn't bother shouting after him this time. Once Eric was fired up, there was often no way of stopping him. He nodded to his islander friend. "Come on, Jam. We better go after him before he gets carried away."

They'd barely taken their first steps before a loud scream erupted from the same direction. Joseph and Jam attempted to catch up. When they did, Eric lay on the ground, his hand wrapped around his foot as he mumbled and cursed.

"What happened this time?" asked Joseph.

"Oh." He looked at the dirt and patted it with his hand. "The ground just looked so *comfortable,* I decided to take a nap." Eric pointed to something nearby.

Joseph sifted through the dirt and rubble until he'd uncovered it. "It's another one of those books."

This one was different from the first. The cover was a deep shade of red, and while the first book had felt cool to the touch, this one put off a strange heat.

"We must be following the world's most clumsy librarian." Eric grunted as he limped.

Jam leaned over to look at the new tome. "They must have some sort of importance to this place, you know? Why else would they be here?"

Joseph pulled the other book from his bag and looked through them both. They were almost identical, even if neither of them was legible. He didn't get to look long, as Eric grabbed the red one from his possession.

"What are you doing?"

"Getting revenge. Let's see how this book likes being stuffed next to my dirty socks." Eric flicked the cover with his finger before he put it away.

Joseph shrugged and placed the remaining book inside his bag. "We'll have to figure it out another time. Come on, I saw something up ahead."

The forest hadn't stirred since the fire appeared. Joseph expected their stunt knocking over the lumbering tree would have caused a reaction. He didn't know if the life in the roots had gone dormant or if it was waiting for the right time to spin them back around. At another small clearing, their path twisted, presenting an entirely new sight.

Buried in the dense jungle of dying trees lay a forgotten ruin. Stone pillars that likely once stood proudly had long since been worn away by the elements. Statues of unknown animals and figures lay toppled and broken where they'd fallen over the cobble brick, encased in dry, brittle vines. Whatever purpose this structure used to hold, whatever civilization once dwelled within, had long abandoned it. Yet even broken and eroded, the ruin still appeared to breathe. Water ran through the base of the stone where channels had been placed, accenting the stillness with the gentle sound of trickling water.

"This looks about right." Joseph set down his bag. He took his sword in one hand and the wand in the other. "Let's split up and check things out. Make sure to stay within eyesight of each other." He didn't like the idea, but they had to cover as much ground as possible.

Eric broke away to examine the left side, Jam took the right, and Joseph climbed up the broken stone steps to the central structure. At the heart rested a monument of some kind. There was a round garden, where a single lifeless tree stood, surrounded by what might once have been a magnificent courtyard. This mighty realm could have held something grand, but he had to imagine what it used to be.

"There's nothing here but a bunch of broken trash." Eric complained. "Usually this would be a great place for a surprise boss battle."

"See anything over by you?" Joseph called out to Jam.

"Nothing much over here," the islander replied.

Joseph's search came up similarly empty until he stepped beyond the deceased garden where a tangle of branches and vines crawled up the back wall. It was carefully hidden and only made visible due to the untimely death of trees that had once protected it. One by one he ripped the appendages from their hold, and the noise drew Eric and Jam over to help. Together they removed the obstructions, revealing a door on the other side.

An intricately ornate stone barrier sealed on all sides, it didn't budge, no matter how they pulled or pushed. The only prominent feature was the center pictograph that showed a small group of figures gathered around a large tree with many different items placed around it, implying some form of ritual. Though beautifully made, it did little to help them.

"No use. That thing isn't moving." Joseph sighed as he wiped the sweat from his forehead.

"I bet this is where they locked away all the treasure." Eric grunted as he kicked the door once again. Nothing happened.

Joseph turned to Jam. "See anything? You seem the master of unlocking stuff."

Jam leaned down to look over the designs but shook his head. "I'm afraid there's nothing here. I guess they sealed this one up tight. Nothing musical about this door, you know?"

It was just another dead end in the great forest maze.

Yet there was something different. When Joseph looked around, he couldn't help but notice the single dead tree, the same one he'd noted in the courtyard earlier, had moved. Its top half curved down and its trunk arched. Weirdly, the branches all swayed in a single direction. The mysterious breeze formed the naked branches into a crude arrow that now pointed to the side, toward something none of them had previously noticed. A giant tree soared over all others and broke through the canopy, extending its crown into the sky beyond. It was a true guardian of the forest.

As they approached, Eric craned his neck. "That's one big tree."

Joseph said nothing, instead trodding silently toward it. The path carried the trio back into the forest, around a small pond and across a teetering wooden bridge to the outside of the temple walls. On the other side waited the large jaws of a vine-choked cavern from which the large tree grew. As the trio tore into the protective sheet of foliage, it fell apart at their touch. As soon as everything had been freed, they nodded to one another and cautiously made their way inside. It didn't take long to reach the center.

It was truly something to behold. Not only did the trunk expand nearly the entire width of the room, but it extended its reach to the sky above. In contrast to the other smaller trees, which had become dead husks, the massive king-tree remained full of vibrant life. The cavern was the throne on which it sat, holding its place as the ruler of the forest domain. An arrangement of stone formed a long central core near the base, where a moat of shimmering water flowed in a circle around it.

Eric raised his phone and snapped a few pictures. "No one is gonna believe this."

An altar had been constructed before the monumental life, as if to honor its existence.

Joseph sighed. "Yeah, it's impressive, but I don't see how it helps us." His sense of optimism crashed again.

Jam waved them over. "Hey, it looks like some sort of offering."

Joseph and Eric joined him and looked where he pointed. There was another set of carvings in the ruin that displayed the images of the same figures they'd found in front of the giant tree. In the first set, the people had been depicted carrying small items into the cave. In the second carving, they were shown leaving these items on the altar. The third set depicted a bounty of plants and other life coming to bloom around them. It seemed an artistic story made by those who'd carried out the same act each day of their lives.

"Looks like they offered things to the tree, and it gave the forest life," Joseph speculated as he looked it over.

"Yuck. Offered what exactly?" Eric winced. "Hopefully not other people."

Jam shook his head. "Hey, I doubt it. This seems to be an offering of *good* nature, you know? The people in this civilization probably brought items from their harvests and gave it back to the land. It must have been like a give

268

and take, in that they returned part of their crops to the forest responsible for the bounty."

"So maybe if we leave something here, we'll find a way in." Joseph glanced around, scanning the chamber before shaking his head. "I don't know what we can offer to it."

Eric snorted and pulled a granola bar from his pocket, then unwrapped it. "Great. What do we do?"

As Eric was about to take a bite of his snack, Joseph gasped, then snatched the snack from his friend and looked to the tree.

"Hey! I was gonna eat that."

Joseph ran to the stone altar and pulled the bar free of its wrapper. He hoped it would be enough. Eric and Jam stood behind as he knelt and placed the food onto the stone carving. Almost instantly, a warming glow filled the air as a bright sense of growth and harmony, like the season of Spring condensed to a single place in time and space, followed. Green sparkles of light danced around them, flickering as if to signal the forest's joy. Small roots emerged from beneath the stone plates and wrapped around the modern food, pulling it down into the earth at its base.

Eric groaned. "We could have at least shared! That was my last one!"

The massive tree swayed slightly as its peak rustled to life. A small branch lowered from above, encased in the same green aura. Joseph carefully extended his arms, took the item into his hands, and held it tightly. It felt alive.

"Hey, do you think that's what we need?" Jam asked.

Joseph glanced down at the tree fragment he held in his hands and turned to the exit of the cave. "Only one way to find out!"

He glanced back at the tree and mouthed a silent thank you before they marched around the pathway to the center of the temple waiting in the distance.

Keeping the shimmering fragment close, he approached the door, then held the glowing object out before him. The branch jerked away from his hand as it gravitated to the sealed frame. A flash of emerald light echoed across the fields before extending farther into the forest, filling the decaying land with fresh air. The gentle blush of the wood faded as it became one with the carvings. Each ornate line came to life as the stone shifted, sliding from its supports before vanishing down into the path beneath their feet.

The trail into the heart had been revealed to them, and Joseph felt a rush of apprehension. "Looks like we found the way. You guys ready?"

"You bet! Let's get in there and take Ryan down." Eric threw a few punches into the air and ran ahead of them.

"Eric, hold on, we—"

Before he could finish, Eric vanished into a rippling wall. Though torches lit the archway on the other side, Eric was nowhere to be seen.

"Eric?"

"Hey, he's gone."

Joseph jolted forward. When he came to the same point Eric had reached, he lost his ability to see, blinded as a wave of light crossed over his eyes. It didn't last long, and when he emerged on the other side, an entirely new sight awaited him.

Eric stood a few feet in front, staring wide-eyed up into the looming tangle of lush woodland. All life had returned to the forest. Beautiful leaves and vines merged into the waves of undulating flora roaming and weaving in real time along the stone. The tall walls of the ruin were quickly rebuilt, and they extended into the center of the temple's home, which seemed to place them in the core of an ancient assembly. Towering stone warriors guarded both sides. Each of the humanoid figures held a massive ax in its crumbling hands. The long chamber top opened to the sky, welcoming in beams of sunlight that reached deep into the forest. The birdsong had returned; their flying shadows rushed through the thick foliage.

At the center rested another garden, but unlike the dying one outside, this one overflowed with the life of flowers that encircled a gleaming sapling with white leaves. With every breath, refreshing air filled Joseph's lungs not only with oxygen, but with a deeper awareness of the life around them.

"This place seems full of surprises, you know?" Jam emerged from the portal behind them. "Did you feel that strange sensation when you came in?"

Joseph nodded but kept his eyes fixed on the path ahead. He knew what Jam had felt. Something changed when they stepped through the doorway, as if time itself had been altered, placing them in an era where the forest still thrived. They appeared to be the only ones there.

"So where is everyone?" Eric said from where he stood ahead of them.

He was right. The revived ruins had become no less vacant. At the back of the long hollow waited another sealed gate. Their course had been set, and it left him wondering whether Ryan had successfully made it to the location. Then an anxious thought struck him. What if *they* were in the wrong place? The forest seemed never-ending. It was entirely possible they'd been led astray.

Joseph shook his head and pointed to the far end of the open room. "No, this has to be the place. Let's keep looking."

They traversed the empty expanse along the stone walkway. Each step alerted the blossoms at their feet, and Joseph would have sworn the flowers tried to move out of the way. He did his best to avoid stepping on them. Against the far wall, the sound of falling water greeted them, accompanied by the tiny stream itself, which trickled down both sides of the ruins. This second barricade was immense, and it left them no way of moving it from their path.

"Is this the seal Ben mentioned?" Eric approached and tapped his fist on the hard stone.

Joseph shrugged. "I don't know what else it could be."

There were no markings on the slab. None of them spoke as they searched for an answer. Only the gentle calls of the forest inhabitants kept the silence at bay.

"I'm going to ask the obvious—what do we do now?" Eric folded his arms.

A deep, echoing voice answered Eric's question. "You step aside, or our power will tear your body from this path."

As a group, all three faced the source of the voice. Ryan stepped into view from the shadows of the wall, followed closely by Boris, who now strode with more confidence.

"Hah! About time you grew a pair and decided to face us!" Eric readied his wand.

Joseph kept his own stance in a tense state, unsure of what Ryan might do.

Ryan barely paid Eric any notice, instead turning toward the stone wall behind them. "The Protection Seal...a creation of the light, broken only by those of the same essence. That light is needed to cast a shadow, and you are here to cast ours. We knew you'd come in search of answers. Your every step has conspired to place you here, in this very moment. You now stand in an era when this forest thrived. A great evil was laid to slumber inside of these broken walls." Ryan raised his arms to indicate their surroundings, but he slowly lowered them. "Our souls are tainted by the oblivion locked beyond its gate, unable to lift the curse that binds those waiting behind the stone. Your light should provide the magic we need. Return the tomes you recovered along your journey. Their only purpose was to guide you here."

"What are you talking about? What's sealed inside this place?" Joseph stepped forward.

Wordlessly, Ryan raised his hand again, and it was quickly engulfed by a dark, spiraling fog. The same fog swarmed the teens' backpacks and pulled. The force jerked Joseph and Eric forward a couple times before successfully tearing the bags from their owners' backs. The strange fog seized the books they'd found on their way and dropped the packs.

Eric growled and jumped back into place. "Oh, that's it! You just earned a beating!"

Joseph tried to stop him, but Eric charged forward. He swung his fist, kicked, and threw out a few slashes with his wand, but Ryan dodged each of them. He retaliated by simply grabbing and shoving Eric's arm. That ended Eric's assault, sending him rolling along the ground.

The teen returned dizzily to his feet. "Like that's going to stop me."

Ryan waved an arm before him. "You bore us. Stand aside."

Boris adjusted his glasses. "Yes, you'd do best to listen to them. I believe it a wise choice, unless you wish your souls ripped apart." He looked down his nose at them and smirked. "The power dwelling within Ryan is the most amazing thing I've ever seen. Hmph, Benjamin would be jealous."

Joseph cocked an eyebrow, and the puzzling statement made him relax his posture. "So there really *is* more than one person inside of him. Professor Ben was right…"

Without answering, Ryan waved his arm again, sending all three of them to the ground using an unseen power. It felt as if a forceful wind had slammed their bodies against the wall and let them crash.

"Move. The time is drawing near. These shackles have grown tiresome."

Joseph tried to stand, but another powerful gust sent him back to the ground. The same happened with Eric and Jam when they attempted to move. They were trapped.

"Ecicia."

With the muttering of that word by those unified voices inside of Ryan, formations of solid ice unexpectedly cracked the ground. The sharp eruptions spread along the stone and encased their legs, freezing them in place as they grew and solidified.

Ryan beckoned Boris over. From a cloth bag, he pulled out six other books, then tore out a selected page from each before he discarded the rest. Joseph watched as the young man arranged the eight pages at the base of the doorway.

Ryan faced the entry. "From pleas of ancient light, we beckon you, break the darkness through our plight. These ancient grounds of times long past, shall be brought to suffer stillness to forever last. We call upon the earth of souls to wake, to let your power come forth, and this seal to break!"

This phrase he repeated multiple times. The words became louder and reverberated in the air like an unseen chime. Joseph grabbed his sword and jabbed at the ice locking him in place. Small chips flew from where he struck, but it was slow going. He looked up as the stone

274

barrier crumbled and cracked somewhere nearby. The pages at Ryan's feet dissolved into a small flurry of differently colored flames, and with a strong, transparent power, the great seal was devoured into the earth at his command.

"Isn't it funny how your every attempt to stop us became nothing more than a catalyst, a simple trick to secure your assistance? We would advise you to remember that no matter how hard the light tries to illuminate everything, it always casts a shadow in its wake. These forces work together and shall bring forth a new slumber. We greatly appreciated what you have done, but we see no further need for your aid. There will be others to harvest."

Ryan turned to one of the colossal stone giants guarding the walls at the side. He placed a hand on its leg and muttered softly. The massive guardian shifted.

His assignment completed, Ryan turned away. "It's a shame. We hoped for more from you. If you prevail, I hope next time you show us what you can do. Or have you forgotten?"

From the glance Ryan gave, Joseph felt the statement had been directed at him.

Boris followed Ryan, and both vanished through the once sealed doorway.

"Ugh, I'm no ice cube." Eric jerked his legs and tried to shatter the frost. "Get back here, Ryan, or I'll...gah!"

Sighing, Joseph slammed his blade again and again into the ice. After much work he was able to shatter the cold prison. Now free, he helped Eric and Jam until all three had been released from the spell.

Eric ran forward and attempted a rush through the doorway, but a strong force repelled him, sending him flying back onto the ground.

"That...didn't...work..." Eric groaned.

Jam pressed forward and placed a hand out until it stopped in midair. "Hey, there's something blocking the path."

Joseph also placed his hand on the obstacle. A strange warm power prevented them from moving beyond it.

"That coward locked us out!" Eric punched the invisible barrier. "This won't keep us out forever. You'll have to face me eventually, Ryan."

The ground suddenly trembled. Eric stopped. He turned to look around, then rubbed his stomach. "Man, I didn't think I was *that* hungry."

The quaking rose again, this time shaking loose small fragments of stone that crumbled from the structures above.

"Hey, it sounds like it's coming from nearby." Jam scanned their surroundings.

It didn't take long for Joseph to make the connections. He gazed to the statue Ryan had stood near before he left. The leg of the soldier twitched, then ripped away from the wall, rose into the air, and crashed down onto the ground.

"You gotta be kidding me!" Eric took a step back. "What the hell *is* that thing?"

With an agitated roar, the hulking giant stepped forward, ripping its body free from its moorings. Its body creaked like a sinking ship, held together by strong, weaving vines that wormed through its joints. Its face had been left with only a blank, featureless stare. It ground its fingers together as it gripped its hulking weapon and faced them, glaring down from its two-story height.

"That dream didn't prepare me for this." Joseph looked at his best friend. "You wanted a boss battle, right?"

"The first boss shouldn't be something like *that*. Where's our tutorial stage?"

"Hey, what if the forest brought it to life?" Jam asked.

Joseph shook his head as he readied his sword and wand. "Ryan must have done something. It's—"

The ground shook, and the group was forced apart as the charging colossus made the first move. It slammed its ax into the ground between them, sending stone and dirt into the air.

The impact was strong enough to make Joseph's legs buckle. He fell to his knees before stumbling into an uncoordinated sprint. "Keep moving! We need to stay out of its reach."

Though it was slow, it was ready to attack again. Each of its steps rocked the sanctuary, causing the pillars to tremble and the stone to quake with each vibration. The great rasping of stone on stone, created by its body as it moved, burrowed into their ears, joined by the thundering impact of its next swing. The shock wave collided with a nearby support, forcing Joseph to slide along the ground to switch his running direction. He dove as the rocky beam smashed into the ground, leaving a cloud of dust where it came to rest.

Shortly after, the stone monster cried out and with an arching thrust of its arm, it threw the great ax toward Jam and Eric to further divide the group.

"Doesn't this thing ever stop?!" Eric hurried out of the way.

The statue strode to retrieve its weapon from a severed section of the wall, and Joseph tried to wave his friends around the perimeter of the chamber.

"Stay near its back."

His sword drawn, Joseph went in for a hit, swinging his blade into the ankle of the living sculpture with a clang. The rock chipped, and he snapped one of the vines, but the attack drew its attention. With a single swing, the golem sent Joseph flying, colliding with the teenager with the force of a running bull. Stars filled his eyes, leaving his head spinning and his body aching. A loud song started to play from nearby.

It was coming from Eric.

Joseph's friend rushed by, frantically dodging the stone soldier's swinging ax. "Crap, that isn't the one I wanted."

The music was still playing, and the song, a recent hit called Up in Our Way by a new boy band named Pop Direction, made for an oddly incongruous soundtrack. The energetic theme radiated through the arena from Eric's phone as he ran.

"Eric, what are you doing?"

His friend gasped as he hurried around Jam, causing both of them to flee. "I was trying to find epic boss music. I swear I don't know how this song got onto my playlist! I must have downloaded it by accident."

Joseph staggered as he ran. The golem had retrieved its weapon and was giving chase. "You think you could worry about the actual problem and stop messing with your phone?"

"Fine!" Eric dove to the side and sliced the soldier with his wand, swinging furiously until an attack forced him to roll. "Dude, we're like ants attacking an elephant."

"Hey, ants are small, but strong, you know?" Jam held his hat as he ducked down to avoid the next attack.

The stone colossus lumbered after them, and though it moved slowly, a strike from its bare fist wasn't anything to be trifled with.

"I could use a little help over here!" Eric dashed ahead, ducked to the right, and then darted under and through the statue's legs.

Working fast, Joseph held his wand and focused on his fire spell. "Come on, come on!" The images—of infernos, blazing bonfires, even the NM27's engines, poured into his mind as the energy gathered. He increased his pace to a sprint, then confronted the beast from the side. "Erif!"

The flames burst forward, encased in a dazzling orb that smashed against the rock monster's shoulder. It veered sideways from the impact, then rolled along the wall, shaving away layers of its own stone body as it did. Its roar of rage gave way to deep, rumbling grunts of pain as its contact with the cavern wall snapped more of its ligament-like vines. The friction was so intense, some of the vines burned away, creating whiffs of smoke and ash. Pieces fell from its body, lifeless and discarded.

Realization finally hit him. "The vines—target the vines!" Joseph called out before he fell back against a chunk of the broken wall.

He was weakened from casting the spell, and Joseph's defenses faltered. He didn't notice the monster was still approaching. It raised its arm, ready to plunge, only to halt as the sharp, rapid notes of a flute filled the air.

The flora along the ground shot upward, wrapping tightly around the creature's limb. The faster Jam played his flute, the tighter the leafy vegetation seemed to constrict. The pause allowed Joseph enough time to slip down and out of the way before the golem bellowed out, pulling its arm upward as it ripped away the plants restraining its movements.

"Hey, come over here!" Jam waved his arms, as if trying to get its attention before he played a few more notes.

Floral vines snared the golem once more, this time controlling its arm and making it punch itself in the face multiple times.

Joseph cringed. He was thankful for Jam's distraction but didn't want the islander to remain in danger. "Be careful!"

The stone soldier broke free and raced at the musician, swinging down hard as Jam swerved out of the way. The blow crashed against another of the supports holding the upper floor in place. When that went down, it took a large portion of the second story of the temple with it. All around, the slab crumbled. One solid chunk after another smashed into the unprotected back of the towering giant until, at last, it fell.

"Hit it while it's down!" Eric ran in.

Summoning his perseverance, Joseph joined his friends in their assault against the monster. He slashed his sword, Eric jabbed his wand, and Jam pulled and tore at the ragged and ripped vines that held the beast together. Chunks broke away, but within moments the enemy regained its vigor. With a trembling cry, it pushed itself to its feet, sending the trio to the ground with a wide sweep of its arm. When Joseph glanced back at the creature, a green orb was glowing in its chest, swirling with sinister energy. Their attack had revealed its core—perhaps revealing its lifesource.

Joseph's voice was hoarse. "Guys, I think I see it! We need to aim for the chest! We need to get it back down again!"

"All right. Time to grind some stone!" Eric cracked his knuckles and charged the rock monster.

Each attack inched them closer to victory. They worked as a team; Joseph would make a move when Eric or Jam lured it in, and they each did the same when the chance arose. They kept to a pattern of moving in, drawing its attention, and backing out to let the next player attack. They destroyed its vines, hacking and tearing, breaking down the magic-possessed statue bit by bit. Their method was going perfectly until a massive sweep of the creature's ax shook the ground, sending them tumbling back.

The sheer force of the attack shattered the giant's cleaver. Its weapon destroyed, it marched to the side of the arena, and its cry echoed through the dense forest before its entire body erupted into a tornado of black, piercing smoke. Enraged, the golem ripped another column from the wall, brandishing it in both hands.

"Oh, crap. It went into its second phase. We must be halfway there!" Eric cautioned.

As Joseph rose to his feet, Eric and Jam ran toward him.

He motioned for them to back off. "We have to stay separated." By breaking apart the group, they might also break away its focus.

"Hit the ground!" Eric warned.

Joseph turned right as the giant's attack swept the entire length of the field. It swung the pillar it had been carrying, and Joseph dove as it slashed the air over his head. It was close enough that the force of its attack blew wind across his face.

Eric and Jam also rolled to avoid the column before it crashed between them. The pillar smashed another of the stationary statues, causing it to crumble into a heap of jagged stone.

"Hey, it's like a deadly version of limbo, you know?" Jam said.

"Yeah, just don't lose your head," Eric's replied.

The monster's assault became more heated. It grew more persistent, following its every fearsome strike with another immediately after. Its attacks shed shards of stone from the pillar-like weapon every time it bashed the temple floor. Holes and upturned slabs of rock littered the makeshift arena. When the top of its columnar club broke, leaving the soldier unarmed, an opening once again presented itself.

Joseph reacted as quickly as he could when the creature recoiled from breaking its weapon. He charged his spell but couldn't cast it rapidly enough. A chunk of stone hurtled in his direction and forced him to dive out of the way. Astonishingly, the giant had resorted to throwing pieces of its own body at them. Playful notes from Jam's flute filled the air again, drawing the assault in a new direction. This gave Joseph the time he needed to prepare his next attack.

His fire gathered, and he approached the monster from behind. "Erif!"

Another flaming orb shot from the gleaming gemstone and detonated along the back of the stone soldier. It faltered, collapsing to its knees.

Joseph was too weak to move in, so he flashed a nod to Eric. "Go for it!" As Eric ran in, he slid his sword along the broken ground toward him.

Eric grabbed the blade by its hilt as he hopped across the shattered battlefield, yelling as he approached the other side of the cavern, where the exposed core of the weakened creation waited.

"You're about to hit rock bottom. Game over, blockhead!" Eric raised the sword, and with an exaggerated battle cry drove it into the giant's open chest.

The blade's point pierced the green orb, shattering it into a brilliant display of broken, glowing rays. Eric quickly retreated when the vast arms of the soldier swung aimlessly at the air. The painful groans of the giant vibrated the leaves of the forest's trees while it clawed blindly around its location. The friends moved to get away as, with one last moan, its body stiffened.

As the great stone figure locked up, the color faded from it entirely. Like a tree to the last strike of a cutter's ax, it tilted forward and fell, getting lost in a pile of rubble and twisting vegetation as its joints broke away. When the clouds settled and the dirt cleared, the remaining pieces lay lifeless on the disturbed earth of the ancient haven.

The trio panted heavily. Music suddenly filled the area. Eric held up his phone as it played a short upbeat tune. It was the victory fanfare from *Timeless Fantasy*.

"Yeah, we did it. Level up, baby!" Eric stepped forward and kicked over one of the smaller chunks before breaking into a short dance. "Hah, it didn't know who it was—" He stopped to rub his shoulder. "Ow—messing with."

"Hey, we did it. That's all that matters, you know?" Jam gave a heavy sigh as he adjusted his torn shirt and bent hat. "It went back to the earth that made it."

Joseph couldn't focus. Something warm dripped from his nose, and when he touched below it, he cringed when his fingers came back bloody. His head throbbed, and he felt lightheaded.

"You okay?" Eric helped him up.

"Yeah, I'm just a bit dizzy." Joseph wiped the blood away and forced a smile.

"Oh, I know." Eric grinned at the sight of his wand. "I can put that healing spell to work. Okay, everyone, gather round. Doctor Eric is gonna cook us up a cure!"

Everything around him was a blur, but Joseph did his best to fight the disorientation. Was it from casting the spell?

Eric focused on his magic, and when the glittering purity formed on the gem atop his wand, he held it out and shouted proudly. "Eruc!"

A soothing breeze blew over them as a white aura encased each of their bodies. Joseph's pain lifted, and his vision returned to normal. The shine remained a few seconds before fading. It left Joseph in a better, more refreshed state.

"Phew, that really takes a lot out of you." Eric staggered but swiftly regained his balance.

"Hey, that's a pretty useful trick there." Jam bent and straightened his leg. "Feels brand new again, you know?"

Joseph's body felt better, but the mental effects were starting to worry him. Maybe Professor Ben was right to say they were novices when it came to casting magic. He looked at his wand, then tucked it away in favor of the scattered books Ryan had left behind. He placed them back inside their recovered bags before returning Eric's backpack to him.

Eric grunted. "Jeez, no wonder I don't like to read. Books are heavy."

Joseph turned away and took his sword back, then returned to the doorway. When he reached out, the barrier was no longer present. "Professor Ben might be able to find a use for those. Now come on, we have to stop them."

The entry led them down a single hallway, alongside which ran many small openings in the damp stone. The entire structure ran deep into the temple and under a cascading waterfall, where the rushing water crashed around their path deep into the cliffs. Near the end, the sound of dark chanting rose over the rushing water. Readying their weapons one more time, they gathered their senses and entered the chamber.

The only detail Joseph observed upon entering was a massive glowing doorway nestled between two arching trees in the center of the room. Roots ran through the earth and rock; the trees had been planted firmly in this small refuge.

A cloud of dark mist rushed at them, then exploded into a painful heat that caused every muscle in Joseph's body to go numb.

"This...is getting...old." Eric fell, gasping when he hit the ground. "I'm tired of playing his punching bag."

Every fiber of Joseph's body burned as if an electric shock ran continuously through him. He rolled on the grass, barely able to control his own reflexes. The sky loomed overhead, visible through an opening where the trees didn't extend beyond the rock.

Ryan stood in the heart of the room, staring the three of them down. He'd swatted them away like bothersome flies. "You and your feeble attempts to delay the inevitable." As if the trio of friends was too inconsequential to fully acknowledge, Ryan didn't face them. "We're impressed to see you still functioning after that. Perhaps you aren't such a waste after all."

Joseph made one last effort to get up, but a foot to his chest kept him down.

"Not so fast, my friend." Boris held him in place. "It seems you have yet to learn your place. Benjamin has instilled in you a foolish bravery. I assure you, it won't take long to break that habit." Boris spoke like he was commanding a pet. "Just stay down where you belong. I wish to see the results of this engagement."

Joseph was too weak to hold his sword, and he winced as it fell from his fingers. Boris had no problem keeping them back. Eric tried to help his friend, but Boris was able to push him away with a single finger.

Ryan resumed his hymn, and bright lights from the runes on the ground came to life. A heavy wind crept into the open chamber, swirling the darkness that gathered over the sealed monument before him. Words lost in translation crashed down on Joseph, slithering through his mind before wriggling back out to be lost. Torches lit around Ryan's circle reignited, replacing their previous orange fires with black and white flames that seemed to vacuum the light from the room.

"Hey, what are we supposed to do?" Jam struggled with his words.

Ryan turned to them, then flashed a sinister grin as the color faded from his eyes. "You came here with a rusty sword, novice magic, and a false hope. You're mindless rats who know nothing of this world or anything beyond. Observe now, as when hardships and suffering grow, the emptiness of this world expands with them. The lives and souls of this universe will soon wither as they recall the terrors of the past. You should have left those objects where they were buried." Ryan laughed, rolling his head as the echo in his tone deepened. "Your kind has dug far too deep, and what's been unleashed cannot be undone. Our power will once again be free, our objectives reset. You can't stop it...you can't undo the path before you. What was forgotten will rise, and all will be consumed in a cold slumber!"

Joseph crawled backward as the symbols surrounding the room ignited one by one and all other sounds were devoured. The chamber grew dark, and the lights from the obsidian and ivory torches gathered with the light of the runes in the air above the ground. Ryan jerked upward like a puppet on strings, and a horrifying glow surrounded his body. Light and darkness danced together around them. The doors of the sealed archway in the center of the chamber blew open as the sinister aura fled Ryan's figure and joined the dark power from the opened frame. The doorway at the center of the room showed nothing on the other side.

Released by whatever had grasped him, Ryan collapsed into a motionless heap. Two silhouettes stood within the shadowy vapor just before the doorway. One waved a taunting finger before it vanished, leaving behind the echo of its upbeat laughter. The other figure remained, however. Time slowed as the figure approached. It remained blurry, devoid of details, but the voice that spoke to him was clear, its tone deeply ominous. "You are a mere shadow of your former self..."

After those few words, it leaned away from him before fading into the curling haze, only to be carried off by the wind. The light of the sun returned as the evil breeze died. The room settled back into the gentle hum of the water cascading behind the chamber.

Ryan's body stirred. He rose and gave a weary stare around the room while rubbing his head. "What the hell just happened?" He blinked. "Wait, I can move my own body again? The voices, they're gone! Those damn entities are finally gone."

Any weakness Ryan had previously displayed vanished. He stood, and a confident smirk spread on his lips as he curled his fingers a few times.

Boris blinked and shook his head. "These events are outstanding. The Sealed Forest came to life right before our eyes. The legends were all true! The theories were no mere myth." He gazed wide-eyed at Ryan and the trio of friends. "This changes everything! Perhaps the power hidden in those seals contained other forces as well. Bah, and Benjamin was willing to let it all slip away."

"Like I care about that," Ryan scoffed. "Whatever those things did to me is over, but they better pray I never find them."

"Yes, I do believe we were under the influence of some dark possession." The older man's face brightened. "However, it appears normalcy has finally returned. Perhaps we may examine this further."

"Drop the scientist act, would you?" Ryan rolled his shoulders and cracked his neck. He finally noticed Joseph when he and his friends stood. "What are you dumb-asses doing here?"

Joseph braced himself as Eric and Jam did the same. Ryan's body tensed, and he raised his fists as he stared them down.

For a moment they shared the heavy silence, until Ryan snickered and relaxed. "Keep dreaming. I don't have the patience to bother with you stooges. You're the least of my concerns right now." Ryan turned away. "Let's go, Boris. The air around here is"—he glanced back at the trio—"starting to get stale."

"Tch, you're the one who's stale! Come on. I hope you're ready to be cleaned out and taken to the trash." Eric grunted as he stepped forward, but he instantly fell to the ground. "Ow! That hurts…"

Ryan mocked Eric's effort with a laugh. "Whatever. Just because I didn't finish you off, that doesn't mean a damn thing. Make sure you tell the crazy professor all about this. I'm sure he'd love to hear it." Ryan folded his arms and stared them down again. His grin returned. "Who knows? If you keep at it, you three might learn a thing or two from me."

"Ryan, wait." Joseph stepped forward but was silenced by Ryan's taunting palm.

With that last gesture, the young man turned and walked away. He and Boris vanished on the other side of the waterfall.

Eric growled and kicked the dirt. "Who does he think he is?"

Joseph set down his weapon and let out a long sigh of relief. He glanced at their tattered, dirty clothes, then up at the small opening through the trees. He gazed at the sky and took in a deep breath. He was exhausted, hungry, and beaten down, but they were all still alive.

"Great, so what do we tell Ben when we get back?" Eric dusted off his pants, frowning at the rips in them. "Are torn jeans still cool?"

"Hey, we just tell him the truth. We were seriously outmatched, but check it out. We came out of this with a new experience, you know?" Jam's bright smile matched his optimism.

Joseph returned the smile. "You're right. That's all that really matters."

"Hey, when we get back, I'll treat us all to a great meal to celebrate." Jam patted them both on the back.

Eric's face lit up to that offer. "Oh yeah, now we're talking."

Joseph nodded, and they grabbed their things before setting down the same path Ryan had taken.

Eric adjusted his backpack as he staggered forward. "Man, I'm not looking forward to finding our way out of here. My feet are killing me."

They crossed the hall and marched back into the arena where the giant stone soldier had fallen. The chunks of its pieces made Joseph think over all the struggles they'd conquered on the journey through the ancient forest and each step they took to reach it.

The magical presence rippled when they stepped through it, but a surprise waited on the other side. Instead of arriving at the dying woodlands they'd come from, they stood before the clearing at the forest's entrance. The roots and trees preventing their exit no longer impeded them. The glowing path of mushrooms and life, the frozen trees—even the trail of burnt, scorched timbers, were gone. It was as if the land had granted them a reprieve.

Eric spun in a circle. "That doesn't make sense."

Joseph was tired. "You're right. It doesn't."

Jam laughed. "Hey, no complaints from me."

As they left, the trees at their backs shifted, creating the protective formation on the outskirts once again. Joseph glanced back as they stepped off the grass onto the sand of the shore. The sound of waves washed over his ears, but through the tranquil crash of water against sand, Kilgan's voice returned.

"Your first steps have been taken. Yet you must travel with caution and keep looking forward. What has slumbered in the emptiness is beginning to stir. Don't let the whispering shadows claim you. Be strong, Joseph."

As quickly as they'd arisen, the words vanished into the slumbering trees.

Eric waved him onward. "Come on, man. We wanna get out of here."

Joseph looked away and ran after them. Ryan's ship was gone, and there was no indication of where he might go next. Joseph climbed to the deck of the NM27 and approached the controls. The engines rumbled to life before they ascended.

They spoke on the deck for a short time while sharing a meal as twilight hours fell. The light faded, and the horizon grew dark. Joseph set the autopilot, and they stumbled downstairs into the cabins, where a much needed slumber waited.

He'd contact Professor Ben when they awoke.

CHAPTER SIXTEEN
RETURNING HOME

They'd been back on the island for a few days. Professor Ben had no more surprises or discoveries to show them. In fact, the man hadn't even asked them about what had happened, insisting instead that they first rest and regain their energy. Regardless, Joseph sensed the apprehension in Professor Ben's tone. There were still places to explore on the island, and Joseph gradually relaxed enough to enjoy the vacation, though the same memories kept playing in his head. His need to relay their experiences grew, until finally the researcher called for them.

"There was no way we could have stopped him. Even with the spells you showed us, whatever was controlling Ryan was too powerful."

"That's quite all right, Joseph." Professor Ben paced the room. "You did your best, and that's all that matters, though I am mostly to blame for these failures."

Joseph cocked his head. "What makes you say that?"

"I rushed the operation based on flimsy hypotheses. Through my own blindness, I allowed the situation to grow chaotic. I should have been more observant, and I most certainly shouldn't have sent you three into the danger zone as recklessly as I did. For that, I apologize."

"You could have gotten us killed for nothing. In fact, it *was* for nothing!" Eric said.

Joseph gave Eric a short elbow in the side.

Eric cleared his throat and rubbed the back of his neck. "Hah, I meant, uh, no worries, Ben. We had it covered!" He looked at Joseph with a look that seemed to say *satisfied?*

"Regardless of what's been done and said, I feel this bridge we've crossed is truly an outstanding outcome. Now, if you wouldn't mind, could you explain what you saw out there?" The professor beamed as he pulled out a pad of paper and a pencil.

Eric's eyes were wide. "Oh, man, you should have seen it. We were at this temple, and this gigantic stone monster came to life and tried to smash us. We totally took it down, though. It was just about to crush Joe into tiny little pieces when—"

"Excuse me, Eric. While all that sounds fascinating, and I don't wish to cut off your exhilarating tale, would it be all right to skip ahead to what happened with the Protection Seal?"

"But I was just getting to the good part." Eric's excitement dwindled.

The professor turned his focus to Joseph and nodded.

Joseph gave a deep sigh. "Once we got past the statue Ryan brought to life, we found him and Boris in the next chamber. We tried to stop him, but he was too strong. He managed to open some sort of gate that didn't go anywhere, but once he did that, whatever was inside him left."

Professor Ben sat and narrowed his eyes. "That's interesting. I've heard of these gateways before, however, my understanding of their purposes is minimal. Was there anything else?"

Joseph remembered seeing the figure that spoke to him, but he couldn't bring himself to mention it. "No. After everything calmed down, Ryan and Boris left. Oh, there's one more thing I wanted to show you." Joseph reached into his bag and pulled out the books Ryan had left behind. "Ryan used these to open the door, but he got rid of them after tearing out some pages. Can you use them?"

Joseph set them on the table.

The older man picked one up to examine it. "My word, these tomes are from the same era as the ones I've shown you! They're thousands of years old. Each is signified by the symbol carved into its cover. Why would Ryan leave them behind like that?"

Eric rolled his eyes. "Who knows? If he would have just given me a moment to catch my breath, I could have taken care of him right then and there."

Joseph laughed. "Yeah, like you did the first time?"

Eric gave a fake chuckle, then stretched his legs. "The forest...I still can't believe it."

"What do you mean?" asked the professor.

"It was so weird. The trees moved, the water had a strange effect on us, it would be snowing and cold one moment, then everything was burned to the ground seconds later." Joseph shook his head. "It felt like we were going in circles. Time seemed to stop, and I swear the land was watching us the entire time."

"Yet here you are, perfectly safe." Professor Ben grinned. "Tell me, did you by any chance find this blue book when it was snowing and this red one near the time of the fires?"

Joseph blinked. "We did, why?"

"While the powers inside these tomes lie dormant, their effects could still radiate into the world around us, especially in a place like the Sealed Forest. I bet it thrived on the presence of magical energies. That would explain at least some of the changes you experienced. As for the illusions you described, they must have been a part of the forest's own roaming life forces. I have no doubt many souls have wandered through the same paths you followed."

Joseph let his gaze drop to the floor. "I guess you're right."

"Joseph, you need to understand that not all things have an explanation. Tell me something. What was your reaction when you first read the letter I sent?"

"It seemed real, and I guess I was excited. Eric and I had been looking forward to that game. I don't like that you lied to get us here."

The professor set down his papers. "Yet you still confronted the unknown and followed your instinct. Does that tell you anything about yourself?"

Joseph chuckled. "I'm gullible?"

"How about instead of the reasons that brought you here, you take a look at what you've done and what you've accomplished. You rolled the dice and took on a baffling challenge even though you knew it was way over your head. That is a victory in itself! The ability to trust your own decisions and follow that intuition to the very end is something I'm quite proud of. You should also be proud.

Each new victory, no matter how small, sculpts you into the person you're meant to be."

Eric spun. "Got that right. This was better than a video game, even if we don't get extra lives. Although, you still suck for all the lies. I had so many hopes for that game."

"That's exactly my point—except about my misuse of your trust. I'm not sure I'll ever be able to earn your full forgiveness."

"It's okay, professor. We're alive. That's all that matters."

"I can see you've grown quite a lot since you first arrived at my door. Soon enough, you'll be able to take any problem thrown into your pot and turn it into the most amazing stew." Professor Ben gave him another hearty slap on the back.

Joseph laughed. "Thrown into my pot?"

"Just an expression, my boy!" The researcher smiled and returned to pacing around his desk. "I must also thank you for gathering information that'll permit me to continue my research. Were it not for you, I never would have been able to delve deeper into these discoveries. You were my eyes on locations I could only dream about. Not that I'm old by any means. Perhaps once my schedule is less chaotic, I might join you both on the next voyage."

"Wonderful. I can't wait for that," Eric teased.

"Oh, speaking of—" Joseph brought out his phone, and Eric did the same. "We took some pictures at the Sunken Caverns, and we're wondering if you know anything about them."

"We also snagged some cool ones from the forest."

The professor peeked at the photographs on their phones, giving a curious hum as he did. "That's truly fascinating, though I can't decipher the meaning of those phrases and pictures just yet. Would you be so kind as to send them to me?"

The professor typed his email address and number into both of their devices.

"There we are. Now you can remain in contact with me should something arise. Also, I believe I promised both of you a vacation. Now would be a grand time for you to enjoy some relaxation on the island while I plot a course for our next move."

Eric jumped, a joyful look on his face.

Joseph couldn't feel the same. Their parents were waiting. Their time on the island had been wonderful, but it had to end. "Thanks, Professor Ben, but I really think we should get back home. I know our parents are worried."

"Ah, yes, I understand. I keep forgetting your lives exist outside this strange new world. Very well. Should anything happen during that time, I'll call you. Until then, you should get some well-deserved relaxation. I shall call and make the arrangements for your return home." Professor Ben nodded and left the room.

Eric groaned. "Are you serious? You can't make me return home after this. I'll be grounded for life."

"We can't abandon our lives. We still have a year of school left."

"Ugh, fine. Guess I'll have to explain everything to my parents. There's no way they can get upset once I show them real magic. Just wait until the others at school see it."

The professor scampered back into the room. "Oh, goodness, no. You mustn't tell anyone else about this! Not your parents, not your best friends, not anyone. Everything you were told here must be kept confidential, and that especially applies to using spells in the open. Those must never be seen by *anyone*."

"What should we tell them?"

"Make something up," Professor Ben suggested. "Do whatever it takes—it doesn't matter! I don't want some stranger to find out about these things. It would blow the entire matter out of proportion." The man frantically searched the coffee mugs scattered around his lab before finding a filled one and drinking its contents. He sighed. "Most importantly, the last thing I want is for the wrong set of ears or eyes to take notice and bring harm to either of you. Especially now that we have this new mystery looming over our heads. Please, can you agree to this for all our safety?"

"I promise," Joseph agreed.

"Man, I'm gonna get it," Eric mumbled as he pounded his head on the table's surface. "Online colleges are cheaper, right?"

They had a few hours while they waited for their flight arrangements to be made. After they returned to the hotel and grabbed their belongings, Joseph took the remaining time to look over the labs. The inventions the researcher showed them still made him laugh. If Professor Ben could find sense in those crazy contraptions, maybe Joseph could make some sense of their own situation.

There was a knock on the door, and Jam stepped inside.

"Hey, you two ready?"

"There you are, James." The professor turned to Joseph and Eric. "James will see you back to the airport. You have everything I gave you?"

Eric rummaged through his bag. "Yeah, my wand's hidden in here somewhere."

"I still need to find a place to put this." Joseph glanced over his sword, unable to fit it into his pack.

"Perhaps you should leave that here." Professor Ben held out his hand to take it from him. "I might be able to pull strings for favors, but the last thing I need is for you to get caught carrying a weapon around the airport." The researcher studied the sword more closely. "I might be able to do something about this rust once I find the time." He placed it on the table. "Ah, yes, and I do have *one* more thing."

Professor Ben walked to one of his computers and pulled a small flat case from the drawer. He returned and handed it to them.

"This is for the two of you. Think of it as an expression of my gratitude for trusting me after all of my unfortunate deceptions."

Eric snatched the case before Joseph could move, popping open the plastic and gasping. "Is this what I think it is?"

Professor Ben chuckled. "It's a full beta test version of the game *Call of Echoes 3*. I felt it was the least I could do after I raised your hopes. I made a few calls while you were away and managed to secure a copy of the game's progress on that disc."

"This right here is the moment I was waiting for. Dreams really *do* become reality." Eric beamed as he cradled his new possession. It looked as if he might start crying. "My online channel is going to explode when I play this baby." He flashed a devious expression. "Wait till Clyde sees this!"

Joseph couldn't believe they'd gotten such an exclusive gift, yet the game was far from the most amazing thing to happen during their trip. Even so, Professor Ben had delivered on his promise; the game was now theirs. It was a small if important reward, but together with their experiences, it made the entire trip worth it.

"Well, then, I guess there is nothing left for me to say. You two make sure to take care of yourselves. It has truly been a pleasure getting to meet you."

Joseph smiled and shook his hand. "Thank you, professor."

"How about next time you give us a little upgrade to first class on our flight?" Eric winked.

Joseph shook his head and nudged his friend in the side.

Eric cleared his throat. "Uh, yeah. Catch you later, Ben!"

"Hey, we should really be going if you two want to catch your flight." Jam smiled. "Unless you want to stay a little longer so we can grab some Maku'ah Mawah on the way, you know?"

Eric grimaced. "Ugh, not the fish guts." He grabbed his things and bolted out the door.

"All right, get going before you miss your flight. I'll contact you when and if I figure something out." Professor Ben smiled and waved them onward.

Joseph waved back and headed for the exit, picking up his things and joining Jam and Eric outside. The door closed behind him.

The only way left was forward.

Jam led them down the same streets they'd walked when they first arrived. The afternoon sun was warm, and the salty air from the sea was refreshing. He was going to miss the view.

"I wish we didn't have to leave." Eric pouted as he looked at the beaches and shops. "No more beach parties, no more food. Why do I have to go home?"

They were back at the airport before they knew it.

"Well Jam, this was a fun trip. I'm glad we got to make a new friend."

"Yeah, it's been cool," Eric added.

Jam tipped his hat. "Hey, no sweat. Just remember that aloha means both hello and goodbye. There's always next time, you know?"

Joseph smiled and gave him a knowing nod. "Well, aloha, Jam!"

Joseph and Eric gave him one last wave before approaching the counter. They shuffled their way through security and after a relatively short stroll reached the gate to their flight.

"Oh, I almost forgot something." Eric smacked the back of Joseph's head.

The smack left Joseph's vision slightly blurred. He rubbed his head and gave Eric a confused look. "Did I...miss something?"

"Don't take that personally. This strange girl in goofy robes appeared in my dream the other night. She asked if I could smack you over the head and tell you to be more careful. I figured since we got the game, I'd make that dream come true as well. Been a good day."

Joseph froze, half expecting the world to shatter, as if he were in one of his recurring dreams, but everything remained the same.

Eric waved a hand in front of his face. "Earth to Joe. Time to go home."

It wasn't a dream, though he was happy to know Eric had seen her as well. He laughed. "You're right. Let's get out of here."

They stepped onto the plane after showing their tickets and found their seats.

"So...what do we tell our parents?"

Eric rubbed his face. "I have no idea. Even when I show them the game, I know I'm gonna get it. Wait—I probably shouldn't show them the game. They'll probably take it."

Joseph tucked his bag under the seat as Eric slumped into his chair. The engines of the plane started and carried them onto the runway before launching them into the sky.

"You've *got* to be kidding me." Eric panicked as he rummaged through his bag. "My pad is missing!"

"You brought too many things. Not surprised you lost something."

His friend's head hung pitifully. "And I didn't charge my phone again. Great. No anime, and my phone will be dead soon."

Joseph chuckled. "You'll be fine."

"Easy for you to say. How am I going to make it through this flight? I think I'm doomed to suffer." Eric flopped back into his seat, much to the annoyance of the passengers behind them.

Joseph thought for a moment, then grabbed something from his bag and tossed it to Eric. "Here."

He lifted the item from his lap and glanced over it. "The Wand of Space And Time? What's this?"

"It's called a book, Eric. People read them." Joseph smirked.

"Hah, that's a joke, right?" Eric flung it back to him. "After all this, if I never see another book again, it'll be too soon. Oh, well. We have an awesome game to play when we get back. I totally call the first round!" He pulled out his phone and started taking selfies with the game.

Smiling, Joseph withdrew his own phone, looking over the photos he'd taken. The island, the caverns, the Sealed Forest; he didn't need technology to remind him of these places. Magic was all around them, and they'd lived the adventure. He'd seen these places in person. He shut off the screen and tucked the device away. Those memories would be with him forever.

He glanced out the window, back to the island, watching it fade into the distance. He felt strange as the sun-drenched beach receded from his sights. He'd come to think of it as a second home over the course of that action-packed week. Yet through his wistful smile, a dark, ominous feeling remained. He wondered what Professor Ben might find in his research and whether they'd see him again. The role they'd played was what bothered him the most. He wanted to know the reasons; no, he *needed* to know them.

With a heavy sigh he ran his fingers along the pages of the book Eric had rejected without opening it. Only time would tell what their next chapter had in store for them.

Until that moment came, there was only one event that required his attention—their return home.

— THE END —